The Dishwasher

Also by Dannie Martin

COMMITTING JOURNALISM
(with Peter Sussman)

The Dishwasher

Dannie Martin

W. W. Norton & Company

New York
London

Printed in the United States of America
First Edition

The text of this book is composed in New Aster with the display set in Madrone and Pistilli Black
Composition by Crane Typesetting Service, Inc.
Manufacturing by Courier Companies, Inc.
Book design by Charlotte Staub

Library of Congress Cataloging-in-Publication Data

Martin, Dannie M.
The dishwasher / by Dannie M. Martin.
p. cm.
I. Title.
PS3563.A723286D57 1995
813'.54—dc20 94-33733
ISBN 0-393-03790-8

W.W. Norton & Company, Inc., 500 Fifth Avenue, New York, N.Y. 10110
W.W. Norton & Company Ltd., 10 Coptic Street, London WC1A 1PU

1 2 3 4 5 6 7 8 9 0

This book is dedicated to my daughter,
Julie René Martin, who decorates
my life with love.

Acknowledgments

I'd like to acknowledge those without whom this book would never have been published:

My companion, Jan Sluizer, for her constant love and support; Ed LeClair, a man whose generosity of spirit is not easily matched, for all the hours he put in typing my manuscripts; and Peter Sussman, without whose superb guidance I would never have become a writer.

Pat Sussman, Machteld Schreymayer, Joanne Guthrie, and Jake and Laurie Fohrer, who took the time to read this book in its various stages and for sharing their comments and criticisms.

My good friends Richard Lee Bostic and Blair Guthrie, who have so generously been there for me through all the ups and downs. And also Dan Capodomo and Mary Ann Bar, who used their professional expertise to help guide me along those bumpy roads.

All my friends who live outside the law both inside and outside of prison from whom I learned the convicts' code of ethics. It is from you I drew inspiration and the characters in this book. Someday society will learn that locking people up for long periods of time is not the key to solving problems.

And last, but certainly not least, my editor at W. W. Norton, Gerald Howard, whose strong belief in me and my work is greatly appreciated; Omar Divina, his assistant; and Fred Hill, my literary agent. Thanks to all of you!

The Dishwasher

1.

The world hit him in the face like a windblown newspaper. The second gate hummed as it slid and clanked shut with the finality of cold iron. The double fences with their rolls of razor wire on top and in between lay behind him now. He craned his head up at the main gun tower, where he could see a shadow beneath the military hat of a federal prison guard. The only easily discernible objects behind the tinted glass were a shotgun and an M-16 rifle standing at ready attention in their racks.

Before him a flag fluttered proudly in the wind on top of a white pole, anchored by an island of concrete that separated the visitors' parking lot from the smaller space for staff cars. He walked on out beneath the flag and sat his flight bag down on the concrete. Reaching into the pocket of his khaki shirt, he pulled out a pack of Camels and a book of paper matches. Turning to face the wind, he lit one, and squatted down next to his bag to wait. The wind felt different somehow as it tugged at him there beneath the flaps and flutter of the flag. It brought a sense of freedom but as yet he didn't feel free.

A station wagon came chugging up the drive, and as it came around the cul-de-sac he noticed the lettering on the faded blue front door, Lompoc Taxi Service. He stood up, bag in hand, and ground out the cigarette on the asphalt. The wagon pulled to a stop in front of him, and a tow-headed boy in his early twenties leaned out from behind the wheel.

"Bus station?" the boy asked around a wad of chewing gum.

"Yes," he replied, opening the door behind the driver,

sliding his bag across the seat, and sitting next to it. The boy turned around in his seat and looked at him.

"Hey, you're the only passenger I got—come sit up front."

He started to reply that he was fine where he was, but he saw an unmistakable shine of fear in the boy's eyes. He got out, walked quickly around, and sat in the passenger seat beside the boy. As he settled himself he could almost feel the release of indrawn breath of the youngster beside him, who was now driving slowly while fiddling with a button on the car radio.

"Hope you don't mind some country-and-western?"

"Country-and-western is fine," he replied.

The boy tuned in a country station and picked up speed, happily smacking his gum.

"My name is Joe," the boy said between chomps.

"Bill," the man replied. "Mind if I smoke?"

"Hell no, Bill, ashtray right there on the dash, don't smoke myself but it don't bother me none."

"Thanks," he told him, and lit another Camel.

Jerry Jeff Walker was singing "Me and Bobby McGee." He listened to every word. The first music he had really listened to in years. The song's definition of freedom–"just another word for nothing left to lose"—was interesting to him. They turned from the eucalyptus-lined drive of the prison onto the main road to Vandenberg Air Force Base and the town of Lompoc, California. He gripped the door handle tightly as they picked up speed. He looked over at the speedometer. They were only going fifty miles an hour, but to him it seemed much faster.

Through the windshield the sky was a marvelous blue bowl, streaked with faint contrails where rockets and jets had left their traces in the cold blue air. He felt good—the wind, the music, the highway. Today was his day, he knew there would never be another like this one. There wasn't enough time left in his life to do it again.

As they eased into the small town of Lompoc, sights and sounds were hitting his eyes and ears. A kaleidoscope of new colors and sights assaulted his vision. He watched a child pushing a tricycle on the sidewalk as his little sister ran to catch up. Their smallness stunned him, the sounds of their voices seemed far away and strange. He glanced at the driver maneuvering the car through the sparse traffic and was startled to see that he was not a bit awed by all this.

A Greyhound bus idled in the parking lot beside the one-room bus station as he retrieved his bag, said so long to the driver, and ambled into the station and up to the counter. A young Mexican girl watched him as he approached. She noted his long-sleeved khaki shirt, khaki pants, and black army-style shoes as he walked toward her, bag in hand.

This one is handsome, she thought to herself. He was taller than he looked at first glance. His hair was dark with a heavy sprinkle of gray, the eyes were hazel/gray under dark sleepy lids. He was clean-shaven, with a good nose and a very light dusting of freckles across the bridge. His generous mouth made her think of John Travolta. His body looked lithe and powerful under the khaki.

She wondered what he'd done and how long he'd been in. She had seen so many of the convicts released from Lompoc prison that she knew them instantly now by their government-issue clothes. She decided to try and make him smile.

"Well, if it isn't Bill Malone," she said with a smile as he reached the counter. "How are you, Bill?"

He looked at her with a slightly startled and wary expression. His eyebrows drew closer together and she saw a muscle twitch in his jaw as he glanced around the room and then back at her.

"I am fine," he replied with no trace of humor.

She held an envelope out to him.

"Here's your ticket, Bill, compliments of the government. That's your bus to Fresno sitting right outside."

"Thanks," he said, taking the envelope and turning toward the door.

She watched him go, knowing that he'd figured out how she knew his name and refused to play her game. Other men usually played because she was pretty.

About a nine or a ten, she thought as she heard the slam of the door and the revving motor of the departing bus. Even if he never smiled.

There were only a few people on the bus. He settled on the long back seat next to the window and watched the town again as the bus hissed, hummed, and grumbled past the stoplights. Soon they were in open country heading for Fresno.

The driver never went to Interstate 5 but took some back road on a shorter route. There was nothing to be seen out the window but manzanita bushes growing thickly, blanketing the hillsides. An older woman just ahead of him traveling with a young boy was unwrapping pieces of fried chicken from a brown paper bag as the boy watched for birds on the telephone wires. There were several Mexican men on the bus with the unmistakable look of aliens to one who knew what to look for. This was mid-August, and he figured they were heading for Fresno for the cotton season. He didn't envy them at all.

Before he knew it they were humming along through the flat plains that approached the San Joaquin Valley and the town of Fresno. Now the cotton and grapes stretched as far, it seemed, as the eye could see. Fig orchards rolled away behind him, and he began to feel a vague stirring deep within himself, a feeling akin to a hope that a destination could be made into a home. Under that feeling was a vague fear that the land would be hostile, and the people on it would put him to flight.

He looked out the window of the bus at the lush earth and contemplated his first day of freedom. His mind shifted back to his first day in federal prison fourteen years ago. He had begun his time at the super-max prison in Marion, Illinois.

He was the only arrival that day, and they gave him his

issue of clothing in the receiving department. A guard told him to carry his bundle of clothes and bedding to a TV room, where he was to wait until summoned by the receiving lieutenant.

There were six other men in the small TV room watching the television monitor on the wall. They merely glanced at Bill as he entered and turned their attention back to the TV. He remembered wanting a cigarette badly and hoped someone would take out a pack so he could ask for one. He took the only empty chair in the room, next to an effeminate homosexual, and put his bundle on the floor beside him.

A big man with an oversized head sat directly in front of the effeminate convict next to Bill, and he had barely sat down when the man next to him tapped the big convict on the shoulder and said, "Could you move to the left or right a little, please? I can't see over your head."

"Fuck you, punk! You move or get the fuck outta here," the man replied without even looking around. The man next to Bill got up and left without saying anything.

Bill felt embarrassed, because he had taken the only chair the man could have moved to. He would have offered it, but the guy left in a hurry. Something didn't seem quite right. The atmosphere in the room became charged, and a couple of the convicts kept glancing warily toward the door. The only one who remained totallly calm was the convict with the big head, who stared blissfully at the Donahue show.

The TV room door opened again, and Bill heard a couple of chair legs scrape as men jumped up to make room for the homosexual, who came back in the door with a ten-inch knife in his hand. Bill leaped to one side as the knife zipped by his head and plunged into the back of the convict in front of him.

The man didn't even know he had been stuck until he looked down and saw the knife sticking out the front of his chest. He tried to rise, but his assailant pulled the knife out and plunged it into him again. He sank to the floor, and the homosexual knelt down and kept stabbing him.

Bill grabbed his clothes and followed everyone else out of the room. As he left he could hear the knife clicking against the cement floor each time it went all the way through the man, who had probably died from the first wound. The killer kept muttering each time he stabbed the man, "Call me a punk, you motherfucker!"

Everyone who had been in the room was locked up in isolation until the authorities could determine exactly what had happened. Like the others, Bill insisted that he hadn't seen a thing. After a week he was released to the general population. But that incident had given him pause to think about the direction his life was taking.

Fourteen more years of violence and noise interspersed with mind-numbing boredom had convinced him he should try a new way of life. That was the main reason he was going to Fresno instead of back to Portland, Oregon, where he had grown up. All his friends in Portland were outlaws. His mother and father had been outlaws. His grandfather had been a bookie and safecracker. The odds against his changing in that environment were slim. Grandpa Malone would probably have made that about ten to one.

These past fourteen years he had taken up reading philosophy. He'd read Plato's *Dialogues* continuously and branched out into Kant and Schopenhauer. Much of the latter he didn't understand, but it all helped to fill the spiritual gap he felt within him. As a lifelong hustler who had grown up among outlaws, he had a profound distrust of organized religion. Philosophy had taught him that one can live an ethical life without religion. The metaphysical reasoning of Kant and Schopenhauer appealed to the outlaw in him. Today he felt that he could leave the outlaw life behind and live free. It was an exciting idea.

The afternoon was hot, and as the bus moved through Chinatown in Fresno he watched the winos stumbling along and the whores picking their way by them as they watched for the obviously out-of-place businessmen who drove by and walked nonchalantly as if they belonged here. The police slowly walked their beat, watching them all. He wasn't familiar with Fresno, but he found it reassuring that he was still familiar with people. The needs of the street people he watched now were simple and basic, wine, money, and sex. Some were just a bit more frantic in their pursuit than others. The police had a calming effect on the more desperate of them.

The late-afternoon sun felt like an oven as he emerged from the bus and walked through the back doors of the huge air-conditioned bus station. As he entered his knees suddenly felt weak, and he sat on a bench just inside the door to catch his breath. Suddenly he was beginning to feel free, and the sensation was a bit scary. A thought fluttered through his mind as he surveyed the room about him. Something Socrates had said about realizing the relation of pain and pleasure once his guards removed his chains.

He was starting to notice the women. All of them. His eyes took in their hips if they were walking, their face and breasts if they were sitting or standing. He began to develop a hard-on. He consulted the big clock on the wall, trying to tear his mind away from women. It was four-fifteen, and he realized he had to be at his parole officer's office by five. He was looking toward the front of the station to see if there were taxis there when his problem was solved by a big, middle-aged, florid-faced man who approached him from the café area of the bus terminal. He wore a blue Sears suit with white shirt and tie, and a pair of thick-soled wingtip shoes—none of which did much to disguise the big square look of a prison guard. They recognized each other at once.

"You must be Malone," the man said, walking right up to him.

"That's right," Bill replied, while rising and taking bag in hand.

"I'm Campbell, your parole officer," the man said, not offering to shake hands. "Let's get on the road."

Bill followed him from the station to a new Plymouth sedan. Campbell kept up a monologue as he drove.

"Not much to do but sign a few papers, then I'll drive you out to the Star Motel. I don't have any big speeches for you. You did fourteen years on a twenty-one-year sentence, so you got seven years of informal parole, which means you send me a report every month and let me know if you move. You know the rules and you know the law. Break either one and back you go. I'm not chickenshit, but I don't give many breaks. You got all that?"

"I got it," Bill replied.

"Fine. I think you will like this town," he said while pulling over in front of the big federal building. "You were arrested here, right?"

"Up the road," Bill said. "Madera."

"Good a place as any," Campbell replied, putting the car keys in his coat pocket.

Campbell's was a bare little office with white walls, a filing cabinet in one corner, a government-issue gray desk, and two metal chairs. Bill took a chair opposite the desk while Campbell removed his file from the cabinet and whooshed down across from him, adjusting his reading glasses. He began thumbing slowly through the file.

"Do you have a trade?" he queried.

"Yes," Bill answered. "Dishwasher."

Campbell looked over the rim of his glasses.

"Dishwasher?" he asked while peering to see if Bill was having a little joke.

"I don't know what else to call myself," Bill replied, looking him levelly in the eye. The exchange gave Bill the feeling of an unsuccessful parole hearing long ago, where the parole judge had gazed at him in almost exactly the same manner.

"Well, I guess that's a trade," Campbell answered, "but not one of the better ones."

"I'm good at it," Bill responded.

"I mean the pay!"

"I'll make enough to live." Bill now sounded defensive, even to his own ears.

"Look, Malone," Campbell said. "I am not deriding your occupation." He stressed "deriding" and "occupation," as if he had just learned them recently. "But I'm lookin' in your jacket here. Your first arrest was almost thirty years ago. This last bank job is the only heavy fall you took, but you got a little dope smuggling and some this and that here. You are now forty-three years old next month. Somehow I can't picture you slaving behind a hot steaming dish machine for twenty years or so for the bare minimum wage."

"I just did it fourteen years for nothing," Bill replied. "The minimum wage looks pretty good to me right now, boss."

Campbell blinked at the "boss," but he accepted it, confirming Bill's assumption that he was a former prison guard.

"Yeah," he responded, "but out here there's things like bills to pay, and I know from your jacket you never got to keep any of that money. How much you got on you right now?"

"About six hundred dollars," Bill replied.

"That won't last long, bud," Campbell muttered under a finger he was rubbing against his fleshy nose. "Look," he went on, "let's don't start off arguin', you want to wash dishes, okay. Just get a job within two weeks, because the Fresno police are complaining about you comin' here anyway and I don't want them on my ass. Now here's the rest of the drill. Don't rob no banks. If you get drunk and blow your money, don't come askin' me for rent money, or I will violate you for panhandling. I don't run no Starvation Army mission here. If you disremember a report and don't hear from me, send me two the next month. Now you got all that?"

"I got it," Bill told him.

"All right, bud," Campbell said, getting up and sliding the file back in the drawer of the cabinet. "I will now drive you to your new home, and good luck to you."

They took an overpass to the freeway, and Bill listened in silence to another of the monologues. He felt grateful that he had an old former prison guard for a parole officer. There was no devious bullshit about the man. He didn't even mind the "bud."

"Now this Star Motel is a good spot," he was saying. "When the new freeway came through, it missed them by a couple miles. They stayed open and they rent these little bungalows for forty-five a week. Even got a little swimming pool. Only thing is, it's about ten miles from downtown and no good bus service, but it's clean, and hell, if I was single I wouldn't mind it myself. I use it for an address for some of my new parolees, but there's none there now. You don't have to stay there over a week if you don't like it."

They pulled off the freeway at the Clinton overpass. Dusk was gathering, and Bill turned his head to watch the big gaudy glittering neon lights of motel row. It reminded him of the Strip coming to life in Las Vegas. A couple of miles on they turned down an almost deserted highway that obviously had died when the new freeway was built. The weeds along the edge had run amok from neglect, and large vacant spaces held the seedy, mournful remains of once busy places. Bill wanted to smell the land about him, but Campbell had the air conditioner on, so he kept his window up.

2.

The motel had a red neon star above the office. The grounds themselves were a well-kept oasis in a desert of neglect. The office was on the left end of a V-shaped drive of bungalows, all connected by their little one-car garages.

They entered the small office, and Campbell punched at a bell on the counter. The blare of a TV game show and the sound of arguing female voices could be heard from the living quarters in the rear.

A woman in her thirties appeared in the doorway. She was wearing a brown peasant blouse and a pair of tight tan shorts that reached mid-thigh. Her face was thin and appealing. Her breasts barely swelled beneath the blouse, but the rest of her body was sleek and voluptuous. Her legs were tanned and smooth, tapering to tiny feet encased in a pair of open leather sandals. Dark and lustrous long hair escaped around her face and shoulders from assorted combs and pins she had stuck in it here and there.

"Hi, you all," she said in a pleasant high-pitched voice.

"Howdy, Gail," Campbell replied, smiling. "This is your new customer, Bill Malone."

Bill clasped her warm hand as she reached for a rental form with the other.

"Well, Bill, if you've got forty-five bucks we're in business," she said while handing him a pen.

"I've got it," he replied. He filled in his name on the form. Below the space for name there was a blank labeled "Occupation." He paused a moment and filled it in—"Dishwasher." Campbell and the woman chatted as he filled out the form. He took a fifty-dollar bill from his pocket, and she rummaged beneath the counter for his change. Campbell stopped in the doorway on his way out.

"Hey, Gail," he said, "when is Tony coming home?"

"Should be the middle of next month," she replied, looking up and glancing at Bill with a slightly startled look in her eyes. He noticed her eyes were green, with big amber flecks close to the pupil, and felt a physical shock as they settled directly on his.

"Tell him hello for me," Campbell said as he left.

Gail handed him a key.

"Your room is 7A," she said. "It's right on the left of the horseshoe here, in front of the swimming pool. There are sheets and blankets on the bed, but you'll have to wash them yourself if you stay. The icebox and stove work, but be careful of the pilot light on the stove."

"No problem," he replied.

She began to move around the counter.

"I'll show you where your room is."

Bill held up his hand to stay her.

"That's not necessary." He smiled. "If I can't find it, you just keep the forty-five bucks."

"Gee, thank you," she laughed as he went out the door.

Campbell's Plymouth pulled out as he turned down the walkway and stopped at the swimming pool. Night was falling now, and the red neon star over the office blazed to life as he put his bag down and squatted near the edge of the water at the deep end. Other lights in amber cages like old gaslamps came on around the courtyard.

Lighting another Camel and drawing the smoke deeply into his lungs, he gazed at the reflection of the lights on the still surface of the azure water. Already a couple of moths were fluttering in long circles from a nearby light coming closer and closer to the light's reflection on the water.

It's just a matter of time, he thought, and no sooner had

he thought it than one of them hit the water like a tiny pelican.

"Jesus!" was the word that ran through his mind in a most unreligous sense. Jesus! I'm free! A calm feeling rose up along his backbone and settled about the base of his skull. Heart and mind began breaking free of gun towers, guards, noise, and turmoil. Fourteen years of mind-numbing tension began to recede from his head, leaving a luxurious peace in its wake.

As another moth ricocheted off the amber light and careened into the pool, he saw the woman coming toward him down the sidewalk. She had a butterfly net in her hand.

He stood up quickly and, taking out his key, turned toward 7A. She wanted to dip around the pool a bit, and chat with him about the bugs in the pool. Maybe ask a few hesitant semipersonal questions. He didn't feel up to it.

Inside the room he dropped his bag, removed the heavy khaki shirt, dropped it on the floor, leaned back against the closed door, and took a deep breath.

The room was old, but it was clean and neat. A doorway led into a tiny kitchenette with a small breakfast nook. On one side was a four-burner butane stove and a miniature icebox. They both faced a counter and sink with cupboards above.

He walked into the small bathroom first and flushed the toilet. Finding that it worked, he checked the shower. The bed was a big double with a box spring and mattress. It was made neatly with two pillows and a plain white commercial bedspread. There was worn carpet on the bedroom floor, and as he walked into the little kitchen he noticed old and torn linoleum on that floor. Everything seemed to work, although some of it just barely. Some old cheese and milk along with a withered carrot sat in the icebox. Another day wouldn't hurt.

When he opened the old creaky cupboard, a family of cockroaches ran for cover. He hated roaches, but he grinned at them. He'd been living with and battling millions of them for years in the dishroom at the prison. These free-world roaches should prove to be tame and timid compared to prison roaches.

He pulled the blankets down on the bed, exposing the clean white sheets. Stripping and dropping his clothes, he turned out the light on the wall switch and made his way to the bed. Heavy curtains across his pool-side window let in just a very faint red glow from the neon sign. He stretched out luxuriously naked between the sheets and drifted off to sleep to a faint sound of a net slurping and slapping water and leather shoe soles padding about on concrete.

He awoke to the sound of a hot rod revving up its motor. A high hot sun beat relentlessly at his curtains. Still the world seemed more peaceful to him than it had been in years. He felt totally relaxed. For fourteen years he had awakened to the sound of mop buckets, steam whistles, and yelling convicts as iron doors banged and work whistles blew.

The car motor revved again, and he sat up and drew his curtains back. A '55 Chevy, lowered in front to a few inches above the ground and shiny with polished chrome and a cherry-red paint job, idled at the side of the street directly beyond the swimming pool. A girl leaned against the driver's window with her back to him as she talked to the driver of the car. He couldn't see either of their faces, but the girl wore only a tiny string bikini, and her smooth tanned legs and valentine-shaped ass were breathtaking in the sunlight. Desire for a woman rose up in him so strong that it settled in his gums just below his teeth, where it throbbed like a toothache. He watched the sheet rise as if it had a tent pole beneath it. Jesus! he thought. I'm going to have to fuck before long. I've got to touch one of these women.

He jumped out of bed and donned the khakis, trying to

ignore his manhood hanging there like a cedar branch. He added a T-shirt and the uncomfortable government shoes, brushed his hair and teeth at the sink, and walked out into the hot sunlight. It looked to be close to noon.

As he locked his door and walked toward the pool, the girl turned from the revving Chevy and came striding toward him. Waiting at the edge of the pool, he saw the driver of the car, who looked to be a middle-aged Mexican with a big Pancho Villa mustache, watching her ass as she walked away. When she drew near him, the car roared away with a spray of roadside gravel.

The girl was beautiful. Her white bikini set off her tan skin and coal-black shoulder-length hair. She had the fully developed breasts and body of a mature woman, but he realized with dismay that she was young, very young, maybe thirteen or fourteen. As she looked at him hesitantly out of big golden-flecked green eyes, he saw a strong resemblance between her and the woman who managed the motel. He also realized she wasn't at all aware of her sexuality.

"Hi," she said, looking him directly in the eyes. "I'm June. My mother is the manager here."

"I'm Bill," he told her, sticking out his hand, which she solemnly took in hers.

"Momma told me to tell you you can swim in the pool if you want, and there's a washer and dryer next to the office."

"Well, thank you, June."

"I'll do your wash for you anytime you want me to for two dollars," she said.

"Well, I may take you up on that." He smiled at her. He couldn't help but smile at her. She was tall, must be close to five-nine. Her body seemed to have run off and left her trying to catch up. As they talked, her full lips kept twitching about her teeth trying to smile, yet she kept looking away with an inherent shyness as she shifted her weight from one foot to the other.

She blushed, and as he saw the spread of color about

her shoulders and her nipples rise like two rosebuds against the thin knitted top, he felt himself getting hard again.

Ashamed at his lack of control, he stepped closer to the pool and squatted there Indian-fashion, pulling a little sprig of clover from the lawn and nibbling at it.

June squatted, facing him, exactly the way he had, picked a bit of clover, and began nibbling it exactly as he was. He smiled at this unabashed mimicry. She snickered as if she were trying to keep from sneezing, and he laughed out loud. He laughed so hard he fell over, and she fell over exactly the same way, laughing as hard as he was. Now even the sun and fluffy clouds looked funny; the more June laughed with her high-pitched snicker, the more tickled he got. They couldn't stop.

"Have you two gone completely crazy?" He looked up and Gail was standing over them, a puzzled smile on her face. She was wearing tight white shorts with a red tank top and shirt and a pair of red sandals over bare feet. Bill sat up catching his breath while June ran and dived into the pool and began splashing toward the other end.

"Your daughter will probably grow up to be a clown." He smiled up at her.

"If she keeps growing, she may be two clowns," Gail replied, looking toward the splashing girl in the pool.

"Do you know how I can get downtown?" he asked, raising himself up off the grass. "I need to buy a few clothes and some shaving gear."

"There's a city bus that comes to the corner down there every hour," she said. "But if you want to go right now, you're in luck, because I'm on my way and I've got all day. So I'll take you wherever you need to go."

"Hey, that's fine," he said. He felt relieved, as the thought of finding a bus and getting to town and back had been intimidating him since he woke up. It was the little embarrassing things he dreaded, like having to ask the driver about the fare, where to get off, and all that. Things the average person wouldn't need to ask. He was relieved and grateful for her offer.

"June!" she was yelling, "you get out of that pool, get some decent clothes on, and cover the office till we get back." They watched as June climbed out the shallow end and began walking toward the office. About halfway across the lawn she slowed, looked back over her shoulder at Bill, and smiled and waved. He smiled and waved back.

"That's how you know for sure when a girl becomes a woman," Gail said to him. "They can't walk away from a man without looking back to see if he's watching."

"She's something to watch," Bill replied.

"Just be thankful you don't have to watch her twenty-four hours a day," she said as they walked along behind June toward the little garage by the office.

Bill wanted to laugh again when he saw her little yellow car. It was a 1968 Volkswagen Beetle, which made it over twenty years old, but it looked to be well kept and pampered.

"This is my baby," she remarked as he tried to settle his long legs in the passenger space beside her.

"Looks kind of like a lawn mower," he couldn't help but say. She looked at him with a hard grin.

"You might make a decent clown yourself," she said as they backed out and she deftly maneuvered the smooth-running Bug into the road.

As they drove away, the red Chevy pulled in near the cabin at the end of the horseshoe-shaped drive opposite the office. A young long-haired man in a pair of Levi's and no shirt walked toward the car from the cabin. A skinny girl in cut-off Levi's and halter top followed behind him.

"I wish that bastard would stay away from here," Gail muttered vehemently as they drove away.

"Who is he?" Bill inquired.

"I don't know his name," she said, "but I know his game. He's a dope dealer. I get a lot of dope fiends staying out here, because it's cheap and out of the way. He comes around two or three times a day, never gets out of his hot rod. I don't care what he's doing, but he keeps trying to mess with June."

"Have you talked to him about it?" he asked.

"It wouldn't do any good," she replied. "But I expect Tony, my husband, will have a few words for him when he comes home next month." She looked over at him and smiled.

They were entering the freeway heading toward downtown Fresno now. They both had their windows down, and the hot air felt good as it wafted through the little car. Bill gripped his door handle tightly every time she passed a truck in the slow lane. He felt as if he were riding in a little fragile plastic bubble puttering around these big iron monsters. It was all he could do to tear his eyes away from her legs as they moved about the floorboard, and her hands on the gearshift and steering wheel. Even the little heat waves ahead rising and writhing from the hot asphalt felt sensual.

"Fresno is a pretty hot town," he remarked.

"In more ways than one," she replied. "But I love it here. It kind of grows on you."

"I hope it will," he replied.

"June's only thirteen," she said to him. "She won't be fourteen until April, so you'll have to be careful around her. She thinks she's sexy already."

As she spoke she glanced over at him, and though she spoke in a light tone he could tell she was concerned about her girl's welfare. He didn't really know how to ease her mind. She was the first woman he'd talked with in a lot of years. Just the smell of her was divine and overpowering to his senses.

"She's safe around me. I don't bother little girls, but I can't guarantee the same with you. You're pretty sexy yourself," he added.

She laughed a sparkling clear sound, and he felt good that she wasn't unhappy at his overture.

"My goodness, a compliment. I haven't had one of those in years. I think my husband has beat up everyone in California, and most men are afraid to even talk to me," she said.

"In that case I withdraw my words," Bill said.

"No, no. He's in prison right now, so you're safe. How much time did you do, anyway?"

"I spent fourteen years in there."

"Fourteen years?" she exclaimed.

He held up his hand to stay her, but she continued trying to look at him and the road at the same time.

"I had a bank robbery conviction, but I couldn't get an early parole because of some charges I didn't get convicted of. I'm out now, and I'll admit I like women, and I'm looking at all the women, including you and June. I'm even trying to see the women in all these cars we're passing. But I'm not a child molester or a rapist or anything else you'd call a pervert, so your daughter is perfectly safe around me."

"I'm sorry," she said. "It's just that she's so damn innocent and naive."

"It's okay," he responded.

"But I knew you didn't have a sex crime on your record, and I knew you weren't an informer of some kind, so I did know a little about you. But fourteen years? My God. I don't see how you kept from going stir-crazy."

"How did you know that much?"

"Because Campbell doesn't bring me any of those." She smiled at him. "Now which is first, the clothes or the shaving gear?" she asked.

She turned off at an exit ramp, and he began seeing so many buildings next to each other that he felt something like claustrophobia, but soon they were driving out Ventura, a street of used-car lots and fast-food stands.

"Let's get the clothes first," he said.

She kept driving out Ventura until they reached a giant K Mart parking lot with a few other stores scattered around the complex. She pulled to the curb in front of a small plain store with an assortment of Levi's and pullover shirts displayed in the window. The sign above the display said "Jeans & Things."

"Come on," she said, getting out of the car. "A friend of my husband's owns this place. We'll get you a fair shake in here."

He carefully extracted himself from the Bug and followed her into the interior of the store. He couldn't help but notice the complicated but intriguing movement of her hips as she walked ahead of him. Just before she pulled open the door, she looked back at him and smiled and waved.

He laughed. She was downright sassy.

A young man with a clean-cut appearance who looked to be in his mid-thirties hurried around a counter and grasped Gail in a bear hug.

"Oh, Momma, where you been all my life?" he yelled.

She pried his hands and arms off her.

"Down, boy," she laughed. "I want you to meet a customer. Bill Malone, this is Richard Avakian."

Richard grasped Bill's outstretched hand.

"How may I serve you, pal?" he asked.

"Listen, Richard," Gail interjected, "this guy is just out of prison and needs to buy a few clothes. You can serve him by not pulling any of your slick 'Ahmed the rug merchant' bullshit."

"Hey," Richard replied, smiling and throwing his arms wide. "I'm your boy."

"I'm going over to the K Mart," Gail said. "Try not to rob him before I get back, okay, Richard?"

"Like I said," he said, smiling at her, "I'm your boy."

They both watched her as she walked to the door. They kept watching through the window as she crossed the parking lot toward K Mart.

"That's one extra-fine woman," Richard said pensively. "I wish Tony wasn't her old man, because I'd love to ask for some of that. Do you know him?"

"What's his last name?" Bill asked.

"Camacho. They call him Tough Tony. He's a biker," Richard replied.

Bill was startled by Richard's remark. He had known Tough Tony well in prison but had never visualized him having a wife like Gail.

"I've done time with him, and he turned out to be a pretty good friend of mine. I wish you hadn't told me, though. I was thinking along the same lines you were," Bill said.

"At least we can keep on dreaming about it," Richard muttered, as they stood watching Gail forlornly like two sailors gazing at land from a departing ship.

"Well, hell, let's find you some clothes." Richard slapped his hands together and walked toward a rack of Levi's. "What size you wear, and what do you need?"

Bill followed along behind him.

"Thirty-one thirty-four. Maybe a couple pair of Levi's to work in and a pair of bon aroos for weekends, if you have any." He used the term "bon aroos," prison slang for dressy clothes, without thinking, but Richard seemed to understand him.

"I got 'em, man. I got another two rooms here stacked full of clothes and shoes. We'll find everything you need here somewhere." He spoke while fumbling through the rack of Levi's. "Are you from Fresno, then?"

"Portland," Bill replied, "but the feds like you to parole to where you were arrested."

"Oh, yeah," Richard said, while extracting two pair of Levi's from the rack.

"These are thirty-two thirty-four, prewashed, but I think they will shrink some more." He handed them to Bill. "You can try them on in that room over there."

He felt good as he dropped the khakis and stood barefoot looking at himself in the dressing-room mirror. The pants were a bit loose at the waist, but not much. The smell of new Levi's and the feel of soft carpet against his feet were wonderful. He left the khakis and government shoes in the dressing room.

As he left the changing room, a big man wearing Levi's and cowboy boots came into the store and walked over toward Richard. Richard acted as if he were brushing some lint off his sleeve near the shoulder, and the man walked on by and stood in front of the shirt rack as if inspecting the shirts carefully.

Richard turned back to Bill and said, "Hey, man, you can tap-dance in them duds!"

When he said that, Bill knew for certain that this man was a thief of some kind, and the store was more than likely just a front. Richard's understanding "bon aroos" had been one clue to his nature, the brush-off had been a second, and the tap-dance remark had confirmed it.

Underworld people use the brush-off as a way of saying "Don't approach me now." That's what Richard had been telling the big man who was about to speak to him. "Tap dancing" is what thieves call blending in with society and passing unnoticed while engaged in criminal schemes.

In using these codes, Richard had been feeling him out. And although Bill was put at ease by learning that he was dealing with one of his own kind, he decided not to respond. He liked this man, but Richard obviously belonged to the world that Bill had made up his mind to keep at arm's length. There was no future in attempting to form a friendship with him.

Richard took the other pair of Levi's from him and walked toward the counter. Bill studied him as he moved gracefully across the carpet. He was lean, with a neatly trimmed mustache, coal-black hair, and dark brown eyes that emphatically declared his Armenian heritage.

"Where did you do your time?"

"Marion and Lompoc," Bill answered.

"Must have been a while," Richard remarked while laying the pants on the counter.

"Fourteen years."

Richard looked at him for a long second or two, dark eyes probing his face as Bill gazed steadily back.

"What was your name again?" Richard asked. "I never catch the name on the introduction."

"Bill Malone."

"Well look here, Bill," Richard said as he walked toward a shirt rack. "These Levi's have a price on them of twenty-eight dollars. You're getting them for what they cost me, which is about twelve bucks a pair, so whatever else of this junk you buy, just figure on paying less than half the marked price. How does that sound from a Persian rug merchant?" Richard smiled at him.

"Sounds real good with my bankroll." Bill smiled back. "I hope I don't wind up washing your windows or sweeping the floor."

"Never happen," Richard replied.

By the time Gail came walking back into the cool interior of the store there was a good-sized pile of clothes on the counter, and Bill was wearing a tie-dyed T-shirt and still walking around in his socks.

"Richard!" she exclaimed. "You'd better not have sold him a bunch of those tie-dyes. You know damn well they're out of style!"

"C'mon, Gail," Richard shot back, "I gave him six of them, for Christ's sake, and they're not all the way out. I still wear them myself.

"Hey, you guys, come on!" he added. "I got something to show you!" He led the way behind the counter and through a small cluttered office to a storeroom at the back and opened the door with a flourish.

Boxes of running shoes were piled all about the room halfway to the ceiling, all different brands. They weren't stacked but were lying about as if thrown there. Some of the box tops were off and shoes spilled out among the boxes.

"These are seconds," he said proudly. "Factory defects. I got 'em for five bucks a pair. Every name brand you can think of, and most of them you can't even find the flaw. You can have a few pairs at my price."

Gail and Bill were already digging among the boxes. She found identical Nikes for herself and June, and Bill picked out two pairs of expensive New Balance running shoes.

When it came time to pay, Richard quoted a ridiculously low price for Bill's stuff, and wouldn't charge Gail at all for her two pairs of shoes. He walked to the Bug with them, helping carry the clothes, and kept standing there after they were seated and ready to go.

"How do those New Balances feel?" he asked Bill.

"Like a million bucks."

"Well, listen, man, you drop back by and see me before long," he told Bill sincerely.

"I'll do that," Bill replied.

"Hey, Richard," Gail said as she got the Bug running, "you sure are being nice today, and I do appreciate the shoes. Is there any special reason or occasion that I don't know about?" She smiled out the window at him.

"It's not every day that Bill Malone comes home from prison and comes to my store."

"Oh, you two already know each other."

"No," Richard replied, "but I've heard about him. He's a fucking legend in this town." He half waved at Bill and walked back toward his store.

"What did he mean by that?" she asked, pulling out into the traffic.

"I don't know," Bill replied. "He must have me mixed up with someone else."

"I doubt that very much, especially when he's giving you a discount on what he believes about you." She grinned.

"I used to come here to Fresno a lot. I smuggled pot, and we flew in some loads to the Tulare and Madera airports. I had a couple of fistfights with these cowboys around here. Nothing on the scale of your husband, but I did win them. These Fresno boys don't think highly of people from Oregon, so it was a bit difficult there for a while.

"Then I robbed a bank here and almost got away with it. It's easy to say 'almost' fourteen years later, but I did come close. This Richard looks to be about ten years younger than me. He comes from a generation that idolizes all those old bandits, I guess. Most people would believe I'm just stupid. He sees it differently. But maybe he doesn't. Maybe he thinks my ignorance is legendary."

She seemed to accept his explanation.

But she kept glancing at him as she drove. Suddenly he realized he was hungry. At the same instant, he realized he could have anything he wanted to eat. Riding in a Volkswagen downtown, with a beautiful woman, all new clothes and shoes that felt like walking on air. He wanted to taste all the smells, even the baking heat and exhaust fumes. Life was good again. In a matter of twenty-four hours he had traveled from hell to paradise. He leaned back in the seat and grinned.

"Gail, how do you feel about pizza and beer?"

"You just said the magic words." She smiled and speeded up some.

3.

Half a pitcher of beer in a dim cool pizza parlor made him a bit woozy, but the pizza was good. They bought a small one for June, and as they drove back he asked her to stop at a supermarket.

The displays that assailed him as he walked into the quiet frigid market were astounding. He felt like Alice in Wonderland. All around were things he had only dreamed about the past fourteen years. Raw oysters, shrimp, clams, artichokes, honeydew melons, fresh pineapple. The list went on and on.

Gail followed along as he loaded oysters and shrimp into his cart. He bought a package of plastic spoons and forks. She watched as he put in a sponge, steel wool, Pine Sol, and laundry soap.

Back in the car he opened a jar of oysters as she drove and began eating them from the jar.

"My goodness," she exclaimed. "Yuck! I hope I don't get sick."

"I can't wait any longer." He grinned at her while raising a large slimy oyster on a plastic fork. When he finished the oysters, he drank the juice and put the empty jar in the sack on the back floorboard.

June came running from the office to meet them as the Bug pulled to a stop in front of the little office. She was dressed in a revealing thin cotton sunsuit that must have belonged to Gail, as it was too tight and too short for her. It was white with big purple flowers. She also had on sandals and a straw hat with a wide purple ribbon around it that fell in the back into her long hair. She was breathtaking. Bill wanted to laugh, but saw instantly that Gail wasn't amused at all.

"Damm it, June," she exclaimed as she jumped from the car, "is that what you call decent clothes?"

Bill began gathering some of his goods to escape the impending argument, but June was an old hand at the game and there wasn't any argument. Before he made the second trip to his room, June was sitting on the office step eating pizza and trying on her running shoes.

Bill took off his clothes and piled them along with his purchases and everything else in the room on the bed. The dresser had a mirror mounted over it, and he detached it with a fingernail clipper and placed it on the bed also. He hacked off most of the legs of a pair of government khakis with a single-edge razor blade, then pulled on the shorts and felt better in the stifling hot room. He opened the door and all the windows and went to work.

Starting with the small kitchen, he scrubbed everything, walls, floor, ceiling, cabinets, icebox, and stove. Then he worked his way into the bathroom and out to his bedroom. The place wasn't dirty but he felt a compulsive need to scrub it completely. He'd scrubbed every cell he had ever moved into in prison. The only space he spared was where a daddy longlegs hung at the corner of the bathroom ceiling near a small window. He'd had a grass spider in his cell off and on for years, so he grew instantly fond of the daddy longlegs. He hoped the spider wouldn't walk on him at night. Such an act would definitely sever their relationship.

When he hit the bedroom wet with sweat and soapy water, June wandered in in her sunsuit and offered to help. He declined her offer while trying to ignore her unconscious provocation. He got rid of her by promising her he'd swim with her when he finished. She lingered awhile, looking carefully at the tattoos on his chest and arms, and finally went out without commenting.

When he'd finished cleaning his rooms, Gail came out with a big pitcher of lemonade and joined him and June in the pool. She had on a bikini exactly like June's. Her breasts were small, like little oranges, and her body was trim and lithe as a dancer's, with a small waist and prominent rib cage. Her hips were full and wider than average, but pleasing to the eye. They gave her a lithe but lush look. She and June both swam without bathing caps, and their long hair floated free in the blue water.

The water was glorious, and Bill floated in it wearing his khaki cutoffs. Then he stood in the shallow end with a glass of lemonade that Gail had handed him. The boy and girl from the end room had been sunning at the edge when Bill dived into the pool. After a few furtive looks at him, they got up and walked to their room. He wondered if he looked somehow menacing to them.

"You're built like a brick shit house!" Gail said to him as he reached for the lemonade.

June giggled from the other end of the pool. He didn't know what to say, so he just smiled at her. The hours in the pool with them stretched into one of the most pleasing afternoons in his entire life. As the sun began to set, so too did his troubled mind. The detritus of the cage seemed to float gently away from him.

Awkward moments arose when the two women tried to play with him or ride him in the water. They were playful girls. He was terrified of their touch, and though Gail caught on right away, June seemed a bit put out and perplexed by his refusal of contact. The first time June sat on his shoulders she hadn't been in the water yet. Her warm thighs on either side of his neck and shoulders was maddening. He dumped her into the water and wouldn't let her back on. Gail seemed to be aware of his predicament and yelled at her daughter: "Leave him alone, June. He isn't a horse for you to ride." June backed off some, but Bill could tell she was puzzled by anyone who didn't like to play. Before long she was riding Gail over her mother's half-hearted protests. It would take Bill a long time to get the feel and smell of those warm thighs gripping his neck out of his mind.

He lay on the warm cement apron of the pool between Gail and June and watched the sun dive like an orange ball into the horizon. Gail got up to go turn on the motel lights, and suddenly hunger overcame him again. Sitting up and looking through a space in the cabins, he saw a sign high above others near the freeway. "Ferraro's," it blinked to the world.

"What's Ferraro's?" he asked June.

"Kind of an Italian place," she answered. "Sort of a smorsg—smorger—" She began to giggle.

"Smorgasbord?"

"Uh-huh," she replied.

"Let's ask Gail if we can all go eat over there."

"Okay," she said enthusiastically, jumping up. He could tell she loved the idea.

Gail had donned a long housedress and stood behind the counter.

"I can't go," she said. "I have to stay here at the office. I was going to ask you to have a TV dinner with June and me, but I'll tell you what. You two can go and bring me back one of their charcoal-broiled hamburgers and we'll call it even."

"That's a deal!" June yelped, and headed behind the counter to change clothes.

"She'll cost you a fortune over there," Gail said to him.

"I don't care," he replied. "I feel rich right now anyway." He went to his room to change.

He waited for June in front of the office, thinking they would walk around the road to the freeway. But June took his hand and led him to the back of the motel grounds.

"We'll cut across the field," she told him.

He looked dubiously at the field of thick weeds and high johnsongrass. It resembled a swamp with old tires, rusty cans, and empty wine bottles strewn around. He didn't want to soil his new running shoes, but he noticed June had hers on also. She was dressed in tight Levi's and a T-shirt.

"Just hold my hand," she said. "I know a trail," and they set off straight for the sign.

4.

Joel Allen Campbell came trudging in from his garden and plopped into an old rocking chair on his screened-in back porch. He'd been in the hot sun most of this Saturday hanging wet burlap to protect his vegetables from the blazing sun.

Standing six feet tall and weighing 250 pounds, Campbell was a square-looking man with big bones. The humid Fresno heat sweated him up easily. With his sixty-second birthday approaching, there were times the heat made him feel old. He'd spent most of the day working in his garden while thinking about Bill Malone. There was something about this aspiring dishwasher that continued to gnaw at the edge of his mind. A complete study of the man's file had only exacerbated his curiosity.

Sally walked out of the kitchen in a thin cotton dress and leaned against the arm of the rocker. He felt a shocking chill on the back of his sweating neck and jumped forward. She laughed and handed him a sixteen-ounce can of Coors beer.

"You'll never get used to that, Big Joe," she said, smiling down at him as he popped the top.

Sweet Sally, he thought. She refused to grow old and only got more beautiful. It seemed that some inner beauty kept etching her features until her age lines became decorations instead of the signs of a lurking mortality. She was still as trim as the day they met.

He'd been a fearsome linebacker at a small Wisconsin high school. Thus the appellation "Big Joe." Sally was a cheerleader. Many local folk thought he was pro material, but caught in the commie scare of the early fifties, Joe took the patriotic route. He married Sally right out of high school and joined the army.

He towed her around the world like a barge from country to country for twenty years, while she told him he was the best top sergeant this man's army ever had. She was still his cheerleader. The only time she ever put her foot all the way down was when he reached the twenty-year mark. He'd decided to re-up. She'd decided he would keep his promise to retire after twenty years. Sitting here almost content with a beer in his hand, he was glad she had been so forceful for a change.

He mustered out at Fort Leavenworth in 1973, walked across the compound, and took a job as a prison guard. Ten more years in government service and he could retire with a thirty-year pension. He didn't much care for being a prison guard, but the work got him interested in criminal justice to the point where he did not retire in '83. He took a job as a parole officer instead. After almost seven years, he was still glad he had kept on working.

The transition from soldier to prison guard was easy. In many ways the work and attitudes of his fellow guards were about the same as army life. The Bureau of Prisons is a vast bureacracy, and it hires all the former—and even failed—soldiers it can get. Men who don't mind obeying orders and have a military propensity to view convicts as captured enemy. Men used to wearing uniforms and getting by on minimal paychecks. The attitude dovetails nicely with BOP aims and goals.

Campbell began as a correctional officer. A private in this new army. Making senior correctional officer was the next step—a position approximating a corporal in the service. He went quickly to sergeant and then lieutenant, which was the end of the line for an old retired soldier. Above lieutenants were captains, and over them associate wardens, deputy wardens, and wardens. These ranks were like higher officer ranks in the military.

The ten years he spent working at USP Leavenworth were sometimes boring and uneventful, but eventually something always happened. Among convicts and inmates, bizarre incidents were bound to happen frequently. About the time he thought he had seen it all, something would come along that would impress on him that he hadn't seen anything yet. He talked to Sally about everything, but some things had taken six months or more to tell her, feeding her bits and pieces until she finally got the picture.

Like the time early in his new career when he heard maniacal laughter from the third-tier shower area in a cellblock. As he walked up the stairs to check it out, he noticed a group of outlaw bikers looking into the shower and laughing like hell. He remembered the time as being around three o'clock in the afternoon. It had been nearing four o'clock, when all activities would be suspended and all inmates would go to their cells for the daily standing count.

When he came off the stairwell, he noticed that only one showerhead was being used in the communal eight-man shower. He also noticed that now there were many convicts milling around watching—some laughing, others just observing with their jaws dropped open.

Big Joe looked in the shower and encountered a scene that would be freeze-dried and preserved in his memory forever.

A huge convict who went by the name Waffle Iron was standing next to the stream of water coming from the shower. He weighed around three hundred pounds, and they called him Waffle Iron because of the scars that a severe case of acne had left him with.

He was standing next to the water with his little dick in his hand, covered from head to toe with soapsuds and baby oil. As he stroked his meat, he had a faraway look in his eye and a long plastic shampoo bottle halfway up his ass. After every few strokes with his hand, he kicked the shampoo bottle with his heel, sending it further with each kick on its journey up his ass. A few convicts began edging away when Campbell arrived, but the majority of them kept laughing hysterically. Especially when Waffle Iron grunted after a particularly successful heel kick. The big, nasty-looking convict paid Campbell no mind at all. Cons were yelling, "Get it all, Waffle!" "Get it, man!"

By this time, Big Joe was a senior officer specialist, or at least that's what his new name tag said. This was a situation that hadn't been covered in training class. But he was in charge of the cellblock and had to do or say something. The shampoo bottle was disappearing at an alarming rate. So what he said was:

"All right, men, don't be gathering up like this, and everyone better be in his fucking cell at count time."

He walked back to the office, wondering if there was some rule on the books about a man kicking a shampoo bottle up his ass. Another rule could be made to fit if there wasn't, but he decided to let this one pass. What really bothered him was the laughter. He didn't see the humor at all, and there was the rub.

It didn't take him long to realize that federal prisons serve a dual purpose. They hold criminals who prey on society from the most sophisticated bank scammers down to the dope fiends who rob tellers. But they are also a dumping ground for the mentally ill. Many of them are so violent and paranoid that they have to be kept sedated with mind-altering drugs like Thorazine and Prolixin. Over the years, he had observed cons who made Waffle Iron look like a good citizen. He couldn't help but wonder what fourteen years of dealing with monstrously sick neighbors had done to Malone's personality. He'd gone in as one of the more sophisticated types. His code was certainly the hard-core convict code, which was the main reason he'd never made an early parole.

That was probably bullshit about his wanting a dish-washing job. He probably knew a restaurant owner who would cover for him by saying he was employed there. Maybe even give him a weekly check to cash and return.

A shuck job, as convicts call it. Campbell had nothing to go on yet, but he assumed that Malone had some kind of score to settle here in Fresno—otherwise he would have gone home. He resolved to watch Malone as closely as possible, but considering his caseload that wouldn't be as close as he'd like it to be.

"Penny for your thoughts, Big Joe," Sally said, running her hand over his stubby hair and ears.

"I'm thinking about a guy who wants to be a dishwasher," he replied.

"My goodness, that sounds like an attainable goal," she laughed.

"Hey, you're sweating yourself." He grinned up at her.

"Let's go have a shower," she replied in a tone of voice he loved to hear.

5.

Richard Avakian was sitting with his cousin, Pete, and Big Alfred Perry in his office at the back of his clothing store. Richard had a gram of crank out on the glass top of his desk, and though the meeting was for a specific purpose, they were snorting it and telling war stories. Big Al was talking about a fight he had had with a fellow biker in a bar recently.

"We're fighting there by the pool table and this fool is giving me a hard time. I mean he was fast and hitting hard, so I used my weight to push him back and I bend him over so he's layin' on the pool table. Then I pull out my buck knife and stab him in the chest. Well, the fuckin' blade hits one a' them Nazi medals on his chest and breaks. I'm standin' there over him with just a knife handle in my hand.

" 'You son of a bitch, you broke my knife!' " I told him.

" 'Don't stab me again and I'll buy you a new one,' he says."

They all laughed, and Richard introduced a more serious tone into the conversation.

"Okay. Here's the deal. We've talked about it some and thought about it and here's what we're gonna do. Al, you're gonna sell all the crank around here, but I want you to get it all from me, or if I'm out, get it locally. No more going to them people up in Oakland or L.A. for supply. If you're dealin' with me, I don't want you dealin' with outsiders, because it could bring heat, and with these new laws, dealin' drugs is no joke anymore. The feds will give you life in a fuckin' heartbeat."

"But what if everyone around here runs dry?" Big Al asked.

"Then you just don't do none until we get some," Pete told him. "It ain't like you're gonna fuckin' go bankrupt."

"Yeah, we've just got to keep all our business here in Fresno where we know everyone," Richard agreed. "It's the safest way. If we run dry, then it's just famine for a while."

"I guess I can live with that as long as I'm the only one doing any crank here," Big Al said.

"That's the other part of the deal," Richard told him. "You have the exclusive rights to sell crank here, and I won't sell it to no one but you. Pete here has the coke and smack and I have the weed, so we won't step on each other's toes."

"Hey, that reminds me, them Sandinistas are selling heroin now," Pete said.

"What? I've never heard of the Sandino family doing any dope," Richard said. He and Big Al were both looking at Pete as if he was crazy.

"Well, they are for a fact. Florence told me."

"The Glove's daughter told you that?" Big Al asked incredulously.

"Yeah, she told me her two brothers, Fred Junior and Joey, are doing business with these Mexicans here. Perfecto is one of their main people. You know him, don't you, Richard?"

"Yeah, I've seen him, drives a red lowrider Chevy. Looks like a gopher."

"That's him," Pete said.

"It's still hard to believe. That family would never touch dope. I'll bet Small Bob ain't in on that play. The Glove could be, but I'll bet those two are on the sneak with that deal," Richard said.

"Speaking of the Glove, how does he feel about an Armenian fucking his daughter? Tuppin' his ewe lamb, so to speak?" Big Al asked Pete with a smile.

"He don't know it yet," Pete replied, looking uncomfortable about the subject.

"You'd better keep it that way," Richard said.

"I guess if anyone should know, you should," Pete said, and put another lump of crank on the tip of his knife and brought it to his nostril. He snorted it with a loud sucking sound.

"It's not something I like to think about," Richard said. "I've got four store-bought teeth and a crooked bite on my jaw to remind me of the son of a bitch."

"How did you get into a fight with him?" Big Al asked. "I mean, you ain't known as a bad-ass around here."

"Ah, it was kind of an accident, you know. All my life I'd been hearing from my dad and uncles how these wops hate Armenians, but I never put much stock in it. I guess there's not enough Jews here for them to hate, so they focus on us. There are more Armenians around here than about anywhere. Just look at the names that end with 'ian'.

"One night I'm up at my uncle Sam Bedrosian's all-night diner. It's about three in the morning and Sam had to go out, so I took over the counter for a while. Well, here comes Fred the Glove and a couple of his guinea buddies. They're all drunk, lit up like Christmas trees. So Fred starts baiting me. At first I think he's being sociable.

" 'Hey, you're Armenian aren't you?' Fred asks me.

"I say, 'Yeah'. He says, 'Man, there's been some really great Armenians. One of the best architects that ever lived was an Armenian.' I say, 'Yeah? Who was that? I don't know of any Armenian architects.'

'Well, he was the greatest landscape architect that ever lived. His name was Erosian,' he says.

" 'Well, I never heard of him,' I said.

" 'You might know him by his first name. His first name was Soil,' he says.

"I didn't catch it at first. I'm standing there with a glass sugar shaker in my hand and him and these two greaseballs are laughin', har, har, har. Soil erosion, you know.

"When I caught on, I hit him in the head with the sugar glass. That's about all I recall," Richard recounted. "He drug me over that counter and beat the holy shit out of me. I thought I'd been hit by a fuckin' bulldozer. A cop happened by and stopped it, and that's one time I'm glad a cop happened by. I woke up in the hospital. Much longer, it could have been the fuckin' morgue."

"I guess he's as tough as they say he is," Big Al said.

"You'll need more than a buck knife on him," Pete mused.

"I ever have any problems with his crew, I got a Uzi for his ass," Big Al said, as he dug his knife blade into the rapidly diminishing pile of crank on Richard's desktop.

"This tough-guy stuff reminds me, did you notice that guy in my store when you came in, Al?"

"The guy was there when you brushed me off?"

"That's him. His name is Bill Malone, smooth-lookin' dude in his early forties. Does his name ring a bell?"

"I don't recall it," Al replied.

"I heard some talk about him off and on, but I was just a sprout when he was around here before," Pete said.

"He just got out of prison," Richard continued. "Been down fourteen years now. I was just getting into weed when he came on the scene. He's from Portland, but I remember when he first hit town. He was bringing in some good loads of pot.

"He was working with Big Ed Arkin up there at Coarsegold in the foothills. Big Ed finally burned him for a load. This guy went up there to Ed's house and tied him up. Ed didn't have the money to pay him, so Malone has him calling all his runners telling them to bring money. As they get there, Malone is tying them up and taking the money.

"By about three a.m., he's got five of them in a pile, and by some fluke, the feds pick that morning to raid Big Ed's house.

"When they bust in, Malone crashes through a plate-glass window and gets away. He left a paper sack there with sixty-nine thousand dollars in it. Most of the guys in the pile had been indicted with Big Ed, so the feds just untied them and scooped them up right there. They caught Malone about twenty miles away, and Big Ed ratted on him.

"He went to trial in Madera for robbery, and while he was out on bail, he robbed a bank in Fresno. He beat the case on Big Ed but got convicted on the bank job."

"His luck was pretty thin right about there," Pete said.

"Yeah, well, that's just background. I remember when he was around here some of these cowboys tested him a few times and he beat up just about every bully around this town. They remember him well."

"He don't look so tough," Al said.

"That's just it," Richard said. "He don't look it at all. I mean, he's well-mannered and polite, but don't let that fool you. That monkey fights like a fuckin' wolverine."

"What's he doing back here?" Pete asked.

"I don't know, and he's playing the ig on me in conversation. Acting like a total square. He's staying out at the Star, that motel that Tough Tony's old lady runs."

"Well, if he gets too close to that, you may see a real good fight when Tony gets back," Al said.

"I doubt that," Richard said. "Malone would go through Tony like a dose a' Epsom salts. We better at least keep an eye on him, because if he's back into weed, we'll have to let him know how things work around here now."

Richard and Pete lingered on in the office until they heard Big Al's motorcycle rev up and go popping toward the highway.

"I don't want to hear any more talk about Florence's pussy," Pete told Richard. "So you pull Al aside and I won't have to."

"Hey, man, we didn't know you was in love, but you know he meant no disrespect," Richard replied. "I'll tell him, so don't get touchy on me."

"Well, I am in love, and we're getting married as soon as

we figure out a way to keep her old man and my mother from killing us both," he said.

"Good luck with that," Richard told him, then he added as an afterthought, "You know, people like Malone and Tough Tony with them old-time values and codes are like dinosaurs now. They still believe in fist-fighting and personal honor, while we're out here dealing with dope babies and drive-by shooters. I think maybe Malone is going to square up. He probably knows his kind don't fit no more."

"I guess that's progress," Pete said.

"We call it that, but I think the dinosaurs did it better," Richard told him.

6.

Ferraro's was a pretty nice place to eat, Bill was thinking as he followed June into the cool interior of the restaurant, which opened onto a cozy TV bar. On the kitchen side was a hickory grill for burgers and steaks. Next to the grill was a buffet counter featuring cracked-crab salad and the day's main courses, chicken and prime rib roast. Interspersed with these dishes was an assortment of salads, pastas, soups, and other dishes, all done up Italian-style.

The tables were covered with long red-and-white-checked tablecloths, and each was decorated with a vase of fresh flowers and a large candle in a chopped-down wine flask.

Bill paid a pleasant-looking woman behind the cash register seven-fifty each for June and him to eat from the buffet counter. Bill told her he wanted a beer with his meal, and she told him someone would bring it to his table from the bar.

Then she noticed June, and her eyes lit up.

"Hey, June Bug!" she exclaimed, coming around the counter to hug June. "Long time no see."

"Hi, Mrs. Ferraro," June mumbled, trying not to be embarrassed by the attention.

"My gosh, you are getting big and pretty," the woman said admiringly. June looked at her new tennis shoes.

"So, who is this handsome gentleman?" the woman asked, looking at Bill.

"Oh, sorry, Mrs. Ferraro, this is Bill Malone. He's staying over at our place for a while."

"I'm Regina Ferraro, the boss's wife and slave," the woman said, smiling and offering her hand.

"Glad to meet you," Bill replied, taking her soft hand in his.

Bill looked her over carefully. She was a short, stout woman of early middle age, very neat and proper-looking in a white blouse buttoned to the throat and a mid-calf-length black skirt. Silver-and-turquoise earrings dangled from her ears, and a pair of black-framed reading glasses hung from a gold chain around her neck.

Pleasant and prosperous was the impression she gave, but a closer look revealed something forceful and intractable in her bearing.

"You two dig in," she said, turning back to the counter as a man and woman entered. "I'll be along to chat if I have time."

Traveling down a buffet line with June was an adventure. He was content with prime rib, cracked crab, and a spinach salad with mushrooms and olives. June loaded enough on her tray for two people, then giggled as she picked mushrooms out of the spinach salad with a pair of salad tongs. Bill left her there and carried his tray over to the table.

As he took his chair, a copper-colored black woman came charging from the bar with a Coors beer on a tray. Stopping at his table, she banged the beer down with a vengeance.

"One cold one," she said. "You pay at the register," and she hurried on without looking at him.

Bill marveled at her rudeness. It didn't seem to fit with the laid-back decor. As she hurried out toward the kitchen, he noticed large sweat stains at the armpits of her uniform and the small of her back. He guessed maybe she was overworked and underpaid. She was certainly good-looking.

June labored under the weight of her tray as she sat down across from him.

"June, you'll never eat all that. There's enough on that tray for a whole family."

"I'm getting a doggie bag for my mom."

"There's a sign on the counter there saying no take-out bags."

"That don't include me," she replied, happily biting into a chicken leg. Bill couldn't help watching her as she ate. She shoveled it down like a hungry convict.

Regina Ferraro ambled over to their table with an empty plastic bag in one hand and a cup of coffee in the other. Bill rose to pull out a chair for her, and as he did, he noticed June chugalugging the last of his beer.

"Here, June," the woman said, laying the bag near June's elbow.

"Hey, Mrs. Ferraro," June said between bites. "Do you need a dishwasher? He's a dishwasher and he's looking for a job."

"Do I ever need a dishwasher!" She smiled at Bill. "Are you really looking for a job?"

"I suppose I am." Bill smiled back at her.

"Well, I need one urgently," she said. "We don't even have one right now, and Leona, my waitress, is having to do them. She's threatening to quit if I don't get one by Monday. Do you think you could start Monday?"

"I can start Monday if I decide to take the job," he replied.

"Well, look," she said. "You will be working for me. I've just had a big argument with my husband, George. He's been hiring nothing but winos and paying them immoral wages, and they have been doing immoral work. We can't keep one over three days, and they usually come to work drunk. George agreed finally to let me hire the help, and I plan to pay a decent wage."

"What do you call a decent wage?"

"Our buffet is open from noon to nine p.m. You'd be coming in at twelve-thirty to eat before you start at one, and you'd work until nine. We're closed on Sundays. I'll pay you five dollars an hour and time and a half if you want to work Saturdays also. The busboys and my waitress all go to the buffet line and help serve people when they aren't busy. I'd expect the same from you, and I'd expect you to show up regularly for work."

Bill thought it over quickly in his mind. The pay sounded as good as he'd probably get anywhere.

"Tell you what I'll do," he said to her. "I'll take the job, and I'll work at least some Saturdays, but I won't serve anyone on the buffet. I'll wash the dishes."

She gazed at him for a long moment.

"I'll see you Monday, Mr. Malone," she said, and got up to go back to the cash register.

"Well, that's it, June Bug. Looks like you've put me to work," Bill said. "Now how about going over there and ordering a burger for your mom?"

"I've got all this stuff," June said, while loading the bag. "She won't want a hamburger with all this."

"Well, go order it anyway."

"There's no need to, really."

"Yes there is, June. I told her I would bring her a hamburger, and when you tell someone you'll do something you should always do it."

She headed for the grill, and Bill wandered into the little bar for another beer, hoping she wouldn't follow him and try to drink this one also.

When June was ready she came to the door of the bar. He hated to leave. The music was mellow, and he'd been exchanging glances with a pretty cocktail waitress. When he paid for the hamburger, Regina wouldn't accept the money for the beer.

"It's on the house." She smiled at him. "You get one a day free while you're on the job."

"He's not a wino, he's a beero," June said to her as they went out the door.

"Well, that's a big improvement, dear," Regina shot back. "You tell your mama to come see me soon!"

They walked across Ferraro's dimly lit back parking area

to the small fence at the edge of the field. After they were over the fence, June took his hand and led him through the weeds and refuse as if it were daylight.

When they reached the motel grounds, June thanked him for the dinner, then shocked him by asking, "Would you like to kiss me goodnight?"

"Goddammit, June!" he exclaimed, stepping back.

She ran giggling up the walk to the office. Her giggle made him laugh. She sounded like a horse choking on an apple.

7.

Inside the motel room he stripped naked and laid his clothes on the dresser. As he moved in front of the mirror he kept his eyes averted from his image. During his first year in prison he'd noticed convicts pausing in front of every mirror they passed to look at their reflection. He'd peer from his window and watch them in the next cellblock as they stood and posed in the reflection of their own cell windows. The weight lifters did it continuously, but most other convicts did it often as well.

They would look for hours in the small mirrors allowed in the cell. He'd watched a few cell partners take up to two hours to shave. It was as if they kept hoping to see something there other than themselves. Or perhaps hoping something would be changed about them from the last time they looked. But what he really thought was that they had lived so long with deceit and lies that they had lost sight of themselves somehow. Outside of prison, criminals feel they have to convince everyone around them that they aren't criminal. They blend with society much as a chameleon changes colors. Perhaps they watch the prison mirror for the return of their true colors. Whatever the cause, he viewed the mirror watch as a sign of weakness and trained himself over the years not to look in a mirror or at his reflection in a window just because it was there. He looked at his image when he had good reason.

Thoughts of women and sex lay on his mind now like a heavy fog. Sounds of female voices, the rustle of a skirt, the strange and wonderful odors emanating from them.

Curious glances from open searching eyes, their softness and their difference.

He needed a woman right now worse than he'd ever needed anything in his life. He needed to touch a woman and be touched by one. Having them all around him now was like a slow, steady form of torture.

He felt utterly helpless about the problem. He went to his flight bag and rummaged around in it, retrieving an old dog-eared copy of Plato's *Dialogues*. The ritual of courtship was as alien to him as the everyday lives of those about him now. Going to a massage parlor or a whore was not out of the question. But he hoped that before long, he could find a woman who wanted the same thing he did. It would be so much better that way. Yet he knew he was walking a thin line by prolonging these feelings of sexual desire. In the core of his being, they represented a form of chaos that had overtones of violence.

Sunday morning he awoke sweating in an unbearably hot room. As he threw open the door and windows he wondered what a secondhand air conditioner would cost. Fresno in August seemed hotter than the precincts of hell.

Stepping out the door in his cutoff khakis and new tennis shoes, he noticed June and Gail standing near the edge of the field. June had some lunch meat in her hand and was trying to coax a dog to come closer. The hot sun stood at its zenith in a burning solstitial standstill, and he guessed he'd slept till noon.

Drawn to the women and their project, he laughed when he saw the dog and drew fierce looks from both of them and from the dog, which stood about ten steps out in the high weeds.

He looked to be part shepherd and part Airedale, but his progenitors were likely more varied than that. He was colored brown, like a shepherd, and stood there expectantly watching every movement of June's hands and the lunch meat she held. One ear stood straight up while the other was flapped down and torn like an old running sock. His nose and lips were scarred, and patches of skin shone through his fur here and there on his shoulders and flanks.

Somehow he still managed to look tough, capable, and self-confident. But his main emotion looked to be caution. His smoky brown eyes were filled with questions about the intent of the people that faced him now.

June threw the last of the baloney near him, and the dog pounced on it, still watching them all warily.

"Here, boy, come on, boy," June pleaded to the indifferent animal.

"He belonged to a homeless man that died out there in the field," Gail explained to Bill.

"A wino," June interjected.

"He was homeless, June."

"He was a homeless wino. If he hadn't been a wino he would have had a home."

Gail looked at Bill with an exasperated expression that told him this was an old argument between them. He hoped his opinion wouldn't be asked, because June's theory sounded pretty valid to him.

"Since his owner died a few months ago, people from the ASPCA and even the police have been out here trying to catch him," she said. "None of them have had any luck. He seems to disappear when they arrive. June's been feeding him every day, but he still won't come any closer than where he is right now."

"Where could he hide out in that field?"

"I think he goes to that wrecking yard up there," she said, pointing up the highway.

Bill looked, and up the highway was a huge wrecking yard. Cars were piled up like mountains of crushed tin cans.

"I wonder why I can't make friends with him," June said.

"He don't trust people," Bill answered her. "He's probably been mistreated pretty badly by someone, and now he won't trust anyone."

"Well, I won't mistreat him. I feed him all the time, and I want to pet him and give him a bath. Look how dirty he is."

"You're going to have to coax him," he replied. "Prove to him you're his friend."

"How do I do that? I've been trying since April."

"What you do is get a plate and put the meat on it and put it out there every day about where he is now, then you move the plate in a little closer every day until you get him eating right up here in the yard. One thing about a dog, if you feed him every day, he will finally be your friend."

"Do you really think so?" she asked excitedly.

"I know so."

Gail stood there watching them talk. This man didn't fit the mold of the ex-convicts she encountered now and then. Standing there with his hands in his pockets talking to June, he looked relaxed and near beautiful. He was one of the finest physical specimens of man she'd ever looked at. His muscles were long and hard, but not bulky like a weight lifter's, more like a gymnast's or swimmer's. The only thing that marred his appearance was the tattoos on his arms and chest, but they weren't like jailhouse tattoos either.

One was a Viking riding a sled pulled by two polar bears. The Viking was on his shoulder holding a sword, while the bears ran down his biceps and forearm. She could see the shadow of the Viking under his T-shirt. It was more like artwork than jailhouse tattooing.

But what she feared about him was what she couldn't see. He seemed awfully nice and well-mannered, but what she knew of his background told a different story altogether. She was feeling a very strong physical attraction to him herself, and June was blooming like a late rose. There seemed to be a certain aura of danger about him. He moved like a big panther, but he seemed gentle enough, or perhaps "tame" would be a better word. She needed some assurance about him that so far hadn't been forthcoming, and she didn't quite know how to go about getting it. This overgrown thirteen-year-old sprout here trying to love a wild, mangy, ungrateful mutt meant more to her than anyone or anything, and she didn't know if she had reason to worry.

The closest she could come to asking him for reassurance was to say, "We want you to have dinner with us tonight, and we insist, don't we, June?"

"Yep, we do insist," June said, watching the ungrateful dog trot away through the weeds.

"Well, since you insist." Bill smiled.

"What would you like to eat?" Gail asked. "How about a nice big juicy sirloin steak smothered in mushrooms?"

She hoped he would jump on that idea, because steak and mushrooms was about all she had ever learned to cook halfway decently, and that was because Tony would accept that three times a day and keep his mouth shut about her cooking. Before he went to prison this last time he had begun calling her Loretta after Leroy's wife in the comic strip. But this aspiring dishwasher threw her a real curve.

"That sounds nice," he replied. "But what I would really like, if I had my choice, is a big juicy meat loaf."

"A meat loaf!" Gail exclaimed. Even June looked at him closely to be sure the sun hadn't addled his mind. Even at her age she knew that meat loaf, or what was loosely referred to as a meat loaf, was served twice a week in prison. Every ex-con in the world hated the very word.

"I can't imagine you just out of prison and wanting meat loaf. Don't they serve it in federal prisons also?" she asked.

"Yeah, they served it, but I never ate a piece of it in fourteen years. I'd like to have one like my mother used to make," he told her.

"Well, I doubt if I could cook one as good as the ones your mother cooked." She felt like adding that she probably couldn't make one as good as those they made in prison, but wasn't quite ready for such a profound confession.

"Let me cook it," he replied.

"I'll help him, Mom," June offered.

"You've got a deal," Gail agreed. "You two cook and I'll

wash the dishes." She felt so relieved she'd have agreed to anything.

"I'm going running for a while," he said. "When I get back, maybe you can drive me to a market and I'll buy what I need to make it with."

"I'll drive you to the store," she replied. "But you aren't buying anything. You're my guest tonight. I'll do the paying."

"He's my guest too!" June offered.

"Oh shut up, June!"

"See you in a couple hours," he said, and took off in a loping run toward the front office.

"Hey, wait till I get my shoes, I'll run with you!" June yelled at his retreating back.

"Another time, June," he yelled back over his shoulder, and turned into the road.

They stood there watching him grow smaller as he covered the distance between the motel and the junkyard.

"June," Gail said thoughtfully, "I want you to stop wearing that bikini around him so much until he's been out awhile."

"Come on, Mom, don't start that again," June responded, and put her arm around Gail as they walked beneath the blazing sun toward the office.

Gail was thinking about Tough Tony when she got back to the office. Malone was the first man who had excited her in a long time, and the more she grew to like him, the more she thought about Tony and their marriage, which she knew was all but dead, even though he hadn't told her for sure yet.

His phone calls from prison were becoming few and far between, and certain weekends when she wanted to take June and drive up for a visit, he'd told her not to come. It was becoming obvious to her that he had another girlfriend, probably a young one. Tony did like them young.

She had been thirteen and he was fourteen when they became sweethearts, and they had been together ever since, what time he wasn't in some jail or other. They began having sex then, and that's why she worried about June so much now.

They hadn't always called him Tough Tony, and part of her love for him stemmed from the fact that she had known him when he was a vulnerable, timid teenager in El Monte, California, where they both grew up. But all that had changed. It changed suddenly when he was sixteen and she was fifteen.

They had been walking home from school and a couple of older boys, obviously drunk, had been following them and making lewd remarks. She had told Tony to ignore them, and he had, until one of them pinched her on the ass and Tony's pride drove him into a rage.

It wasn't much of a fight. The older boy beat Tony unmercifully, while the other one held her away from the fight and mauled her as she tried to scratch his eyes out. They finally quit when passersby began stopping and threatening to call the police. Tony cried that day and the boys called him a sissy, but she knew that the tears were from rage and frustration, not cowardice.

She helped the bleeding Tony to his mother's house and didn't see him again for nine months. He simply quit school and disappeared. Six weeks after he left, she found out she was pregnant. His mother swore she didn't have any idea where he was, and Gail believed her.

Tony's mother was a beautiful blond Scandinavian woman who had married a Mexican named Camacho from the Whittier barrio. He was gone not long after Tony was born. Tony never knew him and as a result didn't like Mexicans very much.

June was born two days before Tony came back to El Monte the following year, riding a Harley-Davidson motorcycle and packing a very big grudge. He tracked down the two older boys who had molested her and beat them both severely. One of them spent two months in the hospital.

Then one after another, he looked up every tough guy in

El Monte and proceeded to beat him up. Everyone began calling him Tough Tony. Gail had loved him more the way he had been, but found she still loved him the way he was now. Even though he treated her and June as possessions more than anything.

Wherever he had gone for that nine months, he had learned to fight. One of his dad's brothers was a fight promoter in San Diego, and she had always figured he went there to the man's gym. She also believed he had landed in prison looking for even tougher men to fight. He now viewed the world and everyone in it as a challenge. It was sad, because she knew that view would one day get him killed. But she still tried to understand.

Her main hope now was that if their marriage was dead he would let go completely. Many outlaw bikers believed that if they had children by a woman, they owned her forever. Even if they left with another woman, they wouldn't let the former wife take up with a man. Sometimes they just never bothered to divorce her, if they were legally married. If Tony had accepted that value from his cohorts, he damn sure had another think coming. If he left her, she would force him to divorce her. She made a mental note to bring it up next time he called and another mental note to learn how to cook a meat loaf. God knew she needed some meat herself right about now.

Bill wasn't used to running on blacktop and it jarred his knees more than usual, but it felt good to be running again. It felt especially good to run without having to go around in a circle on a track. Before he'd gone a mile up the road he was wet with sweat, and the wrecking yard lay ahead and to the right across a field. It was on the same highway that Ferraro's was on.

He cut off the road into the field. He was amazed at the objects and refuse that lay among the weeds. He had to slow down and watch every step. There were piles of trash, broken bottles, and here and there a cement foundation of a building that had long since been removed. Old rusting pipes grew up from the ground among the weeds like deformed mushrooms.

The closer he came to the wrecking yard the more he marveled at the immense size of it. It looked to be about fifteen acres, surrounded by a Cyclone fence with barbed wire at the top that reminded him of the one around the prison. An office faced the highway and there were a few outbuildings in back, but the rest was cars and tires. One pile of old tires looked to be a couple of stories high and lay there in the hot sun like a pile of burned doughnuts. When he'd negotiated the last of the field and emerged on the road, two big dogs ran along by the fence barking frantically at him. As he turned down the shoulder of the road toward Ferraro's, he could smell oil and rubber slowly cooking in the hot sun.

Now his mind broke free of the sights and sounds and began to nibble at his present state of affairs. Running always freed his mind at some point to where he could think about himself. The slap of shoe soles on the road had a calming, hypnotic effect.

The past was of more concern than the future. He hadn't been sure that he wouldn't have an overwhelming urge to call some old friends in Portland, but so far he hadn't had any urge at all. They had all quit communicating with him years ago, so he couldn't exactly call them friends anymore. That seemed okay to him right now. What he really hoped for was a new future and new friends, uncluttered by old habits and obligations from the past. No one expected anything of him now, and he didn't know what to expect from them or himself. All he knew for sure was that he wanted freedom for a good while. If washing dishes would buy it, he'd wash all the dishes in the world.

All his old buddies he'd been smuggling with were dead or in jail now anyway after fourteen years. Frances Logan, his mother's best friend, who had been like a mother to him, was still there. He had left some money with her, and she was caring for some property he had from his mother's small estate.

He felt guilty about not calling her and planned to visit as soon as he got himself lined out. But Portland was shaky right now. He not only had a certain kind of reputation there that some youngster might want to check out, but the police wouldn't be happy to see him back. The ones that had been there when he left, anyway. The last deal he'd done there had left them thoroughly incensed.

Bill and a Nez Perce indian known as Nez had burglarized a DEA warehouse on the Columbia River and taken five hundred pounds of marijuana that was being held as evidence in a smuggling bust aboard a sailboat.

They had gone in on a motorized raft wearing wet suits on a Saturday night, torched a hole through the floor of the building, and loaded the raft up. They lay low on Sunday, then took the rest out on Sunday night. By Monday, when it was missed, they had already sold it in Fresno.

Nez was bad about getting drunk and saying too much. It wasn't long before the DEA got wind of who had taken the dope. They were really mad, because they had to drop charges against the crew of the boat. Bill sometimes thought the fourteen years that he'd done had probably saved him from being framed or killed by the DEA. Nez was doing fifty years in the Walla Walla prison on a charge that he swore was a frame-up.

He cut through Ferraro's deserted parking lot, sprinted across the field to the motel, and dived right into the pool, shoes and all. It felt so shockingly good that he screamed when his head broke out of the water. A man and woman sunning themselves by the pool looked at him as if he were a crazy man. He left his shoes to dry in the sun before he went into his room for another shower and some cream cheese and strawberry preserves on Hi-Ho crackers.

As he showered again he savored the feeling of not being watched in anything he did. The running was much better now without having to pass a gun tower every few yards. A sense of privacy long since discarded in the interest of survival was returning, and the calmness of it drew him to his bed, where he fell into a deep peaceful slumber with his door ajar and all the windows open.

He didn't hear June pull the door open, but when she entered the doorway he came off the bed like a cat that had been dropped onto its back. She looked more startled than he was, standing there with her mouth open and one fist poised to knock on his doorframe.

"I'm sorry I surprised you," she said, gazing at him standing there in his boxer shorts.

"It's okay," he replied, letting out his breath. "I was asleep."

"How did you know I was here? I hadn't even knocked yet."

"The light in the room changed when you stood in the doorway," he replied, feeling at a loss to really explain it to her.

"Well, Mom's ready to go to the store if you are."

"I'll be there in a minute," he replied, going for his jeans.

As they pushed a grocery cart in a nearby market, Gail watched him handle the vegetables. Even the potatoes; he picked up and carefully examined each one before dropping it in the bag. He seemed to treat the vegetables with a reverence as he turned and balanced them in his hands. He reminded her of a farmer admiring the produce of his land.

At the meat department he ordered two pounds of ground sirloin. Then he stopped by the bakery section for two loaves of unbaked French bread and a plastic bag of garlic croutons. On the way to the checkout counter, Gail picked up a gallon of burgundy wine and put it in the cart.

June stood behind the counter when they entered the

motel office with the grocery bags. She wore a pair of bell-bottom cotton slacks with wide strips of pink and mauve running from the waist down the ankles, where just the tips of a pair of semi-high-heel mauve pumps peeked out. A low-cut dark purple pullover and a big floppy purple hat with a pink ribbon around it completed her outfit. Her long shiny black hair was caught behind her neck with a leather clasp.

"My goodness," Gail said as they came in. "I'm going to have to get out of these shorts. This girl of mine makes me feel like a tramp."

June opened the door behind the counter and led them into the living quarters. Bill was surprised by their living room. The entire room was done in black and silver. A chrome glass-topped coffee table stood in front of a black leather couch. The only colored object was a walnut room divider that separated the living room from the dining room. Built into the divider was a large fish aquarium, filled with solid black and solid silver angelfish. It was fitted into the divider so that you could see all the way through. The effect was very pleasing to the eye. Large fake-fur drapes covered the windows. He stood there craning his neck at the room.

"Like it?" Gail asked.

"It's sort of breathtaking," he replied. "You must have a nice boss, to fix your living quarters up like this."

"I'm the boss," she laughed. "I own the joint. June, you take him to the kitchen. I'm going to shower and change my clothes."

As they unpacked the groceries, June held up the wine. "Should I put this in the icebox?" she asked.

"No," he told her. "Burgundy is better at room temperature."

He was prowling around the spacious kitchen, opening cupboards, checking the stove and other appliances. It was a well-laid-out and roomy kitchen. All that marred it was the view from the window over the sink into the weed-choked field between Ferraro's and motel row.

A very pleasant surprise lay behind one of the cupboard doors: a full set of old cast-iron skillets, from the largest to the smallest, one resting inside the other. They must have been her mother's, he thought as he ran his hand over them, savoring the memories evoked by the old cold iron.

He turned his head and saw June standing by the sink watching him. The wine was open, and she had poured three water glasses full. She held one out to him.

"Here," she said. "I'll take one to Mom in the shower."

"June, I think it's a felony for me to give you wine," he told her as he reached for his glass.

"Well, it's not a felony for me to give you some, and Mom lets me have a glass now and then, because I promised her I wouldn't drink anywhere else besides right here at home with her."

"I'll drink to that," he replied, taking a sip of the sour burgundy as she left the room with the two full glasses.

"What kind of music do you like?" she asked over her shoulder.

"Country-and-western, of course."

"Oh boy!" she laughed.

A moment or two later, as he unpacked the rest of the groceries, music from a hidden speaker in the kitchen rolled out at him. It was Hank Williams, Jr., singing "Country State of Mind." He smiled to himself. It looked as if the evening was going to be enjoyable. He drained his glass of wine and laughed out loud. It looked as if the world was going to be enjoyable.

June came back, and to his surprise, she was a willing and able helper. He gave her the croutons and a dough roller to roll them with. But she stopped and watched as he put the ground meat in a bowl, cracked two eggs, and kneaded them into the meat.

"What are these for?" she asked, looking at the crouton crumbs.

"That's the glue that holds our meat loaf together. Now pour me another glass of wine and watch real close how I do this."

It was obvious she was really trying to learn. The way she kept touching him and bumping him as they moved about the kitchen was also obvious, but by now he had figured out her motives. The moves were definitely not sexual. She just wanted to touch someone. He began to touch her shoulder as if to steer her somewhere or rub her head and say "Good job" or "That's it." Once he started this, she stopped the obvious and awkward bumpings. He admired her cleverness at the game and wished he was as smart as she about getting someone to touch him. He damn sure needed some highly specific touching right now. Another glass of wine helped a little.

Gail came in and poured herself a glass of wine while gazing critically at the dent he and June had already put in the jug. June had removed her big floppy hat, and Gail had dressed in exactly the same clothes, color and all. Bill stood and looked at them for a moment.

"Okay, which twin has the Toni?" he asked.

They both smiled.

"I suppose I do," Gail answered. "Tony's my husband's name."

"My dad's name," June said.

"Well, I'll leave you two wine hogs to your meat loaf," Gail said as she took up her glass. "And since I've been outvoted on the music, I'm going to put some real tear-jerkin' George Jones on the stereo," she said as she sauntered out into the dining room.

"Hey! My favorite singer!" Bill yelled after her.

"Mine too," June chimed in gleefully.

"She likes shoplifting music and soft rock," June told him.

"That's awful," Bill replied mournfully. "Now watch real

close while we make a meat loaf like Mom used to make." He was a little bit tipsy from the wine.

He set the oven to 325 degrees, then turned on a burner on the electric range and put June to work frying a half pound of bacon in a small cast-iron skillet.

He mixed the crushed croutons in with the meat and eggs and kneaded it well. He drained two cans of Green Giant sliced button mushrooms and added them, then a small can of chopped olives along with a finely diced onion and half a bell pepper. June watched every move he made, and topped off his water glass along with hers every time they got low.

He put four garlic pods in a crusher and squeezed the juice onto the meat, then added a small can of Hunt's tomato sauce. June had the bacon very crisp now, as he'd instructed, and it lay on a paper towel. He crumbled the crisp bacon into his meat loaf, kneading it well as he added ground pepper and salt.

He took the biggest iron skillet from the shelf and molded his meat into it, leaving a two-inch perimeter between the meat and the outer edge of the skillet.

"Hey, aren't you supposed to grease the pan?" June asked.

He grinned at her as he slid the skillet onto the bottom shelf of the oven.

"Plenty of grease in that meat loaf, girl," he replied. "Now you're the timer, so let me know when exactly one hour is up and let's go see what your mama is up to."

Gail was gyrating in the living room. A fast George Jones song blared out at the room, and she danced seemingly oblivious even to June and Bill as they seated themselves on the leather couch and watched admiringly. She was doing something that looked to be a cross between a jitterbug and a flapper's Charleston and she was doing it beautifully. Every step or move she made seemed molded to the music. They gave her a seated ovation at the end of the song, and she fell between them on the couch looking flushed and happy.

"Do you dance?" she asked him.

"Not lately," he replied.

"I like to show off some," she said. "Dancing was my profession until my husband made me stop."

"He didn't like you dancing?"

"I was an exotic dancer," she replied. "My husband called it striptease, which I suppose in a way it was, but I did enjoy it."

"Oh," he replied.

"His name is Tony Camacho," she said. "They call him Tough Tony. Have you heard of him?"

"I knew him," Bill replied. "He did a couple of years at Lompoc about six years ago."

"That's my dad," June chimed in. "Were you there then?"

"I was there," he replied. "But he hung around with bikers mostly, and that wasn't my crowd."

"That's him," Gail said.

Bill remembered Tough Tony well. He'd been intrigued by the man's last name, Camacho, and his looks. He was blond and blue-eyed, with Nordic features, and he hung around with a tough crowd of bikers. He was built like a big solid oak tree and had a reputation as a fearsome street fighter. He'd served two years on a three-year sentence at Lompoc and Marion for assaulting a park ranger in Yosemite National Park. Bill was hard put to imagine him as the husband of this woman and June's father.

"That's how we met Campbell," Gail told him. "He was Tony's parole officer for a year. Tony's in Folsom now for chewing a guy's ear off in a fight a few years ago. He was supposed to come home next month, but we had a letter from him today. He got into a fight with some prison guards and it looks like he won't be home for a good while yet."

"It's like that sometimes," Bill replied.

"Yeah," she said, pouring some more wine in all their glasses. "With Tony it's like that most of the time. He's not really a mean man, you know, he just enjoys fighting."

"Each to his own," Bill said, raising his burgundy in a toast.

"I'll drink to that," she replied.

"Me too," June said.

He sat back on the couch listening to the music and studying the room. Little prints of Picasso clown drawings in black frames adorned the walls, and the angelfish in the tank had a mesmerizing effect on his senses as they glided and swooped, their fins reminding him of billowing sails on old sailing ships. The ambience of the room and the gentle friendly spirit of the two women were totally alien to what he'd become used to. This scene was more like a prison daydream than a real event. Something vital and exciting rushed his blood and made his heartbeat race for a moment. He felt it pounding in his breast like a little frantic tom-tom.

When the hour was up, June took him by the hand and led him to the aquarium. On the bottom, lazily foraging, were two small catfish with black and white stripes.

"Those are zebra catfish from South America," she told him. "I can't put any fish with fins in with my angelfish, because they eat the fins of any other fish, but they don't bother my catfish."

"They're beautiful," was all he could think to reply, hoping he wasn't too drunk to finish the meat loaf. The mild table wine had hit him like a ton of bricks. Gail and June didn't look much better off.

He washed and quartered six small potatoes, six carrots, and a few stalks of celery. Taking the meat loaf from the hot oven, he laid the vegetables in the skillet around the meat loaf in the space he'd left between the meat and the pan.

"Hey, that smells good," June told him as he worked.

"Tastes better than it smells," he replied. He eased the skillet back into the oven and carefully laid the French loaves on a higher shelf.

"Well, we've got forty-five minutes until chow time, girl," he said. "Let's see what we can do about some dessert."

The kitchen yielded up plenty of fruit for a fruit salad. He chopped it up into a bowl, then drained the juice from a can of pineapple and added it to a can of pineapple juice in a blender. He dropped in a block of cream cheese and let the blender whip it to a frothy texture, like whipped cream. He poured this over the bowl of fruit and inserted it in the refrigerator.

"Now if this was whipped cream," he told June, "we couldn't pour it on our fruit early, because it would get thin and runny, but this stuff here holds up real well."

She didn't seem to hear him. She was busy running her finger around the blender and licking it.

The meat loaf was delicious, they all agreed, but by the time they sat down to it they were all drunk on table wine. Gail and Bill began drinking beer with their dinner, while June ate most of the meat loaf and almost all the fruit salad.

About halfway through dinner, he felt his brain begin to slide off into a muddy ditch and lie there wallowing as he tried to hook it back to his tongue. The remainder of the evening became a series of confused events of a dubious chronological order.

Later he remembered loading some meat loaf on a pie pan and telling June to take it out to the dog, which she did. It really felt good to let himself go and get totally drunk, something he hadn't done in fourteen years.

Gail at one point was asking him if he had family and why he hadn't gone back to his old hometown. He was giving her totally irrelevant answers while hoping if he passed out they wouldn't see any flies crawling around his face.

Sometime in the night, June tried to prop him up and guide him to his room as he attempted to fight her off, proclaiming that he didn't need any help. Drunken luck and her insistence were all that saved him from the cold water of the swimming pool. When he fell across his bed, she removed his shoes and straightened him out as best she could. She leaned down and told him the meat loaf was delicious.

"Smile when you say that, pardner," he replied, and passed out. Angelfish and clowns glided and sauntered through his dreams.

8.

Zero Way was a circular drive off Van Ness Avenue in Fresno near the Fig Garden Village Shopping Center at Palm and Shaw. An appropriately named cul-de-sac that contained three homes, all owned by the Sandino family.

The Fig Garden area was traditionally the home of money and power in Fresno. An old neighborhood of streets lined with sycamore, eucalyptus, and oak trees and large well-tended hedges bordering the grounds of palatial homes.

Everyone knew everyone in the neighborhood, and there was very little crime. It was a place to pass through quietly and respectfully if you didn't live there. A good place to go to jail quickly from if you deviated from that pattern. The police were present and vigilant in the area. This type of ambience had long made the Fig Garden area a desirable neighborhood for the city's well-to-do, along with the better-heeled criminals. Zero Way harbored the cream of the latter crop.

One Zero Way, the first home just off Van Ness, was the residence of Alfredo (Freddy the Glove) Sandino, his two grown sons, and his daughter and youngest child, Florence Sandino.

Two Zero Way, at the rear of the circle, was the home of Freddy's elder brother, Roberto "Small Bob" Sandino, the patriarch of the family. He lived there with his wife, Theresa; their daughter, Rosa, and son, Paul, had married and moved away to live respectable lives elsewhere.

On around the well-tended drive and back at the edge of Van Ness Avenue was Three Zero Way, a large two-story home occupied by old Giuseppe Spilotro, factotum and caretaker of the three combined premises.

The Sandino family was a Mafia family, founded in the early thirties by the elder Roberto Sandino and passed on to his son Small Bob upon his death of old age in the early eighties. Like most West Coast Mafia families, the Sandino clan was small, isolated, and run in a laissez-faire manner. Its members were sometimes referred to jocularly by other mobsters as "them Sandinistas."

The family wasn't connected to the East Coast or even the L.A. and San Francisco mobs, other than by a working, if uneasy, mutual respect. Things were done very differently in Fresno than they were in large cities.

When the elder Roberto Sandino founded the family with the help of Giuseppe in the early thirties, he had the good sense to perceive that he was surrounded by a restless sea of dust-bowl Okies. He referred to them as "fuckin' hillbillies" to his dying day.

The most painful lesson Roberto and Giuseppe learned as young men was that these people could not be intimidated. The only thing they seemed to fear was starvation, and they often laughed and made jokes about that.

When it came to holding a grudge and carrying out a vendetta, their memory was longer than that of a Sicilian sheepherder. Roberto ensured the survival of his family in Fresno by steering clear of these people and their enterprises. When one of his men brought him a deal that required intercourse with hillbillies, his usual judgment would be: "Let's drive around that one." The family prospered by the deals they didn't "drive around."

The elder Roberto Sandino had left New York in the mid-twenties when his father died, because he didn't like cities. His mother had died at the turn of the century in Sicily when he was born. He was an only child. After a year of backbreaking labor on a dairy farm in the San Joaquin Valley, he discovered that he liked working even less than he liked New York City. For a while there he thought about going back to Sicily and herding sheep.

He took a job in Fresno as a bartender for a man named Dick Beltran. There was a dice game upstairs that Beltran paid off the police to run. It wasn't long before Roberto graduated to head of security for the dice game, with a piece of the action.

Fresno being situated in the center of California, most of their dice players were traveling criminals, "crossroaders" they were called, and local farmers and ranchers. There were some monumental fights and more than a few robbery attempts. Roberto took his share of bruises and wounds while keeping the game running. He noticed during these years that Beltran was a very good hustler but also a physical coward.

By the early thirties, they had opened two more bars and Roberto had brought his cousin Giuseppe out from Chicago to help run things. Beltran had purchased a club in Nevada and was spending a lot of time up there renovating it and getting it ready to open.

On one of his trips back from Reno, Beltran discovered that Roberto had moved the dice game to the upper floor of a fenced-in wrecking yard that he and Giuseppe had leased. He found Bob in the bar checking inventory while Giuseppe sat at a table fixing a napkin holder with a pair of pliers.

"Why did you move the game?" he asked Bob, coming right to the point.

"Well, if you gonna build a gambling club in Reno, you don't want it tied to an illegal game you got here in Fresno," Bob told him.

Beltran could see the logic in that, so he began another tack.

"So how's it doin'?"

"What do you mean?" Bob asked.

"I mean, how much fuckin' money did it make in the last two weeks? That's what I mean!" Beltran yelled, becoming impatient. No sooner had the words left his mouth than Giuseppe hooked the pliers on his nose and exerted enough pressure to force him to his knees.

"Don't be yellin' at people in here," Giuseppe whispered, as he put more pressure on the pliers.

A terrified Beltran stayed on his knees there in the bar until Roberto finished explaining that he and Giuseppe were now the sole owners of the dice game and half owners in the three Fresno bars. They let him keep the club in Reno with the provision that he stay up there in Nevada. The Sandino family began that evening, and they started recruiting Italian thugs to stay around Fresno and help with the new enterprises like gambling operations and whorehouses.

In the late fifties, Roberto began buying pizza parlors and real estate along with a Cadillac dealership that Small Bob now ran out on Blackstone. Bob Senior had been so busy building and expanding the family that he had neglected to instill in his children the necessary values it took to run a Mafia family. The more legitimate it became, the weaker the entire structure. Their main source of revenue had been from the illegal operations. A lack of vigilance in that area was now causing money problems. He noticed the dry rot after Giuseppe became senile but didn't have the will or energy to correct it before he died.

Small Bob sat in an easy chair on his opulent screened-in front porch, watching old Giuseppe trim the hedge bordering his property along Van Ness Avenue. The old man kept up a running conversation with persons unknown as he wielded the pruning shears, but the talk didn't detract from the quality of his work. The hedge looked as neat and uniform as a surveyor with a plumb line could have made it.

Small Bob was worried, and part of the worry came from the fact that old Giuseppe had entered the land of incoherence. There was no one left to seek advice from. It wasn't so much that he needed the advice as he needed to know how to make someone listen to his own advice. Old Giuseppe was far beyond a concept as complicated as that.

Bob's main worry was Freddy and his two sons and that crazy fuckin' daughter of his, Florence. They were all completely out of line, and none of them would listen. When he tried to remonstrate with any of them they got a blank, faraway look in their eyes. Though they seemed to listen and make the appropriate respectful gestures, he could tell they didn't hear a word he told them.

It was Fred's fault, and the harm seemed to be done now. His kids just never had a chance to learn to be human beings. But now the culpability edged more and more onto Bob's own shoulders as they began to influence the family, and he wondered at times if the fault wasn't his all along. Fred's wife, Angie, had been a kind and gentle woman who ostensibly died of a brain tumor. But everyone in the family knew that Fred had beaten her to death. He did it little by little over the years, but everyone in the family, including the kids, knew he was doing it, and watched in terrified silence until he finally finished her off. A black eye here, a broken jaw there, all finally added up to a "fatal brain tumor." Now, as bad luck would have it, the unfortunate spectators were the future leaders of this family. God help us all, Bob thought, as Theresa sat a tray before him on a snack table and said in a low voice, "The Glove is here with Mr. Stubbs."

"Show them in, honey," Bob replied.

Raymond Stubbs entered first. Bob stood and shook his hand and motioned him to a chair across from his own. Fred entered and remained standing near the doorway. The way the chairs were positioned, Fred stood just behind Stubbs's left shoulder.

"Coffee, tea, and juice there, whatever you want." Bob motioned at the tray and watched Stubbs's shaking hands as he built himself a cup of coffee.

He was a small compact man of middle age. His graying

sandy hair was well barbered, and he was impeccably tailored and turned out in a lightweight linen suit. He owned a Dodge dealership on Blackstone Avenue not far from Bob's Cadillac dealership. They had been friends and business associates for years now, but it looked as if all that was about to end.

"You owe us one hundred and twenty thousand dollars, Ray," Bob said to him as he took the first sip of his coffee.

"Hey, I know that, Bob," Stubbs replied, sitting his cup down on the saucer and spreading his hands wide, trying to appear cheerful and open. "I know you guys didn't bring me over here to tell me I owe you."

"No," Bob replied, "it's how you are going to pay us that we want to talk about."

"Hey! I've always paid before. You never had any problem about my money, right, Fred?" He said this while craning his neck around toward Fred, who just stared at him in antagonistic silence.

"Look here, Ray," Bob said to him. "You've got serious problems. I don't mind you getting this deep, because you've been a good player of ours for a few years now. But now you're plunging on exhibition football and everything else."

"Well hell, I'm stuck, you know," Stubbs interjected.

"Let me finish, Ray," Bob replied, raising his hand in a pushing motion. "That beauty queen you married is suing you for a divorce."

"Well, Sally and I have had a few problems, and she's talking divorce, but I'm sure we'll work it out. I don't see what that's got to do—"

"It won't get worked out, Ray. She talked to my lawyer on Friday."

"She what?"

"Look, Ray. What I'm about to tell you is a violation of attorney-client privilege. It's a fuckin' felony, do you understand?"

"Why sure, I uh . . ."

"Listen close now. Any of what I say to you gets back to your wife for any reason, you will get hurt."

"Your head will get separated from your fucking neck," Fred droned from the corner where he stood, arms folded across his chest.

"Hey, Bob, you got my word. Now what's it all about?" Stubbs asked.

"She comes in on Friday to Vic Fraschetta's office," Bob replied. "Tells him she wants a divorce and plans to take you for a bundle. Seems she's had private investigators watching you comin' and goin' to motels with these bobby-soxers and all your other little immoral habits."

"Jesus Christ!" Stubbs exclaimed.

"Fraschetta knows you and I are friends," Bob said, "so he calls me while she's there. I told him to stall her until I could talk with you, so he told her to hold off until he could check your financial situation, and she agreed to that."

"Hey, I appreciate that, Bob," Stubbs said.

"Well, Ray, it ain't what you appreciate or don't. This is about me getting paid my money and you keeping your nuts out of her purse, do you understand that?"

"Why, sure, I—"

"I'm glad you do," Bob said, "because we're going to milk your business and put you in Chapter Eleven bankruptcy."

"Bankruptcy!" Stubbs exclaimed.

"That's right," Bob said. "It's your only out."

"We want our fucking money, Ray!" the Glove roared from the corner behind Stubbs.

"Take it easy, Fred," Bob said, thinking that his brother had about the same type of personality as Frankenstein's monster.

"Look, Ray," Bob said to the obviously agitated man. "Your business hasn't been doing all that good for a few years now anyway. Your wife is getting ready to nail you to the wall. If you listen to me, I'll tell you how we can pull a minimum four hundred thousand cash out of your business in a year. Maybe five or six hundred thou. You pay me off, pocket the rest, put the business in Chapter Eleven, and let your wife have it on the divorce settlement."

"How do we do all this without going to jail? I mean, without me going to jail?" Stubbs asked. Bob could now see a definite spark of interest in his eyes.

"Simple," he replied. "You have a deal with the bank where you sign recourse for certain people who don't have the proper credit; right?"

"Yes," Stubbs replied, "but I have to know them real well, like an old friend or something."

"Well, when you cosign them you get your money right then from the bank, right?"

"That's right," Stubbs replied. Bob could see he was getting the drift already.

"Okay. What we do is you sign recourse this year for every flake and squirrel who wants a car, advertise them for twenty-nine dollars down, get all the cash, and then file for bankruptcy. I'll fix it on paper where you can show you lost the money on a bad investment. I'll have Fraschetta stall Sally until we get the scam done. I get my one twenty plus the juice and you get the rest clear. What do you say? You make an easy minimum two hundred thou."

Stubbs glanced back at the Glove.

"Hell, let's do it," he said. "This town's getting on my nerves anyway."

"Honey!" Bob yelled. "Bring us that Campari and some glasses. We're gonna drink to a deal here!"

When Stubbs walked out to the car, Bob motioned Fred to hang back for a moment.

"Fred," he told him, "you've got to talk to them boys of yours. Fraschetta told me Fred Junior had another assault charge filed on him yesterday."

"Ah, it was just some punk in a bar," Fred replied. "It won't come to nothin'."

"He pistol-whipped the guy, Fred. Sure, he'll probably beat it, but if I've told them kids once, I've told them a hundred fucking times that fighting with these hillbillies is bad news." Even as he said this and watched Fred gaze dolefully at the floor, he got the feeling he was talking to the wall.

"I hear they're selling a little dope these days, also," he added.

Fred looked up at that. "That's bullshit," he replied. "Look, I'll talk to them about the fighting, but you know, boys will be boys."

"Yeah, you talk to them, Fred, but not about fighting. It's about these Okies having twenty-nine cousins and twenty-six of them don't ever forget anything. It's about dying, Fred. They keep this shit up they gonna wake up dead one of these days. That's what you need to talk to them about."

"What about this guy's wife?" Fred asked. "What if she files for divorce and ties up all his money before we get the scam done?"

Bob blinked and looked at him for a moment. This was just like Fred to totally change a disagreeable subject. It didn't really matter—as usual his advice was wasted anyway.

"Fraschetta can handle her," he replied.

"How do you know that for sure?" Fred insisted.

"He fucked her on his desk on the first visit," he replied.

9.

When Bill awoke and tried to open his eyes, the right eye wouldn't cooperate. The lashes seemed to be glued together with mucus, and he had to pry it open with his fingers. He lay there bathed in sweat as the hot sun beat at the closed window, but all the moisture seemed to be on his outside. The insides, where it was needed, were dry as desert sand. From all available clues, a mule had visited him in the night. He felt that it was an awfully ill-mannered mule that would shit in a man's mouth and kick him in the head while he slept. He made it to the shower and lay against the wall while the water revived him to the point where he was ambulatory. There was an hour and a half left until work time, but he decided to go early. Might as well make a good impression.

As he started across the field, he noticed the pie pan June had put out for the dog. It was a little closer than where he had first seen the dog. That young lady was showing signs of becoming a serious seductress, he thought, and smiled at the thought in spite of a hammering headache that the blazing sun didn't help at all.

He was startled a few steps later to see a pair of feet sticking out from under a clump of grass and weeds. They were still as the feet of a dead man and Bill wanted to skirt them and keep walking, but curiosity made him take a closer look. An old man in torn and tattered clothing lay sleeping on his back beneath the bush. His face was covered with a wiry growth of gray hair, and his nearly toothless mouth was canted open so that it looked like the coin return on a Coke machine. His old creaky chest rose and fell in a seemingly peaceful slumber, and his right hand was curled possessively around an empty quart wine bottle. For some strange reason he reminded Bill of a baby bird fallen from a high nest. The prospect of washing dishes began to look a little brighter.

Regina Ferraro seemed glad to see him and ushered him right over to the serving line.

"Just help yourself," she told him. "The help all eat back in the dishroom."

He loaded his tray, cutting a good chunk of rare prime rib, and made for the dishroom, which was situated so that he had to walk through the perimeter of the kitchen. The steamy feel of the place and smell of good things cooking felt wonderful. Three cooks bustled about. Two of them looked young and eager, and none of them even glanced his way.

He turned into the dishroom and stopped and stared in amazement. The room itself was much larger than he had thought it would be. Along the wall directly to his left was an industrial-size Hobart dish machine exactly like the one he had used for the past eight years or so in prison. It crouched there along the wall like a wary alligator and looked totally out of place in an Italian restaurant.

At its far end stood a rinsing tub, and mounds of dirty dishes and silverware were piled higher than the machine itself. Soggy napkins leaked from piles of trays and plates.

Down the wall directly before him ran a row of stainless-steel tubs for washing pots and pans. Assorted wire brushes and scrapers hung on the wall next to extension hoses with varied nozzles. A large Hobart mixing pot with remnants of mashed potatoes lay on the cement floor in front of a steaming tub.

He glanced to his right, where Leona and two busboys were eating at a table while furtively looking him over. Leona sat at the head of the long rectangular wooden table like a queen presiding over her court. Regina Ferraro walked in as he pulled out a chair opposite Leona and sat down.

"After you eat, I'll tell you what I know about the dish machine," she said.

"Won't be necessary," he replied. "I know all about it already."

"Well, it's way too much machine for us," she said, "but it looks like we're stuck with it. Are you sure you can handle it?"

"I can handle it," he replied, cutting into the prime rub. His headache was almost gone now and he felt much better. Something about the thought of the big Hobart machine resting there behind him was comforting.

"Don't forget you get a free beer every day, so just tell Leona when you want it, or walk over to the bar when you get some time and they will fix you up."

"I won't forget," he replied.

She fidgeted at his shoulder for a moment as if she wanted to add something, then turned and left. Both busboys carried their empty trays to the pile near the dish machine and left behind her.

He was almost finished eating before he became aware that Leona was sitting quietly staring at him. He looked up and gazed directly into her big brown eyes. They locked eyeballs for a good minute or so while each waited for the other to speak. She finally broke the ice.

"Who might you be?" she asked him insolently.

"I'm the dishwasher," he answered in the same tone.

"I axed you who you was, not what you is. I don't see how in the hell you can just sit right down to eat with a bunch of strangers without even a how-de-do or nothin'."

"Well, I apologize if I have offended your highly tuned sense of etiquette and protocol," Bill replied. Inwardly he shuddered at a mental image of himself walking up to the table with his tray in his hand and saying, "Hey there! Hi, everybody, my name is Bill Malone and I've been retained to wash all your dirty dishes."

"You look scary, man," she said. "You scared my friends off. What's all them tattoos? You a merchant marine or something? You ain't crazy, is you, man? You want me to just call you D.W. or what?"

He gazed down at the frayed tattoos on his inner forearms, wishing he hadn't been as foolish at sixteen as he had been. Answering her seemed futile. She'd asked about five or six questions in one spurt, and answers to them would probably lead to about fifty more. He didn't feel like getting into his life story with a strange woman.

Gathering his utensils, he got up and placed them on the pile at the end of the dish machine. He could feel her watching him all the way. He turned and met her gaze again.

"Yeah, just call me D.W.," he said to her, and began pulling a food trap from the side of the machine. The trap was fouled and encrusted with old food and looked like it hadn't been cleaned in years. He dropped it on the floor and began prying on the next one. He heard Leona's footsteps as she approached him but didn't look up at her.

"Okay," she said, "I'll call you D.W., and you call me Leona, but if you start any of that mean macho bully shit around here, I'll bust yo' fuckin' head." With that, she turned and left.

He stood frozen, leaning over with a dirty food trap in his hand. "Stunned" was a mild word for what he felt, and his lower jaw dropped open slightly. The hard part was believing she had said what she'd said to him. It was so ridiculous that in a moment or so his slack jaw realigned itself in a smile and he shook his head in amazement and began prying out another trap.

After scrubbing and replacing all the traps, he closed the drain and began to fill the machine. He'd hoped a big utility closet on the opposite wall held a rubber apron and boots, but all it yielded was a ripped pair of rubber boots not worth wearing and an empty Gallo muscatel bottle. He was glad he'd worn his steel-toed prison hightops and resigned himself to getting wet the first day on the job.

Soon he was absorbed in getting the big Hobart ready for action. The machine was close to twenty feet long and was capable of washing the dishes for an entire army base. He still found it unbelievable that this one was sitting here in a small Italian restaurant.

As he turned on water and heat gauges he found this one to be in good shape but for some small problems caused by years of neglect. The apparatus on top that administered the rinse would need some work when he got time, and when he ran the first load he noticed a primary pump was completely out near the front. He'd have to fix that before long, but the dishes came out clean as a whistle.

It was a two-man machine. As the dishes moved out the other end from where he loaded, there should be someone to unload them, but there was a bar on the belt that stopped the machine automatically when dishes reached the end. Soon he had a rhythm going whereby he staggered his loads and caught them on the far end before the machine stopped. A table stood against the wall with racks for the drying trays and dishes near plastic cups for silverware. It all kept him busy, but soon he was caught up and ahead of the game.

Cooks walked by and skidded used pots and pans toward the steaming sinks. Bill found time to scrub a few of their pots for them while the busboys brought him dirty dishes and retrieved clean ones from the drying table. Sometime around four o'clock when the lunchtime rush was over he found himself almost idle. Catching Leona walking by the doorway, he told her he'd like his beer now, Heineken if they had one. She glared at his wet T-shirt sticking to his body and showing more tattoos before stalking off without answering.

This is one mean bitch, he thought to himself as she walked away. But that assessment was tempered somewhat when she returned carrying a tray with a half-gallon pitcher of beer and a frosty glass on it.

"They got Heineken on tap. I thought you'd like it better like this than in the bottle." She grinned at him.

"I'm glad you're not stingy with the boss's beer," he said, taking the tray.

"Don't get drunk and lose your job, D.W. We need your talent around here," she said on her way out.

He put the tray on the floor behind the dish machine and poured a foaming glass full. It tasted delicious. Things were certainly looking up. As he worked on a second glass, one of the cook's helpers walked in the door to retrieve a pan and approached him with outstretched hand.

"Howdy," he said. "I'm James, and the other helper is Sam. We appreciate your washing those pots for us."

"Bill," he replied, taking the man's hand. "I don't mind helping out when I have time, but I'm hoping you'll think of me when you cook something good. I like to eat."

"Hey," James replied, "just name it and you got it." He was a man of average height with brown hair and long sideburns framing a clean-shaven face. He looked sincere, and Bill judged him to be in his early thirties. He wore a white cook's frock over a pair of pants with small black-and-white checks.

"I like sandwiches, and I'd like to have a sandwich every evening," Bill told him.

"What's your preference?" James asked.

"Lots of meat, mustard, and you do the rest." Bill replied.

"I'll catch you about eight o'clock," James said on his way out.

"Eight will be fine," Bill responded.

Business picked up around six, and at one point Bill saw Regina standing in the doorway watching him work. But when he looked at her she just smiled and left.

He found time to do a few more pots, and at eight o'clock James came in with a big juicy corned beef on rye on a platter with chips, assorted condiments, and a salad. No sooner had he sat it on the table and left than Leona walked in and put a cold bottle of Heineken beside it. He wondered if she'd had a change of heart but was cautious about the thought. Both busboys still acted leery of him when they came to retrieve dishes and silverware. He tried his best to glare when one of them glanced his way. They both had the look of college freshmen about them.

He got a paper sack from the locker and began putting pieces of leftover meat in it for June's dog. He was amazed at the volume of meat left on these plates. In prison the rare times steak had been served there was very little thrown away. Some of these plates contained a generous slab of prime rib with only one or two bites cut away.

It got busy again, and before he knew it Leona came to the door and yelled, "Quittin' time, D.W.!" She pronounced the second initial Dub-You.

He drained the machine and filled the soak tub for any dishes that would come in between now and tomorrow. Finding an old rickety squeegee, he began to clean up the floor while wondering if there was a possibility that the cocktail waitress could be seduced by a smelly dishwasher in wet clothes. That remote dream was shattered when he turned to find June standing there eating the remaining chips from his sandwich plate while gazing wistfully at the empty beer bottle. She smiled at him.

He couldn't help but grin back at her. She smiled with her entire being, and the refulgence of it bathed him in a warm glow.

Regina walked in, and Bill noticed her disapproving glance at June's tight T-shirt where her nipples pressed like grapes against the fabric.

"You weren't kidding when you said you could handle that machine," she said to Bill.

"No problem," he replied.

"I want you to know everyone here is relieved," she added. "When we don't have a dishwasher it takes Leona, both busboys, and sometimes myself to get them done."

"You can all relax," he replied. "I'll be around awhile. But this is an awful lot of machine for a restaurant this size."

"That bullheaded husband of mine bought it from the navy base out at Lemoore Naval Air Station," she said. "He got it cheap, but it's so hard for one person to operate."

"It's a good machine," Bill told her. "But it's been neglected. There's a primary pump on the blink, and it needs some new wiring and bulbs for these lights here," he said, pointing at on and off indicators on the side of the machine.

"I don't even know what a primary pump is, but can you fix all that if I get you the stuff?" she asked.

"I can do it, but I'll need some tools, and it will cost you a few hours of overtime and some rubber boots and a rubber apron," he replied.

"Write down what you need and I'll get it all for you," she replied.

"Come on, June," she said as she left. June followed her out and was back in a moment with a pencil and a note pad.

He sat down at the table and made a list of everything the machine needed as June looked over his shoulder. He added squeegees and cleaning detergent at the end of the list.

"This is gonna cost her," he said to June.

"She'll get her money's worth," June replied, and ran her hand through his wet hair.

Embarrassed, he jumped up and retrieved his sack of meat.

"Here's something for your dog," he said, handing it to her. "Be careful and hold it by the bottom or it's liable to break." He'd put much more in the sack than was needed.

He dropped the list off at the counter while Regina gave June a handful of foil-covered mints. They left the near-empty restaurant and went into the warm muggy night.

The old wino was coming over the fence into Ferraro's

back parking lot. June spotted him and yelled, "Hey, Cabbage Head!"

The old man stood there on one foot like a bird looking their way, then he grinned and shuffled toward them.

"Well, if it ain't Betty Boots, got her a rich boyfriend and a sack full of money," he said, nodding toward the sack.

"This is Cabbage Head, and this is my boyfriend, Bill," June said by way of introduction. The old man wiped his hand on his pants and stuck it out shakily. Bill took it, and could feel the shaking become a spastic trembling below the surface of the skin. He couldn't help but feel pity for the poor old fellow. He noticed that the sparse gray around the old battered face did resemble a head of cabbage in a surreal kind of way.

"Where you headed, Cabbage?" June inquired.

"Oh, I thought mebbe I'd go to a fancy ballroom downtown and waltz with some a' them highfalutin ladies," the old man replied with a shaky toothless grin.

Bill had already dug a couple of crumpled dollar bills from his pocket.

"Here," he said, holding them out. "You can buy one of the ladies a drink."

"Much obliged," the man said, taking the money.

"You want some prime rib?" June asked him, opening the top of the sack.

"Prime rib?" the old man replied. "Sheeeiiit!"

"You do like prime rib, don't you?" June asked, holding out the open sack.

"I like prime rib, spare ribs, barbecue ribs, and short ribs," the old man muttered as he extracted a few choice pieces from the bag. "Only kind of ribs I don't like is broke ribs."

He tore off a piece of meat and began enthusiastically gumming it.

"It's been a pleasure meeting you folks tonight," he mumbled around a mouthful as they took their leave.

"What's the story on him, June?" Bill asked when they were halfway across the field.

"Him and Bullfrog are hobos," she replied. "They live right here in this field, and they leave next month and go somewhere for the winter and come back in March or April. They come and go every year."

"How can they be hobos? They don't even have blankets. I saw that one sleeping on the ground today," he said.

"Oh no," she said. "They have bedrolls and cooking pots and everything. Sometimes they just drink too much wine and go to sleep wherever they are. They're pretty clean, too. I let them take a bath in our swimming pool now and then."

"You what?" he asked incredulously.

"Well, don't tell Mom," she replied, looking down as if she had said too much already. "She doesn't know them as well as I do."

"I'll bet she doesn't," he said as they emerged onto the motel grounds. Gail was standing in front of the office and began to walk their way when she spotted them.

"We've got a surprise for you!" June whispered before Gail reached them where they stood waiting for her.

"How was the first day on the job?" Gail asked.

"Just a bunch of water, garbage, and dirty dishes," he replied.

"Oh, I bet it wasn't bad," she replied as she led the way to his room. "Those are real nice people that own that place. I've known them for years."

"Where's the husband?" Bill asked.

"George? Oh, he's around somewhere. He's usually there every day. They have a beautiful daughter, Sophie, that goes to college at Fresno State."

"I can't wait," Bill said, unlocking the door to his room. The surprise June had mentioned became obvious as soon as he opened it.

A table had been installed at the foot of his bed and a

portable color TV was sitting on it. A Pioneer tape deck and a box of tapes were on the table beside the bed. A large portable fan was sitting plugged in against the wall opposite the bed.

He didn't know what to say or why they thought he deserved to be pampered like this. But he knew it would be difficult to accept this kind of charity, even though he was grateful to the point of feeling choked up.

"Gail, I can't—" he began.

"Wait a minute," she broke in. "Tony called today and I told him you were staying here. He said to let you use all this as long as you're here. It was his idea, not mine. I even asked him why he wanted you to have his things and he told me you would understand."

Bill had an idea why Tony had done this. When Tony had first arrived at Lompoc, he had been housed in Bill's cellblock. Bill had heard a lot about the man's reputation as a fighter. But Tony could also be vicious. Convicts talked about the time he had buried a hatchet in a stool pigeon's head at San Quentin and deposited the man in a garbage can.

There was an unspoken hope among the convicts in Lompoc that Bill and Tony would get into a fight with each other because of their reputations. People spent a lot of time speculating on the outcome of such an event. But Tony and Bill, being old hands at doing time, were very much aware of that sort of speculation and became good friends. They both understood that there was no percentage in fighting each other. Being friends made them that much stronger in a dog-eat-dog environment.

Bill had lent Tony a big radio and a pair of earphones. Tony loved hillbilly music. He got drunk one day while Bill was at work and slapped a new guard around in the cellblock. The goon squad finally subdued him and put him in isolation, from where he was to be shipped to the prison at Marion, Illinois.

Tony sent word out of the hole that he would have a property officer return Bill's radio. But Bill sent him word back to just keep it, as he would be locked down twenty-three hours a day in Marion and would need it.

Tony was now showing his respect for Bill and his appreciation of that gesture. Bill couldn't help but feel there was more at play here. Tony seemed to be also pushing him and Gail closer together. That would be just fine with him, but he couldn't afford to take the chance of being wrong about that kind of reasoning. It was probably just wishful thinking.

Gail had a defiant tone in her voice, and as he looked into her eyes, a defiant look there also. He could discern that she was prepared to get mad if he didn't accept these things as a loan.

"We're hoping you will stay here awhile," June put in.

"Oh, shut up, June!" Gail turned her wrath on her.

"Both of you get out of here and let me shower," Bill said before June could say anything else. It was as close as he could come to saying thanks.

When they were gone he stood looking at the TV for a minute or so. He hated television, and except for the evening news now and then, hadn't watched any for the past fourteen years. It was a nice color portable, but a gift he could have easily done without. He was drawn to the tape deck, however, and delighted to find a box of hillbilly tapes. He slid a David Allan Coe tape in, turned on the fan, and opened his bedside window a crack for draft. As he headed naked for the shower, he was thinking about June's last remark. She didn't have much to worry about. This little place was beginning to feel like home, Cabbage Head and all.

As he stepped into the shower, David Allan was singing:

I lost her lipstick one night on a strawberry daquiri,
Jack Daniel's whiskey and rum couldn't help me that time,
I lost her hair and her eyes in a glass of tequila,
I lost her heart and her soul in a bottle of wine.

He was in bed asleep before the last song on the tape played. His last thought before drifting off was a hope that he hadn't lost anything other than his youth in a prison cell.

10.

He slept late on Tuesday, and by the time he made himself a cup of instant coffee and drank it, it was ten o'clock. He wanted to get to work early in case Regina had the things for the machine that he needed. He hoped she had the boots, anyway. The steel-toed government high-top shoes were uncomfortable.

June was standing by the field watching the dog eat. The pan sat only about ten feet away now. The dog was uneasy about it but he was nevertheless eating. June was wearing a pair of white short shorts with a red halter top and red sandals. Her raven hair was tied back by a white ribbon and spilled down her back in a waterfall of curls. Something about this girl and dog in the sunshine instilled in him a heady feeling of pleasure. He stood watching as the dog snatched another piece of meat, then sat back on his haunches warily watching June as he chewed it.

"You're reeling him in pretty quick there, girl," he said.

"Oh hi, Bill." She turned toward him. "I thought he would come closer for prime rib than he would for baloney."

"No doubt about it," he laughed.

"What do you plan on naming him?" he asked.

"I hadn't thought about it," she replied.

"Well, if he's so hard to catch, how about Shadow?" he asked.

"Hey, that sounds good," she exclaimed.

"Think about it," he said, and walked on into the field, being careful to give the wary mutt plenty of leeway.

"Don't work too hard," she yelled at him.

"I won't," he shot back.

The restaurant door was locked when he arrived, so he went around and entered through the bar. The bartender nodded at him as he walked through while fiddling with a TV mounted high on the wall. Two men in a corner booth looked up warily from a pile of paper as he walked by. For a moment he thought they were tallying the previous night's receipts. Then he realized the slips of paper looked more like betting slips.

James and Sam were lethargically moving between the kitchen and the service counter in the dining room. The head cook, a big bear of a man, stood in the corner of the kitchen at a wooden table. He was dipping onion rings in a batter while glaring at everyone who looked his way. Bill figured him for a hangover and avoided his eyes.

The dining room was dim and cool, with the drapes drawn and the door closed. A man stood behind the open cash register.

"Can I help you?" he asked as Bill approached.

"I'm the dishwasher," Bill replied.

"Oh, hey! You must be Malone," the man replied, walking around the counter with his hand out. "I'm George Ferraro, and my wife's had me runnin' around town all morning finding stuff for you."

"Glad to meet you," Bill replied, as he returned the firm handshake. George Ferraro was a short man with coal-black hair and the olive skin and strong features of many southern Italians. His tendency to overweight was slight enough to make him look good in his clothes, and even in the dim light of the room Bill could see that he dressed well. He was wearing a white-on-white shirt with brown trim over a pair of tan slacks and two-tone brown-and tan-loafers that were probably made by Bally. A big diamond glittered on the ring finger of the hand he held out, and his appearance managed to be casual but impressive.

"Come on," he said, turning toward the dishroom. "I've got everything on your list except the motor. I've got all the tools."

Bill followed him into the dishroom, where the things he'd ordered were piled on a drainboard near the garbage disposal at the head of the big machine. A new pair of irrigation boots were there with a rubber apron draped over them.

"I got this machine cheap from the naval air base," George said. "But I was too stupid to realize it takes two or three people to operate it. It was so cheap I couldn't resist, and I figured I've got a big dishroom here, so what the hell."

"I can handle it," Bill told him, as he jumped up to sit on the drainboard and remove his shoes. The boots were exactly the size he'd ordered, and everything else looked to be precisely what he'd asked for. A complete box of electrical tools sat alongside a box of machine tools on the floor by the sink. Bill was impressed. George saw him eyeing them.

"You can keep those tools in the big utility closet," he said. "They came with the machine. I've had them stored to keep the winos from selling them."

"Winos will do a bit of bartering at times," Bill replied.

"You're not kidding, mister. I even hired a couple of illegal aliens, and they were drunks too. You don't drink a lot, do you?"

"Not on the job," Bill replied, as he began looking through the supplies.

"Well, about that motor," George said. "They will have to order it, and they told me it takes about five hours to install at sixty dollars an hour."

"Just get it, and I'll install it in three hours at seven-fifty an hour," Bill replied.

"Hey, I'll get it," George said as he started out. "You need anything else, you let me know. Anything at all."

"I'll do that," Bill told him as he left. He was a bit stunned at how happy these people were to have a dishwasher. As he unscrewed the rinse dispenser on top of the machine he began wondering how long he should wait before he asked for a raise. Sixty days seemed about right.

The next few days went along fine, and he began to feel at ease around all these new people. Leona ran hot and cold and he couldn't quite get a fix on her, but they worked out an uneasy way of communicating, and she kept plenty of beer coming his way.

The head cook was a big surly rascal who spoke very little to anyone. He roamed the kitchen like a big bear growling now and then at James and Sam, but he was a competent cook, and Bill noticed he steered way clear of Leona.

Gail and June took him to the Roeding Park Zoo on his first day off, both flirting shamelessly with him the whole day. The animals were awe-inspiring, but seeing them in their cages reminded him too strongly of his recent past. Most of them seemed resigned to the cage and content with the security. But here and there a bewildered rage gazed back at him from unfathomable eyes. To him they seemed much like convicts.

A big gorilla walked down to a little stream, pulled a handful of grass, and rubbed it in his chest as they stood looking at him. Bill looked at the red-rimmed eyes and thought he could discern the feelings of this caged animal being stared at by passersby. He knew the gorilla wasn't happy or content in this situation.

The wolves were especially pitiful to him. They ran back and forth in their cages with their tongues hanging out and their eyes brimming and bloodshot with the rage of frustration and confinement. He found himself checking their cages looking for a possible way out, but security was tight. They didn't have a prayer. Still they ran and looked.

Only the monkeys and bovine mammals seemed at home in this environment, but to him they also seemed deformed somehow by their confinement. He didn't envy any of them.

They didn't even have the option of drugs and alcohol as humans did to help them survive the killing boredom of the cage.

June began to grow on him like a barnacle on the bottom of a ship. He felt sad for her in a way he couldn't quite define to himself. She had almost no young friends, and he hoped that would change when school started in September. But she was wonderful company.

Almost every evening she brought a Scrabble board over and beat the hell out of him. Sometimes Gail played, and he couldn't beat her either. He found it amazing, because he possessed an extremely good vocabulary. But they both knew more three-letter words than he had ever dreamed existed. Words like "xyl," meaning wood, which he foolishly challenged. Or "xen," which meant a stranger. They both seemed to know a thousand such words.

The motel attracted mainly pimps, whores, and dope fiends along with the occasional truck driver. The women liked to lounge around the pool in bikinis, and that kept his mind on sex. But he was growing calmer about that.

The pleasure he felt in the company of June and Gail was like a balmy warm oil bath in the lee of a turbulent world. It was such a change from the last fourteen years of hatred, violence, and chaos that he found himself becoming addicted to it. In the mornings he ran for long distances, often miles past the junkyard in the grass along the freeway.

The Mexican in the '56 Chevy became his alarm clock. He showed up every morning between seven and eight o'clock. The sound of the loud mufflers never failed to wake him up. Sometimes Bill would pull his curtain back and watch as the dope fiends straggled out to the car in various states of undress to score their morning fix. He was amazed at the brazen attitudes about something that years ago was done in total secrecy. But he also noticed a prowl car cruising by more often now, and figured the Mexican's days were probably numbered. He never left his car. Just drove up and waited, and he never had to wait very long. His business here was usually done in five minutes or less.

The work at the restaurant was smooth and easy for him. The amount of dishes he washed was tiny in comparison to the dishes of the twelve hundred convicts he'd been used to washing for. Often he would look up from the machine to see Regina or George standing in the doorway watching him. But they said very little and asked no personal questions at all. It was as if they had ceded the dishroom to him and were afraid of losing his services. He had begun to put the leftover meat in two sacks now. One of the sacks he left each night on the inside of the fence where he'd met Cabbage Head. The sack was gone every day, so he figured the hobos were getting it. The other he kept for June.

George brought the pump in during Bill's third week, and he decided to wait until Sunday night to install it. There was some sort of banquet or party that night, and as he tore the machine down, Leona came in with a stack of dishes and dumped them in the sink.

"Man, I'm glad you tore that thing down tonight, otherwise I'da had to wash all these dishes," she said, looking down at him where he lay near the front of the machine disconnecting the conveyor belt.

"Well, get me some beer and we'll call it even," he replied.

"You got it, man," she said.

When she walked back in carrying a tray containing a pitcher of beer and a glass, Campbell was right behind her.

"Gentleman here to see you, D.W.," she said. She put the tray on the table and left. Bill noticed there were two clean glasses on the tray.

"Hey there," Campbell said as Bill got up off the wet floor. "I didn't want to come where you work, but you hadn't come home at the usual time and I didn't want to make two trips. Hope you don't mind."

"I don't mind," Bill replied. "What's up?"

"The old bottle trick, buddy." Campbell smiled as he took a small cardboard box out of his coat pocket and fished a urinalysis bottle out of it. Bill saw Leona walk by the doorway and look in as he took the bottle from Campbell's outstretched hand.

Bill had to piss anyway, so he walked behind the machine out of sight and opened the bottle.

"Do you want to watch?" he asked Campbell from behind the machine.

"I trust you," Campbell responded.

He filled the bottle and finished relieving himself in the drain behind the machine. The bottle overflowed as he screwed the top back on, so he carried it to the rinse sink and washed it off before handing it back to Campbell.

"Thanks," he said as he put the bottle back in the box. Bill noticed him eyeing the pitcher of beer on the table. He walked over and poured the two glasses full enough that foam ran over the sides.

"Here's one for you," he told Campbell.

"Well hell, I don't mind if I do," Campbell replied, putting the bottle back in his pocket. But Bill could tell he was uneasy about drinking a beer here.

"First time I've ever drunk on the job, but I'm a beer lover. Is this bottle going to come back clean?" Campbell said after draining half his glass and wiping his lips with the back of his hand.

"Clean as a Safeway chicken," Bill replied after a healthy drink from his own glass. The beer was so cold it made his head ache right between his eyes, but it carried a wonderful coolness straight to his blood.

"I received a letter from a woman named Frances Logan in Portland. She told me you own half the property she lives on and she wants you to get in touch."

"That's my mother's friend," Bill replied. "I'll call her."

"Well, I hope so, because you know, of course, that I can't give her any information about you at all, but she seems concerned."

"I'll call her," Bill told him again and refilled the glasses.

"Looks like with all that property business and all your

friends in Portland that you'd parole up there. You can if you want to, you know."

"I don't want to," Bill replied.

"I'm having a tough time figuring you out, Malone." Campbell adopted a serious tone.

"Don't strain yourself," Bill replied, looking him levelly in the eye.

"Part of that is my job, but on a personal level I'd really like to know why you'd rather wash dishes in Fresno where you don't know anyone and live in a fleabag motel when you have your own property and friends in Portland. Can you just enlighten me that much?"

"It's what I want to do," Bill replied.

"Well, can you explain why? You know, give me some logical reason?" Campbell prompted.

"I don't explain myself on a personal level to people who carry my piss around in their pocket," Bill answered in a resigned but polite tone.

Campbell stood there a moment looking at him before he replied.

"Okay, bud, if this bottle is clean, I won't see you for a while, so get your reports in."

"I will," Bill replied, glad to have done with the conversation.

"Did you give a phony name here when you went to work?" Campbell asked as he turned to leave.

"No, why?" Bill asked.

"That woman called you D.W.," Campbell said.

"Stands for dishwasher," Bill replied with a smile.

"Don't work too hard," Campbell said on his way out.

As he lay back down near the front of the machine, Leona walked back in with another load of dishes.

"Man, that looked like an FBI agent," she said.

"Parole officer," Bill mumbled, knowing it would be futile to try to sidetrack her curiosity.

"D.W., you ain't one a' them secret witness guys, is you?" she asked.

The blood rushed to his head, and he sat up and looked at her standing there with her hand on one hip. He had to take a deep breath before trusting himself to reply.

"No, I'm nothing like that. I'm just an old jailbird trying to mind my own fucking business, and stool pigeons are the one thing I don't make jokes about." He tried to control his tone, but she could tell he was mad.

"My my, ain't we touchy tonight," she replied and started for the door.

He watched her as she walked away. She had high and well-defined hips, and their movement tonight was just a bit more pronounced than usual. At the door she stopped and turned back toward him and with a half-smile remarked, "No wonder you look so horny all the time." She dropped the smile and added, "I hope you ain't one a' them white-power fuckin' nazis," and was gone before he could reply.

All he could do was go back to grappling furiously with the sprocket on the conveyor belt. Five minutes of this had him mumbling, laughing, and muttering to himself.

Leona didn't fit in with his image of modern-day women. A few minutes after he'd met her she'd threatened to bust his head, then brought him beer like it came from a waterfall. Now she'd walked in here and asked if he was a stool pigeon, implied he might be a nazi, and told him he looked horny.

Her game wasn't really that difficult to figure out. She was intensely curious about him and too proud to just ask. She probably thought if she kept accusing him of being all these unsavory things he would throw in the towel, let his hair down, and tell her all about himself. He really wouldn't mind doing so, but there wasn't that much to tell, and what he could tell her she had no frame of reference to understand. When it reached that point he'd be spending all his time explaining and attempting to justify himself to her. Better to let her speculate on his nature and politics.

11.

His thoughts settled on Frances Logan, and he felt guilty about not calling her. She had been his mother's constant companion as long as he could remember. One of his earliest recollections of her was a weekend morning when his mother, Rita, and Frances readied him for a drive to visit his father in the Oregon State Prison.

As they dressed in demure but fashionable clothes, they constantly posed and asked each other, "How do I look?" One would have thought they were attending a gala event. They were beautiful women, and both belonged to his father. By the time he realized they were both prostitutes also, it didn't bother him that much, because many of the women he had met in his life were in that game.

Frances was childless and tried to spoil him as much as she spoiled Fifi, her insufferable poodle. Bill had fought her tooth and nail on that issue. But the pampering did have its moments.

They drove to the prison in their old '46 Ford Club Coupe, which Bill thought was the finest car in the world. He could still remember the smell of the new seat covers mingled with perfume, and the wonder of the treasures he found in the glove compartment. Frances sometimes took the batteries out of the flashlight in the glove box and stuffed it with candy for him to find. Other times she'd lock it and pretend she'd lost the key.

Sometimes she would haul him up on her lap and sing an old silly song to him, and though he squirmed and blushed he loved every minute of it. Rita would join the singing as she drove. Bill could remember the words to this day and how good it felt to look out at the tall trees and the world flowing gently by as the women sang to him.

Oh where have you been, Billy boy, Billy boy?
Oh where have you been, charming Billy?
I have been to seek a wife, she's the charming of my life,
She's a young thing and cannot leave her mother.

At the prison itself they were treated like touring royalty. The staffs of prisons view most convict visitors with red-eyed suspicion and treat them as potential criminals. But Rita was one of those rare women who possessed the right amount of wit and beauty to charm even the most dour of bureaucrats. Doors and gates opened quickly and smoothly for their entourage.

Visiting was in a basement room of the prison where a long counter with stools on each side divided visitors from convicts. A guard sat in a high chair at the end of the counter observing every move. No touching or reaching across the counter was allowed.

Bill remembered his father as a good-looking, dark-haired man sitting across the counter in a white cotton duck prison uniform. Sometimes laughing and other times being stern with him and the women, but always mild-mannered and easy to talk with. It was always Rita's job to get up and divert the guard's attention for a moment while Frances slipped his dad some money across the counter. He sometimes joined in their elaborate ruses. When he asked them why his dad needed the money, they would reply vaguely, "Oh, this and that."

Rita and he lived with Frances in adjoining apartments in downtown Portland. The women did their entertaining in Frances's place and they all lived in Rita's apartment.

By the time Bill was ten, they had bought him a shoe shine box and he was on the street shining shoes after school and weekends. They lived in a seedy part of town.

A place of poolhalls, pawnshops, sex stores, and hat cleaning and blocking establishments.

Whores would sometimes have Bill clean their shoes and would pull their dresses up to show him their crotches.

"Do you like that, boy?" they would ask, then laugh when he blushed and stammered.

Pimps and whores would pay him to keep their dope stash in his shoe shine box among the polish and rags, picking it up when they needed it. He made good money. He was in high school before he fully realized that most women were not prostitutes. They were in a minority, but from his experience in life, he'd thought it was the other way around.

Two years before his dad's parole date, he was murdered at the prison. Stabbed in the back as he stood playing dominoes at a table in the yard. A tragedy that almost drove Rita crazy and one she never completely recovered from. It changed her somehow from a confident, assured woman to a tentative and hesitant girl. Bill came to view the diminishment of her spirit with as much sadness as he did the unreasonable death of his father. When Bill himself went to prison she was terrified and had insisted that he call her twice a week right up to when she died of a sudden and unexpected brain hemorrhage.

He decided he'd have to call Frances, but it was kind of nice in a way to have something to feel guilty about. There certainly wasn't much debauchery or profligacy in his life these days.

He finished installing the pump just after midnight and left through the bar, carrying the two sacks of meat. The cocktail waitress smiled at him but directed a concerned gaze to the sacks he carried as if she thought he was taking food home to eat. Her disapproval didn't bother Bill. She was brought to work every day and collected every night by a big burly husband.

The night was still, warm, and muggy. As the warm air

pressed at him he felt the usual sense of surprise and delight. In the Northwest where he'd grown up, when night fell it was time to put on a warm coat. Here in Fresno it often stayed warm all night.

An old black man leaned patiently against the fence by the field with his arms crossed over his chest. As Bill drew near, the man became so animated that it was obvious he was waiting for the meat. For a moment Bill felt chagrined at the thought that his largess hadn't been getting to Cabbage Head, but then he realized this was probably the Bullfrog June had mentioned.

"You must be Bullfrog," Bill said as he drew near.

"Yes suh, that's me." The man smiled and reached for the heavy sack Bill was extending toward him.

He was a short, frail man with a full head of wiry gray-and-black hair. The gray looked white, like balls of cotton caught up in a black wire brush. Bill couldn't see any resemblance to a frog. The brown eyes didn't protrude, and were calm and steady as ball bearings. His face, though worn and battered, contained a bearing of dignity. His only pronounced feature was a nose that looked as if it had been broken twenty or thirty times. In the dim light of the parking lot it resembled a half-skinned catfish hanging from its tail between his eyebrows.

Bill was impressed by the cleanliness of the man. He wore a pair of clean overalls beneath a light denim jacket, and a plaid shirt buttoned to the neck. A pair of worn but clean black hightop shoes completed his outfit.

"My name is Bill," he said, extending his hand.

"Bullfrog, and pleased to meet you, suh," the man replied, taking Bill's hand in a firm grip.

"How did you get the name Bullfrog?" Bill asked.

"Ah, it was in a 'bo camp a few years back, suh. White boy drunk on wine he looked cross a campfire at me and says, 'Man, your nose look like a squashed African bullfrog.' Old Cabbage Head hear that an' I been Bullfrog ever since."

They stood there grinning at each other until Bill laughed

out loud. Bullfrog flashed strong even teeth and laughed right along with him.

"Don't call me sir, I'm just a dishwasher. I don't own that place. I should be calling you sir; you and Cabbage Head are the first real hobos I've ever met personally."

"No suh—I mean Bill—I'm no hobo. Now Cabbage Head, he a hobo, but me, I'm a retired brain surgeon."

"A what?" Bill asked incredulously.

"Yes suh, Bill suh, just a old retired brain surgeon out seein' a piece of the world."

"That must have been interesting work." Bill grinned at him.

"Nah, I didn't work on no white folks," Bullfrog replied and grinned back at him.

Bill took an instant liking to the man and felt like talking awhile with him. He suddenly realized how terribly lonely he felt. It was the same kind of loneliness he'd felt in prison with people packed around him like cattle, more a feeling of total isolation and alienation than anything else. But he didn't have time.

"It was good meeting you, Bullfrog, but I've got to go—there's a girl waiting on this other sack and it's way past her bedtime. Give Cabbage Head my regards."

"Same to you, suh, and we do appreciate the groceries. Old June Bug start school tomorrow. Tell her to come to see me and Cabbage 'roun the weekend, 'cause we be takin off 'fore long."

"I'll tell her," Bill said, and as Bullfrog turned to go he added, "Now don't you go practicing no brain surgery on Cabbage Head."

"Cabbage ain't got nothin to practice on," Bullfrog replied over his shoulder.

Gail was waiting for him near the back of the motel. He was glad June hadn't stayed up this late before her first day at school. But as he drew near it was obvious just by looking at her that something was amiss.

"Is June with you, Bill?" she asked anxiously as he walked

up to her. There was a pleading tone in her voice as if she wanted him to say yes.

"No, I haven't seen her today," he replied.

"I haven't seen her since before dark," she said. "She knows she starts school tomorrow."

Bill didn't know what to say. Her tone alarmed him as well. He walked over to where June had the dog dish and began piling meat on it while trying to think of where she might be. Gail walked over and stood beside him.

"What about those homeless men out in the field?" she asked hopefully.

"They haven't seen her in a while. I just talked to one of them," he answered.

"Well, she has a sixteen-year-old girlfriend across town that has a car. I can't stand the little rich bitch, but that's probably where June is," she said.

"Can you call over there?" he asked.

"I already did, but there's no answer. There's a little house out back they use for parties, but I just don't understand June doing me like this. I wonder if you could watch the office and stay by the phone while I drive over there."

"Sure, no problem."

He followed her to the office and stood behind the counter as she got her car keys. The night had just begun to turn cold, but he felt much colder inside. He didn't believe Gail really thought June was off with a girlfriend. It was more like she just wanted to do something to alleviate her own fears. He felt the same way, but there was nothing for him to do but stay here and worry.

"If you want to eat, help yourself. I'll call you if I find her," she said on her way out.

He listened to her car start up and pull out. He didn't know what to do with himself. There was a chair behind the counter, but he didn't want to sit down. From all he knew about June and her behavior, something was terribly wrong. It wasn't in her nature to pull a stunt like this. She was hardheaded and stubborn but very considerate of her mother's feelings.

He found himself pacing up and down behind the counter and was relieved when the door opened and a pimp he'd seen around the two women next door to him entered. The man was tall and good-looking, with curly black hair and big liquid brown eyes. He was dressed in lizard-skin cowboy boots, silk slacks, and a tan leather jacket over a beige silk shirt.

"Hey! How you doin'?" The man spoke with an Oklahoma accent.

"Pretty good," Bill replied. "Yourself?"

"Ah, I'm okay," the man replied. "Came to pay the rent."

Bill watched as he extracted a huge roll of bills from the front pocket of the slacks and counted out $140 onto the counter.

"There you are," he said. "That brings me up to another week, so I'll catch you next Monday."

"You want some kind of receipt?" Bill asked as he gathered up the money.

"Not me," the man replied with a smile. "I can't read anyway, so it wouldn't make me no difference."

Bill opened a drawer and put the money in it. He was wondering why this room was $140 when his was only $45 when the man spoke again.

"Hey, I want to apologize for Paula bothering you last week. It won't happen again. She didn't know you and Gail were hooked up."

Bill had to pull his mind back to figure out what the man was talking about. Then he remembered a few days back a woman in a very short robe had knocked on his door asking to use an iron. It was obvious she intended to sell him some pussy. She was good-looking and he had been thinking about inviting her in when Gail suddenly appeared by the office and called the woman over. Bill had thought no more about it.

"Gail and I aren't hooked up. I just rent a room here," he replied.

The man laughed and looked closely at him.

"Well, Paula sure got her ass chewed for bothering you, but she's okay. Most girls work at night. Paula wakes up on the job."

"It's okay," Bill replied.

While they were talking, Bill heard the Mexican's Chevy pull up out in front. He couldn't keep his mind on anything but the phone at the end of the counter. He would probably feel like he was swimming under water until it rang.

Just as the pimp went out the door, he heard the car door slam and the motor rev up and drive away. He guessed the Mexican must have had an emergency customer, as he usually didn't come by this late at night.

The door opened again, and the pimp stuck his head back in the door.

"Hey, man, there's a broad passed out on your grass out here. Looks like she's drunk or something."

"Thanks," Bill replied and began to walk around the counter. His feet felt as if there were lead in them, and a tight band began to grip at his chest. Hair stood up at the back of his neck, and there was a feeling of relief mixed with fear as his mind began putting things in perspective. He wasn't going to have to wait for the phone.

The pimp was walking briskly away, and Bill heard the tap of his heels on the walk as he came out the door and saw June lying at the edge of the lawn nearest the road. The light was dim there, but there was no doubt it was June.

He ran to where she lay and kneeled down over her. Her hair was matted and looked wet. She lay on her side curled in a fetal position. Strands of hair lay across her neck and cheek, and relief flooded him when he saw a strand or two rise with her breath. At least she was alive.

She had on a pink-and-white short cotton skirt and a low-cut white peasant blouse. A lone black leather sandal adorned her right foot. The left foot was bare, and there was blood on the front of her blouse. The chill of the night air and June's condition sent a shiver up his spine.

He grasped her bare shoulder and tried to turn her toward him.

"June?" he said.

"No!" she exclaimed, and pushed feebly at his hand while trying to roll away from his grasp. Her actions were pure reflex and had no force or strength at all. He kept the grip on her shoulder and shook her gently.

"June, it's me, Bill," he said as he shook her.

"Bill?" she mumbled into the grass. Her words were slurred, as if she'd taken a big dose of sleeping pills. He rolled her onto her back and lifted her off the grass. Her eyes fluttered open for a moment and looked at him, then she rolled her face in against his neck like a small sleepy child.

"Help me, Bill," she breathed against his neck.

"Don't worry, girl, you're okay now," he said reassuringly. He walked with her in his arms back to the office. He hoped he could keep from crying and was amazed to feel tears stinging at the back of his eyes and his throat muscles being forced closed as if in the grip of a vise. A pounding ache was starting at the base of his skull.

She wasn't passed out. It was more as if she was conscious and made of rubber. Her eyes were dilated, and all he could think of was Valium or PCP. There was something vaguely familiar about her state. The blood on her blouse was just a big splotch with little dabs and drops beneath it, so she wasn't bleeding now. He hoped she hadn't been cut.

"Where's Mom?" she mumbled against his neck as he carried her into the office.

"Out looking for you," he told her. She seemed to relax more in his arms when he said that.

The only light on in the living quarters was the bathroom light. He carried her in there, placed her on the toilet in a sitting position, then held her there with one hand while with the other he turned on the sink faucet and held a towel under it until it was sopping wet with cold water. He mashed the wet towel against her forehead and let the cold water run over her face and onto her shoulders.

She spluttered and came alive, pushing at the rag with one hand.

"Wait," she said.

"Wait hell," he replied and dropped the towel back into the sink, raised her arms above her head, and pulled the blouse off.

"Shit," he exclaimed as he looked at her breasts. Her left nipple was swollen, and there was a gash in the areola covered by a glob of half-dried blood.

"He bit me," she said, looking down at herself. "Please don't tell Mom," she added.

"We'll see," he replied, getting on his knees and removing the one sandal. He then caught the stretch band of her skirt and, lifting her slightly, pulled it off. As it came away, he noticed for the first time that there was dried blood on it also. Blood was smeared on her upper thighs as well. She pressed her legs together and turned slightly sideways, attempting to hide herself from him. The gesture relieved him somewhat, because it showed she was lucid enough not to be in danger of an overdose of something, but the sight of the blood mingled with a faint bad odor almost nauseated him.

"Jesus Christ!" he breathed as he rose off the floor. "I'm going to call an ambulance." He knew he didn't have the guts or the nerve to look any further to find out the extent of the damage that had been done to her.

"No!" she yelled emphatically, and seeming to come alive she tried to rise shakily from the toilet seat. He pushed her back down, and as the life seemed to ebb from her again a distant memory flickered at his mind and he became reasonably certain of the drug that had caused her condition. She'd been given a mickey. Probably chloral hydrate. All the signs and symptoms were there.

"I'm okay," she said, making an effort to raise her head and look him in the eye.

"You're covered with blood," he replied.

"That's, that's—I'm just on my period," she said, waving her limp hand toward her clenched and bloody thighs.

"Help me into the shower," she added.

He went to the shower, turned it on, and adjusted the water until it was good and hot. Then he put his hands under her armpits, lifted her up, and walked her on stumbling feet to the stall.

"What happened?" he asked as he put her under the water. There were large blue bruises on the backs of her thighs.

"He raped me. When he saw I was on my period he got mad and then raped me in the wrong place," she mumbled as she gratefully let the water run over her head. He took a washcloth from the soap dish, soaped it up good, and handed it to her. She took it and dabbed feebly at the blood on her nipple. He reached across her and turned off the hot water and watched her gasp and jump as the cold water hit her. She tried to fight her way out, but he held her under it for a minute or so, then turned the hot water back on. She was spitting and spluttering, but it woke her up quite a bit.

"I feel dirty," she said as she began to soap her hair. He let her go, and she wobbled slightly but kept her feet.

"Lean against the wall," he told her, and she did, letting the spray hit her in the face. Bill's breath was short, and he was almost overcome by feelings of rage, fear, and sadness, but he was successful enough at suppressing them all so that he couldn't be sure what he felt. He had to think now—not feel.

He rummaged around in the medicine cabinet over the sink and found some alcohol, iodine, and hydrogen peroxide. Pulling June away from the water, he had her cup her hand under her nipple while he poured the peroxide and alcohol over it. The glob of blood was gone now, and it was obvious she'd been bitten. A rage overtook him that made him weak in the knees.

"Did you take a ride with the Mexican in the Chevy?" he asked as he put her back under the water.

"Yes," she mumbled, looking down toward the floor.

He hit her with the cold water, and she came alive again. As he turned the warm back on, he heard the insistent ringing of the telephone in the office.

"The phone's ringing. It's probably Gail. I've got to leave you here for a minute," he told her.

"Don't tell her!" she yelled pitifully as he left the bathroom.

"I won't," he replied. "You try and get washed off."

It was Gail on the other end. "Bill! She's not over here!" she yelled frantically into his ear.

"She's here," he replied, hoping he sounded more calm than she did.

"Oh my God, is she okay?"

"She's okay," he assured her. He could feel the relief that flooded her and wished he could feel it also.

"I'll be right there," she said and hung up.

June was out of the shower and drying herself when he returned to the bathroom.

"Did you tell her?" she asked defiantly.

"I told her nothing. She's on her way. You tell her whatever you want to tell her." He grabbed another towel and began vigorously drying her long hair. She wrapped her towel around her waist and grabbed up a Kotex that she'd laid out by the sink.

"That's enough," she told him. "I've got to get in bed before she gets here." He stopped rubbing her hair.

"Will you get rid of these clothes?" she asked.

"Go ahead, go to bed," he answered.

She left the room walking slowly, and he began to clean

the bathroom as best he could, trying to put things back as he had found them. One of the towels had blood on it, so he rolled the bloody clothes and the one sandal up in it and carried the bundle out to a Dumpster at the side of the office.

Gail came driving up right after he got back inside.

"Where is she?" she asked as she came in the door.

"She's in bed," he replied.

"What happened? Where'd she go?" she asked, looking intently at him.

"You'll have to ask her. She just came in, took a shower, and went to bed," he replied as he walked around the counter and toward the front door.

"Goddammit, didn't you even ask her?" she demanded as he reached the door.

"None of my business," he replied and went off.

When he made it back to his room, his head was bursting with pain. He found a Bayer aspirin bottle in his nightstand drawer, took four, and lit a cigarette. Taking down a saucepan, he put some water on to heat for coffee. He'd never had a headache that aspirin with a cigarette and coffee wouldn't cure, but he knew it was going to be close with this one. He stripped naked, made the coffee, and carried the cup into the shower with him.

As he dried himself off, his twelve-dollar Casio alarm clock read 3:35 a.m. He put on clean Levi's and a long-sleeved cotton pullover shirt. An insistent throbbing persisted at the base of his skull. He knew it would be no help going to bed. He put on socks and his steel-toed government work shoes and took a seat on the easy chair by his bed. Perhaps if he could sit here awhile his mind would clear.

An insistent knocking at his door informed him that his night was far from over. He went to the door and pulled it open. Gail stood there breathing hard, her leopard eyes red-rimmed and angry. They now held the look of a cobra, and they fastened right on his. He didn't move or invite her in, but she pushed past him and turned to face him in the dim room.

"I want to know what happened, and I want to know right fucking now," she demanded.

"You'll have to ask June," he replied as calmly as possible.

"Well, where are her clothes? I can't even find her clothes! You know something, dammit! Where was she? What happened?"

He took her by the shoulders. Now a tear leaked from her eye and skittered down her cheek. She seemed on the verge of violent hysteria.

"Gail, go home. Ask June in the morning. I don't know anything to tell you." As he said it he eased her toward the door. She didn't resist, but she turned at the door.

"All right, I'll go home, but you don't forget your rent runs out this Friday."

"I'll be gone by noon Friday," he said and shut the door firmly. He felt so drained of energy that the chair seemed to swallow him. The ease with which chaos had entered his life in spite of his most careful efforts to keep it at bay overwhelmed him.

How in hell, he thought to himself, does a square plan his life out for years ahead of time? Just lay it all out there in a neat line like a road map and travel happily on his planned route? There was something terribly amiss here when he couldn't even wash a few dishes and mind his own business. Now the only thing he could see in his future that was absolutely certain was that he was going to kill a Mexican if and when he could find him. The rest was up for grabs. But how does murder just enter a man's life as if to walk in and say, "Howdy, here I am, let's get it over with"?

What he guessed a workingman—a good citizen—would do right here is find a good justification for not killing the son of a bitch. But what could that possibly be? "That, my friend," he mumbled to himself, "is the question."

Call the police? It's the Mexican's word against a girl who can't stand any more of the ugly scene and an ex-convict hearsay witness. That wasn't likely to play well in court, and even if it did, would a few years of the bastard's life pay the tab? Wouldn't that just put another little girl in more jeopardy down the road somewhere?

He realized that much of this kind of thinking was futile. His own ethics prevented him from telling the police about anything or taking a witness stand to testify against someone.

The Mexican's world and his operated under the same code. Whatever justice he could find for June would have to be found without courts and laws. What was done to her was outside laws. Anything he could do for her would have to be the same. There was just no use in trying to turn it any other way. Much as he would like to.

If there was a justification to try to roll with the punch, Bill knew he wouldn't be able to find it. The answer, if it existed, lay off in another world. That beautiful little girl that fed stray dogs in the sunshine and hobos in fields, that had the power to bring joy to a bitter convict, lived in this world, and the creep that hurt her was not going to share it much longer.

There was another option. He knew he could have his clothes packed in a few minutes and be in another state before today was done. But he'd rather spend another fourteen years in prison than live the rest of his life with the memory that would follow him from this place. A past that would reside in all his mirrors and patiently wait for him to gaze upon it each day. Sitting like a vulture in a gilt frame waiting to peck and pull at his diminished and dying spirit.

His rage washed over him now in waves, beginning with goose bumps at the base of his spine. Daybreak found him walking and pacing with clenched fists and gritted teeth. He stopped himself and took a few deep breaths. In the condition he was in he didn't trust himself to leave the room. He was pretty well certain the Mexican wouldn't come back here.

He figured to get what information he could about the man from the two young addicts who lived in the room at the end nearest the street. But if he didn't calm down somehow, he'd be liable to hurt one or both of them if they said or did anything he didn't like. Sitting back down and deep breathing helped some.

It was some consolation that he knew his mind was made up as to how he would proceed. But every time his mind began to calm a bit, he thought of some words he'd read by Albert Camus: "Perhaps this world is a place where children suffer, and if we do not alleviate the suffering, who will?"

He seemed to be in a trance when he heard the sound and for a moment thought he must be dreaming. The drone of the Chevy's pipes reverberated in his ears like a bee coming closer to his head. He heard them faintly when the car turned the corner, and they revved and popped even more loudly now as the car drew up to the front of the motel. He arose from the chair and, kneeling across his bed, pulled the curtain back an inch or so. The Mexican was sitting there in his pretty idling car while the young couple were leaving their room in the morning sunshine. They must have been waiting for him, Bill thought to himself. But they certainly weren't the only ones.

The only window at the back of his living quarters big enough to crawl through was above the kitchen sink. It screeched as he forced it up. Then he jumped up on the counter and slid out feet first onto the dew-laden grass in the field. He was glad he'd put on his steel-toed shoes. The night had been chilly, but as he turned and walked along behind the rooms toward the street, a plangent orange sun lay above the horizon.

The two addicts were leaning against the car door talking to the Mexican when he came walking around the side of their room. No one noticed him until he was at the front bumper of the car. Then the male addict saw him out of the corner of his eye. He jumped back from the car, obviously startled, as Bill kept coming. The Mexican saw him a second later, muttered something under his breath, and very quickly popped something into his mouth. Then smiled as Bill drew up to the car window and muttered between clenched teeth, "*¿Qúe pasa?*"

This scene was so obvious to him. The Mexican had been about to sell the couple some dope, and thinking Bill was an undercover cop, he had popped it into his mouth to swallow. They always kept dope in rolled and tied balloons for this purpose. It would come out intact later with normal body wastes. The Mexican was about his own age, with small eyes and a protruding overbite that a Zapata mustache did little to hide. Long shaggy black hair hung beneath a porkpie hat. He resembled a smooth-shaven beaver.

His little eyes widened in shock and surprise as Bill's right fist hit him in the mouth so hard it knocked his teeth through his upper lip. He went over sideways and yelled something in Spanish as his head slammed the inside of the passenger door. Bill felt the shock of the punch in his shoulder, and it felt wonderful.

"Hey!" the girl outside the car yelled, and grabbed his shoulder with both hands. He slammed his elbow back across her jaw as he drew his arm back out of the car and went for the door handle. The Mexican was scrambling around in the seat trying to open the passenger door.

Bill grabbed one of his kicking feet and jerked him until his shoulders cleared the seat, then let go and kicked him in the groin with the same force he'd once used to dropkick a football.

"Aiyeeee!" the man screamed, and the pain and terror in his voice reverberated in the still morning air. He lay doubled up beside the car, and Bill took careful aim and kicked him again in the small of the back. He then began kicking him in the kidneys, the knee, anywhere he could see, and alternately stomping him on the neck and head just as he would have stomped a rattlesnake.

The man had long since become silent, and the force of the kicks edged him toward the front of the car. The ground was soaked with blood beneath him. Bill's foot was hurting by now, and he reached down, grabbed a handful of hair, pulled the man's head up to the hood, and tried to pound him through the metal with his fist. Something had snapped inside him like a dam bursting, and he couldn't stop. He tried to make every punch harder than the last. He was in a slow-motion zone and could hear faraway screaming around him like bees buzzing in his ears. Suddenly a clawing banshee was on his back pulling at his hair and grabbing at his arm. He reached around, grabbed her, and pulled her around, slamming her onto the bloody hood of the Chevy, fully intending to bust her head, and when he saw it was Gail he heard her voice at the same time.

"Goddammit, Bill! You're killing him!"

He stood breathing hard and looking at her for long seconds before he took his hand from her neck. He took a few deep breaths and looked down at the Mexican lying crumpled and bloody in the dirt. The man's face was a swollen mess of blood, dirt, and torn flesh. A splinter of jawbone poking through his bloody flesh was the only clean-looking aspect of his face. Both doors of the Chevy were open and the motor was still idling. Bill felt some of his reason returning with the sound of the motor.

The girl was lying on the lawn, and the kid was pouring water on her face from a hat. She was sputtering and coming around. Bill looked again at the Mexican, and Gail stepped toward him and put both hands on his heaving chest.

"Bill, please don't," she said softly.

He felt overcome with pity for her. She was standing there in a bloody bathrobe, strands of hair adhering to pale cheeks wet with tears and drawn with terror. It had been a bad night and day for her as well.

"I'm all done," he assured her.

With relief he looked around and saw that no cars had driven by or stopped. A man stood on the stoop of a unit near the office looking at the carnage, but when he saw Bill turn toward him he ducked back into his room and shut the door. The only ones outside were Gail and he and the two youngsters on the lawn. He could feel his right hand throbbing and swelling now.

He crawled across the seat of the Chevy and slammed the passenger door. As he backed out he noticed five balloons lying on the seat like little red and yellow marbles. He scooped them up, noticing they weren't wet, so they weren't the ones the man had popped into his mouth. He was in a hurry now. He walked fast to where the kid was helping the girl off the grass, and they jumped back as he approached.

Throwing the balloons on the grass, he said to them, "Take those and pack your stuff and get out of here."

They eagerly scooped up the balloons and were headed for their room almost before he finished speaking. He felt relief that he hadn't hurt the girl badly.

He grabbed the Mexican and threw him up into the car seat. He saw bubbles forming and bursting in the blood around the torn lips and for a moment thought about finishing him off.

Instead, he slammed the door, put the car in drive by reaching through the window, and by holding the steering wheel guided it out into the road. He walked along beside it for ten steps or so, then let go of the wheel, and it eased off down the road edging toward the field on the opposite side. By the time he got back to Gail, the car had left the road and edged up against a chain-link fence in the field opposite the motel.

"We've got to get this blood off the ground or cover it up," he said to her.

"It's too late," she replied, and pointed up toward the main road.

He saw the aerial of the prowl car cruising slowly up the street a half block from where it always turned onto the road fronting the motel. He ran around the end room and was walking in the grass behind the rooms before it made the turn. With considerable difficulty because of his hurting and swollen hand, he crawled back through the window into his own room.

Looking out through the curtain, he saw that Gail was gone also, and he couldn't see the prowl car. But they were sure to find that Mexican. Close to a half hour later as he stood under the spray of a hot shower, he heard the siren of an approaching ambulance. They had certainly found him now.

12.

By the time he left the shower, his right hand was swollen so badly he couldn't see the first two knuckles. He poured some aftershave on the cut where the second knuckle had been, hoping the slimy little bastard didn't have AIDS or some kind of hepatitis, diseases that needle users constantly expose themselves to. He had an impulse to warn June of the danger but decided not to. It would be too late anyway if either of them were exposed. Best to just hope they weren't. Slipping between the cool sheets, he was surprised to find himself drifting steadily toward sleep despite the throbbing hand.

In the early afternoon, Gail used her master key to slip silently into his room and woke him up. By the time she sat on the edge of his bed he was looking expectantly at her. He'd slept well, but the sleep had been visited by an old, unwanted anxiety. The vague expectation of the heavy knock at his door.

"I can't believe it, Bill," she said in a low voice. "I watched them today until they took him away. The first two cops there called the ambulance, and after it left they sat in the prowl car writing up a report or something. Then they just took off. I mean, they didn't even come across the road. Didn't ask anyone anything—I couldn't believe it."

"What about that blood?"

"I covered it up right after they left. I acted like I was watering the edge of the lawn. I hosed it down good and kicked dirt over it the best I could," she said.

"Good girl," he said, and slid up to sit against the head

of the bed. He could feel the warmth of her through the sheet, and he was getting aroused in spite of himself.

She gazed directly into his eyes and said, "Look, Bill—I know this is about June, but I also know you won't tell me anything. I just want you to know it's okay. I've already figured out she was molested by that Mexican. She won't talk to me about it. I'm keeping her out of school for at least a week, or until she feels better. She's not in a very good state of mind right now but she's really tougher than she looks."

She looked down at the bed, and he could tell she was close to tears. He felt pretty close himself.

"But I do need to know why you tried to kill that man, and for all I know you have killed him. I mean, I can see you wanting to beat him up, but what you were doing was going so much further," she said, looking down at her hands in her lap.

He hoped she could stand the truth. "I intended to kill him. I didn't have a gun to shoot him with, so I decided to beat him to death," he told her.

She whipped her face around toward him, green eyes wide open and startled.

"But why? I mean, you don't have the right to just kill someone."

"I didn't have the right to beat him up either. I did what I had to do. It was either him or me."

He hoped she wouldn't ask him to explain what he meant by that, and she didn't. She just sat there for a long time looking at her hand.

"Get out of here and let me get up and go to work," he said gruffly, but there was a gentle edge to the words.

"I'll be here when you need me," she murmured as she left the room. As he got dressed he wondered what that statement really meant. He also wondered if women mean anything other than exactly what they say.

With the advent of fall, his working hours had been changed. He now worked a four-to-midnight shift to accommodate the emphasis on family dining. The buffet was less popular during the winter months.

On his days off, Leona and the busboys along with James and Sam did the dishes. They had a system so confusing that Bill hadn't tried to figure it out. Regina even pitched in at times. They usually left about as many dishes as they washed, but Bill didn't mind.

He tried to take as few Saturdays off as possible so as not to strain them too much, but he had never really liked working on weekends.

When he walked into Ferraro's over an hour early, Regina was adding receipts at the register and barely glanced up to greet him. No one but the surly-looking hungover cook was in the kitchen. He opened the door of the utility closet at the end of the dishroom where he hung his apron and kept his boots and tools, and it seemed as if every breath he had ever drawn had remained in his lungs.

Leona was reaching up for something on the wall and, startled, turned to face him when he pulled the door open. All she had on was a pair of white cotton bikini briefs; she was holding a white waitress frock in her hand but made no attempt to cover herself. Calmly, with no discernible expression, she gazed into his eyes as he stood paralyzed with the doorknob still in hand.

She was a long-legged, slim-waisted vision in pure copper. Her breasts were heavier and fuller than he had visualized them to be and extended outside her rib cage like full gourds that tilted slightly upward. They trembled like shaken Jell-O from the suddenness of her turning, and he felt a corresponding tremble in his lower abdomen.

Plum-colored nipples set in golden areolae rose up and bulged like wine grapes as he stared, unable to tear his eyes away. Finally she smiled and spoke.

"Shut the door and lock it, D.W. We can't stand here like this all night."

He began to back out, trying to stammer an apology as he pulled the door shut.

"Hey!" she yelled, and he froze again.

"Bring your ass back in here. That door only locks from the inside," she said in a lowered voice, and she bestowed on him the most radiant smile he had ever seen in his life.

He came back fast and rammed the bolt home, because he didn't want to do any thinking at all about this. Her arms went around his neck before he faced her squarely. His mouth ran her jawline until it found her big, soft lips, and when their tongues tentatively touched, the nerve ends in his brain and down his spine became an orchestra.

His hands roamed her warm slender back, coming to rest under the panties on the high soft buttocks, and she began grinding her pelvis against him, fumbling at shirt buttons while their lips and tongues were still locked together. He began to worry that he might come before he got his pants off. She didn't help any by reaching down and gripping him firmly in her hand and whispering against his mouth, "I've got to have that on mine, God, I've got to have it." As she spoke she squeezed him fervently.

He reluctantly tore himself loose from her long enough to jerk his clothes and shoes off. As he performed record-time gymnastics, she stood there smiling and taking the panties down her legs very slowly. When she'd kicked them off, she laid a coat she'd been wearing on the floor and put his shirt on top of it.

The second his shorts came off, she sat gracefully on his shirt, and he kneeled beside her, seeking those soft lips as his fingers pinched her hard nipples.

"God," she groaned urgently, taking him in her hand. The next thing he knew her legs were up like the handlebars on a Harley-Davidson motorcycle. Her eyes fluttered when he entered her. She felt like a tight glove coated with warm butter and honey, and he couldn't control himself enough to make love to her.

Her eyes widened as he began fucking her in much the same manner as he had fought the Mexican. She didn't resist, and though his trancelike long battering strokes were hurting, she opened her legs wider and raised them higher to try to accommodate the assault.

A storm gathered at the base of his skull and whooshed down his spine like a hurricane, and he came pounding at her like a fighter on a heavy bag. As fourteen years of sexual tension and frustration poured out, he came to rest atop her feeling as if a flock of pigeons had flown out of his asshole.

"Jesus Christ, D.W.," she whispered. "You sure works a mean ass."

He went from his stiff-armed hands down to his elbows and looked closer into her brown eyes.

"I'm sorry, but it's been a long, long time," he told her softly.

She bit and kissed at the Norseman tattoo on his shoulder.

"I never fucked a Viking before," she said. "So I should have been ready for that. But you stay right there, honey, because Leona wants hers."

She bit harder into his shoulder, closed her eyes, and began working her pelvis against him. He remained all the way in, and her frantic stroking of his still-hard member was warm ecstasy. She came quicker than he had, and he had to clamp one hand over her mouth when she began a series of loud agonized groans that sounded like a cat fornicating in a garbage-strewn alley.

As they reassembled their clothes and put them on she said, "I thought you hadn't had any for a while, D.W., and I don't mind getting fucked like that, but if you want to make love to me we got to find a bed. I ain't gettin' down on that floor no more."

He smiled at her and said, "Are you married, Leona?"

She raised her left hand and looked at the gold band on her fourth finger for a moment in contemplative silence, then cut her beautiful brown eyes back to him.

"Yeah, I am. Ain't every fuckin' body married someway?" she asked as she went out the door.

Bill stood there naked for a long time savoring the immense pleasure and relief he felt while wondering what Schopenhauer—woman-hater that he was—would have thought of a woman like Leona.

13.

Detective Martin Torres sat behind a mahogany desk on the edge of a gray county-issue roll-back chair, looking at the two patrolmen shifting from one foot to another while sliding their eyes anywhere that wouldn't meet his own hostile glare.

He was impeccably dressed as usual. His stocky frame was draped in an olive-drab double-breasted suit, powder-blue shirt, and silk tie with navy and olive-green stripes. The ensemble went well with his dark skin and brown Florsheim loafers.

Torres silently regarded these two cops while trying forcefully to calm the rage he felt after reading their field reports, which really didn't report a fucking thing. Patrolman Jewell was a tall, slim black, and Torres didn't really expect a lot from him, as he seemed inexperienced in spite of his seven years on the force, and not at all cerebral.

But Fitzgibbons, beer-belly fucking Fitz—his report was a disgrace. His dad and grandfather had been cops and he usually did better work than this, and Torres had just told him so.

"The fool died, goddammit!" he yelled again at both of them. "I got a homicide dumped in my fucking lap here and all these reports say is 'Hispanic victim of severe trauma found behind wheel of lowrider Chevrolet.' It don't even say clearly where you found the fucker, much less if any weapon was found or what any potential witness or neighbor may have volunteered. Now would it be asking too fucking much to ask you exactly where you found this fucked-up greaser?"

His invective was directed at Fitzgibbons, who blinked at the "greaser," Torres being a Mexican himself.

"We discovered the lately decadent in a vacant lot opposite the Star Motel behind his steering wheel beaten badly, and that's all in them reports there," Fitzgibbons replied obstinately.

"That's dec*ed*ent not dec*ad*ent," Torres shot back.

"The motherfucker was both," Officer Jewell chimed in.

"Goddammit! That's what I'm talking about," Torres yelled, slapping the paper-strewn desk with both hands and jumping to his feet as if to square off with these two hostile adversaries. "We're all cops here, for Christ's sake! I'm a homicide detective and you two are deputies and here you don't seem to give a flying fuck about a savage killer running around loose out there. I get a call from the coroner this morning that I've got a homicide on my hands. Fine. I go to the D.A. for some reports and I find this shit. That blowhole was dead when you found him, or as good as. He's laying over there, takin' his time about dying, and this trail is getting colder and colder. Over three weeks, man, and nobody tells me shit. One of you birds could have at least let me know I had a pretty sure corpse on my hands.

"Now would that have been asking too much? I might as well try and track down Jack the Ripper as some shit this old."

"Medical diagnosis and patient prognosis is not part of our job," Fitz said.

"Damn sure ain't," Officer Jewell agreed.

Torres stared down at his desk as air leaked from him like a punctured balloon. He made an effort along with some deep breathing to get himself under control as any good detective would. Something is wrong here, he thought to himself. I've got to start over.

He looked up, smiled, spread his hands in supplication palms up, and said, "Come on, you guys, what's going on here? We're all cops, so give me some off-the-record input. I mean, wake me up man. If one of you killed Perfecto

Salazar, just tell me and I'll close the case and write 'unsolvable' all over the fucking file. But if neither of you did it, well, help me, huh—huh?"

"Well, since we're off record here, it's sad to say neither of us did the deed," Fitz replied. "But if I find out who did, I'll take him out and buy him beer till he pisses blood. I'll mortgage my fucking house and buy him more beer if my paycheck runs out."

"I'll buy his ass scotch and water if he don't like beer," Officer Jewell put in.

"Let me tell you something, Torres," Fitz took up again. "We been following this little troglylip, liver-brained gopher around for two years watching him sell heroin and taking reports on him raping underage girls. I mean, that's all his job is, you know? He does that kind of shit full-time, and it's like he was assigned to our area. When we pinch him, he swallows the smack and gets that bozo shyster Carter and pleads out to a misdemeanor for no time. We jail him on a possession or something, go off shift, and he's selling dope before we get back to work next day, for Christ's sake.

"So you think we feel sad or get indignant when we roll up on him after some citizen beat his headlights out? You wanna solve the case, get the rape reports, not ours. One of the fathers probably got sick of them misdemeanor plea bargains."

"Okay, okay." Torres nodded in agreement. "But I've got the case now, and I'll just put it all out here. This *cabrone* was my boy. Three different times people robbed banks around here and drove to Perfecto's house to score. When that happened I had their names by that night. The feds are still wondering how I performed that magic.

"He also helped me a lot in two murder investigations. Yeah, he was bad about taking that pussy, but the only broads I know of him forcing were dope-fiend whores who had probably been raped a couple times that same week anyway, and I did intercede a couple times with the D.A. But like I say, he was one of my stoolies, and I'm going to find out who did him in, because that may have been the reason he got his lights put out."

Fitz had been looking down at his feet while Torres spoke.

"Well hell, Jaysus, I had the poor guy all wrong," Fitz interjected sarcastically. "Somebody should have told me he was only raping dope fiends. Man, just to think that probably all he was selling heroin to was dope fiends, and here I thought the guy was a real crook."

"You guys watch your mouth—my thirteen-year-old daughter is a dope fiend," Officer Jewell put in.

"I give up," Torres said, beginning to straighten papers on his desk. "You guys get out of here, and if you ever turn in another police report like this, I'll try to get you transferred to the graveyard shift at the county jail."

Jewell went out putting his uniform hat on, but Fitz hung back by the door and said to Torres, "Look here, Martin. You didn't do that little shithead no favor by keeping him on the street. He'd've been safe in jail. I'd rather you let the bankrobbers rob banks if they tell on creeps like him. The taxpayers would be a lot better off."

"Goddammit, Fitz!" Torres exploded, but the door slammed in his face before he could say anything else.

He stood looking down at the papers on his desk until the throbbing at his temples subsided. The report did contain one small pitiful lead. He could begin at the Star Motel. He left his office thinking it was a good thing those two clowns had never thought of that. They might have left off the area where the murder actually happened. He made a mental note that if he ever solved the case, he'd ask the D.A. if there was a way to try it without their testimony.

14.

Malone started reading the *Fresno Bee* after Gail told him the detective had been around asking if anyone had seen anything. There he saw a small front-page story that said a Perfecto Salazar had died from a beating at the hands of persons unknown. The article speculated that the beating could have been gang-related.

It felt good to be reading the paper again, because he had read the *L.A. Times* every day in prison. But other than Leona, he didn't feel good about much else. Somewhere in the city there were two skinny little dope fiends who knew he had killed Salazar. They even knew what room he lived in. He thought of packing his few things and running, but dismissed the idea almost as soon as it entered his mind.

Flight is evidence of guilt in a court of law. By running he would only lend credibility to their testimony if they ever did tell on him. If he stuck it out, he could argue that they had probably killed the man over a drug deal and were trying to shift the blame to him. If Gail kept quiet, as he felt she would, then he had a fair chance even if they told what they saw. In a strange way he was glad it was the addicts rather than the whores or someone else.

Heroin addicts are misunderstood by almost everyone. They must commit four or five felonies a day just to use heroin. Buying it is a felony, having it is a felony, carrying it is a felony, and almost anything they have to do to get it is a felony. As a result of living constantly on the wrong side of the law, they are farther out in the cold than anyone else. Any cop determined to arrest a heroin addict can do it just by following him around for a day or two. The cop knows his quarry has to commit crimes every day.

That's one of the main reasons other thieves hate junkies. It's the kind of heat they bring around, not so much the kind of people they are. Statistically there are fewer stool pigeons among junkies than among any other group of criminals. Addicts know they will be going to jail a lot. They expect to be caught now and then. Because of the sheer number of crimes, their odds are worse than anyone's, and they know it's just a matter of time. By that same reasoning, they don't relish the idea of becoming informers.

Their main incentive not to become snitches is that a lot of dope comes into prisons. They still get their share even when they are locked up. But if they get put in the prison within a prison, they no longer have access to the drugs that other convicts do.

What prison officials call "protective custody" is actually isolation. Heroin addicts aren't ever housed in honor camps where white-collar informers go, because their records make them ineligible for such places. So Bill felt better knowing it was two dope fiends that saw him do it.

His hand was completely healed now, and Leona was stopping by his room at least twice a week for an hour before she went to work. Their lovemaking was just as near perfect as it could get. He looked forward to seeing her again soon.

Leona's husband was gone for the weekend and she came to Bill's room after work on Saturday night. They made love almost continuously until Sunday morning, when they took a short nap and shower before going at it again. When she woke him up before noon, he told her he had had enough for one night.

"I had enough myself, D.W., but I bought me some new things and I want you to tell me how I look in them." She went into his bathroom and put on a pair of white satin bikini briefs, a white see-through bra, high heels, and a white garter belt that held up cream-colored stockings with a pink carnation pinned mid-thigh on the garter strap. Then she walked around, primping and posing. The blood began pounding in his ears until he thought he was going to faint.

"Come over here," he said in a voice that was between a croak and a groan.

"Come get me, D.W.," she cooed, and kicked off the high heels, throwing one at him. The chase was on. She laughed and eluded him until he caught her and threw her on the bed, fumbling at the catch on the bra as she squirmed around giggling. Suddenly she became very still.

"Tear it off me, man, tear it all off," she breathed.

He rolled her over onto her back, grabbed the bra between her breasts, and jerked it off. She eased her fingers beneath the waist of the bikini panties and pulled it away from her body. He gathered them in his hand and ripped them away in one motion, causing the strap holding the carnation to pull loose.

He caught one ankle in each hand, pulled her to the side of the bed, jerked her legs apart, bent them back, and entered her still standing up. She was sopping wet.

"Ahhh, lover, lover!" she groaned, and arched to meet him, digging her nails into the back of his arms. Still standing, he lowered his upper body until their faces were very close and gazed deep into her eyes as he stroked her soft yielding body. Fucking Leona was physically luxurious, like making love to a large, perfectly molded satin pillow.

Gail thought she had finally figured out what schizophrenia was. Or possibly manic depression, because all morning she had been going from feeling good to feeling bad like a yo-yo going up and down. Part of the time she felt good and bad at the same time. Tony's early-morning call had started the ball rolling.

He wasn't going to live with her and June when he got out. It had taken him almost an hour to tell her, but that was the bottom line, their marriage was over. He hadn't even admitted having another woman. Just said he wanted to go live in San Diego for a while and be on his own and that was that. Gail didn't have an idea in the world of how she was going to break the news to June. June idolized the fucking Neanderthal.

Malone was the source of the good feelings. It was hard for her to believe the strength of her attraction to him, especially with the unfinished business of Tony and the Mexican standing between them like a prison fence. But it was a feeling she couldn't reason herself out of. Reason and logic had very little to do with it. She loved him, and the loving was even more exquisite because she didn't know how he felt about her, although she knew he was sexually interested.

He was also an outlaw, and she had promised herself there would be no more outlaws for her if and when Tony left her or vice versa. But she was pretty sure that Bill was tired of the whole "us against them" thing. If he was willing to wash dishes for a chance to come in from the cold, she would help him any way she could, even if they never became lovers. She figured the best thing to do right now would be to seduce him and see where things went from there.

She would have to force the issue. He didn't know how things were with Tony and her, and she knew he wouldn't make the first move. He liked to eat, and he was probably over there still sleeping right now. She decided to fix him a country-style breakfast of eggs, sausage, gravy, and biscuits and carry it over to him. She knew he liked his eggs soft scrambled. She would serve him breakfast in bed. What could be more romantic than that?

Bill was buried all the way in Leona and they were tongue-kissing and nibbling each other's lips when Gail knocked on his door. His first instinct was to jerk out of her. He didn't know if it was June, Gail, the police, or his parole officer. But Leona dug her nails into his hips and clamped on to him, whispering, "No, D.W., not fast."

She had told him before not ever to jerk out of her fast.

That she couldn't stand the way that she felt to her. So he always pulled out very slowly, even though the lips of her vagina closing slowly over the supersensitive head of his penis right after he came was like being tortured. The knock became more insistent, and Gail was now yelling; "Bill, wake up. I'm loaded down out here."

The tray was getting heavy, because she had put a quart of orange juice, a melon, ice, and a quart bottle of milk on it, along with everything else.

"Just a minute," he yelled, and she felt relieved to know he was in there. But the relief was short-lived. He didn't swing the door wide as he usually did, and she heard a rustling of bedclothes the same time he cracked it and peered out at her. She looked down and saw a pair of torn white panties lying beside his bare foot. Mortification sucked like quicksand at her feet and filled her mouth with foam rubber. But she recovered enough to move. She prayed he wouldn't invite her in, but from the look on his face, that fear was groundless. He didn't know what to say either.

"I fixed you some breakfast," she said, and carefully placed the tray in front of his door.

"Oh, uh, thank you," he stammered.

For some reason his stupid attempt at helping her disengage mortified and maddened her more than she already was.

"Tell the bitch I'm sorry I didn't know how she liked her eggs," she said, and walked back to the office with as much dignity as she could muster, which wasn't very much.

After she left, Leona ate almost all the food, because he wasn't very hungry. "That woman seemed very unhappy that I was here, D.W.," she commented.

"I don't believe it was your visiting here that she was mad about," he replied.

"Maybe I shouldn't come over anymore," she said, as she got dressed to go.

"Let's not go that far," he told her. Still he felt very ambivalent, because in his mind he wished it were Gail here instead of Leona. Bill got into the shower for the second time that morning, thinking about the confusion he'd gotten into so quickly.

The Friday before Thanksgiving began well. He woke up thinking that he might take a trip to Portland and visit Frances over the holiday weekend. June was home from school early, and they played Scrabble for an hour before he walked to work. Shadow lay outside his door whining occasionally the whole time they played. When Bill and June came out the door, the mutt took off for the high weeds. He wouldn't associate with anyone but June.

"You gave him a bath," Bill remarked.

"Swimming pool," June giggled in reply.

He laughed and walked off through the weeds to work. The day was cold and clear. He'd cut down the smoking and picked up the running and felt good, but this day would always stick in his mind as the day chaos once again opened the door of his life as if to beckon and say, "Come on in, my friend."

They came in on him around ten o'clock. He had just walked over and retrieved a large iron skillet from the pot tank. After he'd been on the job a week, he'd been doing over half the pots and pans. Since this was the cook's and the assistant cook's job, they all liked him and he could get anything he wanted from the kitchen.

He was scrubbing at the skillet with a wire brush when they entered the dishroom. He thought it was a busboy and only looked up when one of them closed the door and stood against it with his arms folded across his chest. The other came walking straight toward him and said, "Hey, Malone, we need to talk with you a minute here, if you can spare the time."

The move startled him, because the door to the dishroom had never been closed in the few months he had worked there. If these two were cops, they damn sure didn't look it and would have to be from vice or somewhere. He didn't reply, just straightened himself somewhat and went on brushing at the skillet as he looked from one of them to the other and tried to figure out what the hell was going on.

The speaker stopped just out of range of the dripping pan and looked at him expectantly. He was of medium build and just about exactly Bill's height and weight. His hair was black as a crow's wing, cut short and neat, combed straight back with the comb marks preserved by a heavy gel. He wore a two-toned brown wool cable-knit sweater with the collar of a white silk shirt showing and tan silk slacks that fell just right over a pair of black-and-tan ostrich-hide cowboy boots.

This one's features were heavy almost to the point of being a caricature, and scars on the outer edges of his heavy eyebrows suggested an early foray into boxing. Bill couldn't put his finger on it, but something about the man lent him a sinister aspect.

The one by the door was very similar in appearance but had a heavier build and wore a light green wool suit and brown loafers. Despite his heavy frame, his features were refined in comparison to the other's.

"Hey, man, I just said something to you. Don't you hear good?" the man said, and Bill could hear utter contempt behind the words. He felt those old chills of fear and anger beginning to gather at the base of his skull and fluttering down his spine.

"Well, uh, sure I hear you. What is it you need to talk to me about?" he stammered, trying to sound like the wino dishwasher that they obviously thought he was.

"Hey, Freddy, you hear that? He can hear me," the man nearer him shouted to his buddy by the door. Freddy just nodded his head and smiled. Then the man looked back at him and said, "Do you know Robert Odum?"

"Can't say as I do," Bill replied.

"Well, you know, he's that guy who lived in the end room

over there at the Star with his old lady. The one who saw you beat old Perfecto Salazar to death. We finally found him yesterday, told us what room you lived in, where you worked and all that good shit."

Bill caught his jaw as it tried to fall open, and his heart began pounding like a bass drum gone haywire.

"You've got me confused with someone else," was all he could think to reply.

"Look here, man, we're not cops. And Robert Odum ain't no snitch—he sort of told us this between friends. We really don't care about the fool getting himself snuffed. But we gave him a pound of something about thirty minutes before you lit his ass up, and we do care about that. Are you getting my drift here?" As the man spoke, Bill could see him studying the tattoos on his arms and taking a very close look at him.

"I'm telling you, you've got me mixed up with someone else," he said again, trying to make his voice sound convincing.

Someone pushed at the door from the outside, and the one leaning against it turned, jerked it open, and spoke rapidly to someone, then shut the door and leaned against it again. Bill figured it was one of the busboys or Leona, but he thought he saw the flash of George Ferraro's coat before the door shut.

"Look here, man. The shit was still in the car. Now, I'm talking fourteen thousand dollars here that we're out. You beat the fool up and took it. And we want our fuckin' money, simple as that. I know you probably didn't know it was ours, so we will just forget the disrespect. You just kick back the pound or our money and we'll be on our way. But you ain't leaving here or washing another fucking dish until we make some satisfactory arrangements. So just get off this shit about us having the wrong guy and let's talk sense about our money, okay?"

As the man talked, he turned his palms up, spreading them away from his body, and edged closer. Bill, still holding the skillet, shifted until his body was at a forty-five-degree angle to the man. It's a defensive posture for a convict, because it's difficult for a person with only a knife or his fist to get a good shot at you when your left shoulder is angled slightly toward him. The shift was automatic, even though Bill knew that it wasn't that strong out here where guns are the weapon of choice. But so far these two had not displayed weapons or even implied that they had any.

That thought contributed even more to his feeling that he was suddenly in some *Twilight Zone* episode on television. If what the man said was true and they had this information, why not confront him at the motel? Why brace him here in a busy restaurant? The whole thing just didn't make any sense. It was as if they were trying to impress the rest of the help. But what kind of gangster would want to impress a hungover cook? The thought entered his spinning mind that they could be cops trying to con a confession out of him, but that supposition was full of holes.

If they were on the level, then they were so stupid as to be extremely dangerous and there was no telling what they might do next. He made the decision to act as if they were on the level, but he'd waited too long to reply.

"Look, punk, do you know who you're dealing with here?" the man demanded and edged closer as a menacing look took over his heavy features and his hands began falling to his sides.

Just then someone pushed at the door again, and as Freddy angrily jerked it open, the man advancing on Bill glanced that way for a moment.

Bill swung the heavy iron skillet, and it connected with the man's forehead. The bong of the skillet meeting bone resounded like a tuning fork in the closed room. A splotch of blood hit Bill's T-shirt at the right shoulder just before the man hit the floor like a sack of cement dropped from a truck bed.

As the man at the door wheeled around, Bill threw the skillet backhand and rushed him. By the time he could duck the skillet, Bill was on top of him. The man threw his arms up to ward off the attack, and Bill drop-kicked him in the knee. The rubber boots diminished the force of the kick somewhat, but the man gasped as his leg went out from under him. In that second, the man looked at Bill, and he could see not only surprise but naked fear in the look.

As he fell awkwardly to the floor, he reached beneath his coat. Bill now had him by the coat collar with his left hand and reached along with him with his right hand. They both touched the gun at the same time. The fellow was mumbling frantically, "Motherfucker, motherfucker," as Bill jerked him around by his collar to keep him off balance and they fought for a good grip on the handle of the pistol.

When the gun came clear, they both had a grip on it, but Bill's grip was weaker because of the way the handle was turned. Bill let go of the coat collar and grabbed the wrist of the hand the gun was in. He jerked the gun toward him, being careful to keep the barrel pointed away from his body. When the man's arm straightened all the way out, Bill drop-kicked him again in the elbow. He didn't hear the crack of bone as the elbow broke because the gun went off at the same moment. It was a short-barrel .357 Magnum, and it sounded like a cannon in the closed dishroom.

The gun fell to the floor, and the man's head lolled back against the wall when Bill let go of his wrist. His face was now white as a sheet, and as Bill reached down for the gun he could see a look of pure agony on the man's face. A band of sweat drops had broken out across his forehead and he looked as if he was in shock. The one he'd hit with the skillet still lay where he'd fallen, his head surrounded by a small pool of blood.

George Ferraro peeked around the door tentatively and saw Bill standing over the man with the gun in his hand. He entered the dishroom and closed the door behind him.

"Did you shoot him, Malone?" His voice was so low as to be almost a whisper.

"Nobody shot. The gun went off," Bill told him.

Regina was pounding at the door and yelling, "George! George! What is it? What's going on in there?

"Give me that fucking gun," George said, taking the gun from Bill's hand and dropping it into his coat pocket. Bill was glad to be rid of it and went over to take a look at the man he'd hit with the skillet.

Before he reached the prone form, the door blasted open and he heard a bellowing voice yell, "Freeze! Police officers!" He turned, and since he was looking at the gaping hole of a riot shotgun barrel, he froze.

15.

Fitz and Robert Jewell had pulled into the parking lot in front of Ferraro's at 9:45 p.m. They had just been changed from the graveyard shift to the swing shift and were feeling pretty good about that.

"Yeah, it's all about getting home, a little TV, a shot of pussy, and having breakfast with the kids," Jewell said.

"You got to quit that lying, Jool. The only time you get any pussy at home is on payday, if then," Fitz said as he turned off the motor and lowered the volume on the two-way radio.

"Sheeeiiit!" Jewell replied and got out to go into Ferraro's for their coffee. They both hated doughnut shops, and neither was into socializing with citizens on their breaks. So they always got coffee and drank it in the prowl car. Ferraro's made good coffee and wouldn't let them pay for it.

"What about that fucking Torres? Fucking fig-orchard Columbo," Fitz remarked when Jewell got back in the car.

"Yeah, they solve about one out of twenty murders around here that aren't domestic homicides and he's all pushed out of shape about a victim that should have been in the gas chamber anyway. I don't know what the hell he expects us to do," Jewell said.

"Whoever did that, I'd hate to run up on him in a dark alley," Fitz said as he took a sip of the coffee.

"Say, Fitz, what are we going to do with that pound of dope?" Jewell asked in a low voice.

"Ah hell, I don't know. Maybe we could trade it for pussy," Fitz replied.

"Well, no thanks, bubba. If I wanted to get AIDS I'd just start shooting the shit. But that stuff has me worried, man. You ain't never took a nickel in bribes and all of a sudden you go to your lunch bucket with a pound of heroin we find in a dead man's trunk. We can't sell the shit. I really can't figure why you took it."

"Well, you can quit worrying. I put it in some coffee grounds and sent it off in the garbage two weeks ago. I ain't sure why I took it either, but I can tell you what was on my mind when I did it. I think we're pretty much agreed on how we felt about old undercover agent Perfecto Salazar."

"No doubt about that," Jewell responded.

"Well, in the first place, I didn't want who done it to get caught, so I figured I'd eliminate some evidence. I don't think you'd argue with me there, because that damn sure wasn't no oil slick in front of the motel."

"Hell, it could have been," Jewell said.

"Yeah, but then I got to thinking if I turned this stuff in they're going to put it up there in an evidence locker and then break it out one day and run one of these reverse stings with it."

"A reverse what?" Jewell asked.

"It's a new thing these narcs do these days. They sell dope to someone, then come back later and bust them for buying it. If the fool has property, they take it. But however it goes, the dope gets back on the street. Myself, I'd rather it get put in the dump or down the shitter. I guess I'm old-fashioned."

"Goddam, do they really do that?" Jewell asked incredulously.

"If you quit begging your wife for pussy and opened a fuckin' paper now and then, you'd know they do it. I think they done run out of dope pushers, so now they push it and bust the buyers. They got to keep them paychecks coming in, baby. You think them longhair prima donnas want to admit the drug war is over and go back to riding in prowl cars and fighting drunk, violent husbands every weekend like we do? Shit!" Fitz spat out the window.

A gray Lincoln pulled into the lot near them, and two men got out and started for the front door of Ferraro's.

"Well look here, the local wise guys. You want to put them up on the wall and shake 'em down, Fitz? I'll lay two to one there's a hogleg on one of the punks," Jewell said.

"Nah," Fitz said, watching Fred and Joe Sandino enter Ferraro's. "Not on my coffee break. Maybe we'll shake them up some on their way out. I wonder what they're doing way out here?"

"Maybe they're gonna ask George and Regina to invest in a *Godfather* movie," Jewell said.

"They probably own that bookie in the bar here. Another thing I could never figure about this town is how these yokels let these cigar-chomping wops terrorize them and take their fuckin' money. I grew up in Chicago, and believe me, these slickos wouldn't make a pimple on a real Mafia man's ass," Fitz said.

"Ah, but they carry that mystique, that aura, you know, and they use words like 'being connected.' These country folks is happy to give them their dough. Makes them feel like they're a part of something secret and dangerous," Jewell responded.

"That's the problem, as I see it," Fitz muttered. "There ain't nothing secret about these assholes, and a fucking rattlesnake is not dangerous as long as you can see it, for Christ's sake." He drained the rest of his coffee.

The radio crackled with the code number for a domestic dispute, but it was over on Belmont, and two other cars were called.

"Phew, that was close. You want more coffee, or you want to roll?" Jewell asked.

"Let's get on the road awhile," Fitz said. He was reaching for the ignition when they heard the gunshot. They jumped out of the prowl car, and Fitz took the riot gun off the rack as Jewell unholstered a fourteen-shot 9mm pistol.

"Sounded like it was around back," Jewell yelled.

"Nah, it was inside," Fitz said. He ran for the front entrance to Ferraro's with Jewell right behind him. They ran through the restaurant, where a few diners had dived under tables. Regina was still knocking at the dishroom door with Leona behind her.

Fitz shoved them out of the way, kicked the door open, and yelled, "Freeze." He saw Joey Sandino lying on the floor looking like a dead man with someone standing over him, but as he traversed the room with the shotgun, he couldn't locate a weapon.

"Where's the fucking shooter?" Officer Jewell yelled as he ran by Fitz and took up a position to the left of him.

"Take it easy!" George yelled, holding up his hand. "No one is shot. I don't know where the gun is or even if there is one."

Jewell edged carefully behind the dish machine while Fitz cautiously probed the utility closet at the end of the room. As the two cops looked around, George handed the gun to Leona, who wrapped it in a table rag and went back out the door. Regina was bending over Freddy, who was whispering something to her. She began helping him take off his suit coat.

Jewell holstered his gun and gave Bill and George a quick frisk while Fitz covered them with the shotgun.

"How did you get that blood on you? he asked Bill.

"I tried to help that guy there off the floor," Bill replied, nodding at Joey, who by now was twitching his fingers and moving slightly.

"What happened here?" Fitz asked George.

"Joe and Freddy got into an argument in the bar, came in here, and ran my dishwasher out," George explained, nodding at Bill when he said "dishwasher." "A couple minutes later we hear what sounded like a gunshot, ran in, and this is what we see, but no one is shot. If someone had a gun, he went out the back or something."

"My God!" Regina gasped as Freddy's coat came off, and George had to grab her as she stumbled backward.

A bone protruded through the skin near Freddy's elbow, and his arm was swollen to near double its normal size. Freddy looked at his arm and fainted dead away.

"Run to the car and call an ambulance," Fitz yelled at Jewell, who was stooping down looking carefully at Joey's head. As Jewell took off, Fitz laid the shotgun on the dish machine and pulled a notebook from his pocket.

"What's your full name and address?" he asked Bill.

Freddy came around before the ambulance crew arrived, and when Fitz sought to question him, all he said was, "On the advice of my attorney I have no comment." Joey was still twitching and groaning when they rolled him onto a stretcher.

Before the cops left, Fitz told George to be sure anyone present would be available for questioning, but that it would probably be Monday before anyone called, and given Freddy's attitude, even that was iffy. Fitz looked long and hard at the skillet on the floor and cast a contemplative eye on Bill before he followed Jewell out the dishroom door.

Leona had led Regina away while the paramedics loaded the men onto a stretcher. When the cops departed, only Bill and George were left in the room. George became much more visibly shaken after everyone was gone. Bill could tell he was having a hard time comprehending the situation but decided that it wouldn't help anything to enlighten him.

"What the hell happened?" George asked.

"I guess it was a misunderstanding that ended up in a fight. I hit Joey with a skillet and broke Freddy's elbow when he pulled a gun," Bill told him.

"That's not good enough, pardner," George shot back. "Do you know who these guys are? They are from a mob family. You're in trouble, man, serious trouble, and if I can't get this straightened out, I may be in trouble right along with you."

"Look here, George, you just straighten your part of it out with them and I'll take care of my part," Bill replied.

"Jesus, Malone, you don't listen too good. I told you these guys are mobbed up," George said. His voice was becoming fearful and plaintive. Bill felt sorry for the little man.

"George, you haven't done anything to these guys. In fact, you just saved them a gun charge. So give them back their gun and tell them you were glad to be able to help. Let me worry about the rest of it."

George looked at him for a long time, and Bill could see that the words had a calming effect.

"What are you going to do?" George asked him. "I mean, I'll help you get out of town, but I don't want them to know I helped you."

"Right now I'm going home to get some sleep. I'll call you tomorrow, and if you want me back here I'll be here to wash the dishes. I'm not going anywhere," Bill told him.

"I don't believe this. I don't fucking believe it," George said, grabbing his head with both hands.

Bill put on his Levi jacket and took the sacks of meat from the end of the dish machine. George stood silently watching him as he carefully checked all the knobs and switches and made sure the machine was draining properly.

"I'll talk to you tomorrow," he said to George. He went out the back door, leaving George standing there as if in a trance.

Bullfrog was standing by the fence.

"I thought you guys were going south for the winter," Bill said to him as he handed over the sack.

"We usually does, suh," Bullfrog said softly. "But it don't get too cold here, so we just decided to winter it on out right chere in Fresno. 'Sides that, ole Cabbage Head and me, we gets the feeling June Bug needs us to stay around even if she don't say nothin'. So we figured to go on and keep her some company this winter. Maybe her daddy be home in the spring."

"Maybe he will at that," Bill said, looking over toward the motel. "But I think I just got laid off, Bullfrog. This may be the last of the prime rib."

"Well, suh, don't nothin' last forever."

Bill started on across the field, then turned back.

"Hey, Bullfrog!" he yelled.

"Yo," Bullfrog responded.

"Don't call me sir!"

"Yassuh," Bullfrog replied and kept walking with the sack.

By the time Bill reached his room, he had decided not to spend the night there. There was another motel within walking distance, and it seemed a good idea to not be here until he saw how things were likely to shape up. But he felt totally exhausted and sat down on the edge of the bed to rest for a minute or two. He lit a Camel and took a deep drag. Looking through the curling smoke at the stark walls of the room, he began to wish that somehow he could get a firm grip on the rudder of his life.

His plan had been to come out, hold down a steady job, live a normal law-abiding life, and work his way up through the ranks of whatever established pecking order there was. All he had wanted was some order and peace in his life. He knew he had made a pretty good effort in that direction, but he also knew he hadn't even come close to getting there. But perhaps the fault lay somewhere within him that he couldn't see clearly. He had the feeling that he didn't really know what normal was.

He didn't like TV, and everyone else out here seemed to. He didn't go to movies or bars. He hadn't socialized or made any friends out here other than Gail, June, and Leona. Maybe that's where he went wrong. The room he lived in wasn't much bigger than his cell, and it seemed to him that his time on the streets was just an extension somehow of the time he'd been doing in prison. But try as he might, he couldn't think what might be the key that would break the cycle. He didn't see anything he could have done differently and still be able to live with himself. There was no doubt what would lie at the end of this journey. Either a graveyard or another prison cell.

His thoughts were interrupted by a knock on the door. He recognized Gail's knock and got up and let her in.

"Are you all right, Bill?" she asked breathlessly. She was dressed in a dark green terry-cloth bathrobe, her hair was done up in curlers under a scarf, and she wore no makeup.

"I'm fine," he replied, and at that moment he felt a huge sadness in his bones. He realized how much he had missed her company these last three weeks, during which she had been acting cool and distant toward him. A lingering smell and feel of Leona here in the room only intensified the feeling.

"Regina called and told me what happened, or what she knew about it anyway," Gail explained. "She said those were some really bad guys, and she's hoping you aren't involved someway in whatever happened."

"I am involved," he said, and their eyes searched each other for a long time.

"I kind of thought so. So what do we do now?" she asked.

"I can't stay here anymore. If I stay in this room, you and June could get in the way of some violence. This scene is far from over, and I don't know how it's going to wind up. I've got another problem with the parole officer—I'm supposed to get permission to move. But that's minor. I'll call him tomorrow. But I've got to pack and get out of here right now. Maybe you could drive me somewhere."

He turned toward his dresser and started gathering items for his flight bag.

"You're not going anywhere," she said in a firm voice that startled him. He had heard her use that tone of voice with June, but never with him. He looked at her, and she seemed determined.

"This is no time to start acting crazy, girl," he said, and went to the closet for his flight bag.

"Bill, I'm in love with you. I don't know any other way to say it. This bullshit started over June. I don't know what it is with these other guys, but I want to be with you now and with you when it's over, and I'm sure June feels the same way."

Her voice broke, and when he looked at her, tears were streaming down her cheeks and dropping to the bathrobe. Her pale lips trembled, and she reminded him of a little girl who had been hurt by something beyond her understanding. He went to her and folded her in his arms.

"Gail, I care about you, but your husband will be home in a few months. I can't repay his generosity by trying to steal his wife," the dishwasher said as she laid her face against his neck and moved closer to him.

"We have both agreed that our marriage is over. I knew that before you started fucking that nigger."

"Don't call her that. You don't even know her," he said, and disengaged from her.

"I'm sorry," she said. "It's just that it hurt so fucking bad. Tony has a little twenty-two-year-old sweetie and he's joined the San Diego chapter of the Hell's Angels. I told him I was in love with you and he told me I'd made a good choice, and before I knew it, you were seeing Leona. I mean, she's married, so what's the big problem about me being married? I don't understand how you fucking guys think."

"Tony and I are from the same world and we share the same values. Rule number one, we don't fuck with each other's wives. It's hard to explain, but if my values were different, I wouldn't be in this fucking mess I'm in. I could have dropped a quarter in a phone a long time ago and asked the police for help. But in the world Tony and I live in, the police are enemies, not protectors. I can't go to them for help."

"Well, I'm in your world too. So can you ask me for help?" she asked, looking him right in the eye.

"Well, sure I could," he said.

"Then let's get that stuff packed and move it over to my place. If anyone comes around, I'll tell them you took off. That way you won't have to worry about the parole officer and June and I won't have to worry about where you're at and what is happening to you."

"Gail, this shit is going to get very hairy before it's over," he told her.

"I've got something hairy I want you to think about tonight, and the rest we can deal with tomorrow." She looked at him and smiled.

He laughed and put his arms around her again. His life was so fucking ridiculous right now, it was funny. It was just all good or all bad, but she was right. The ugly could wait until tomorrow.

Her room was feminine right down to a doll on the bed pillow. He expected her to be soft and clinging, but she came hair down and naked into his arms with an animal urgency that rivaled his own excitement. She wanted the light on, and that was fine with him.

She was double-jointed, and just before he entered her the first time, she effortlessly lifted her legs and placed both heels behind her head. It was the most lascivious posture he had ever seen. When he entered her it was all right there. Buried deeper than he had ever been in a woman, he looked at her face thrown back on the pillow, eyes closed, lips pulled tight across her teeth, and the veins swelling and throbbing in her soft white throat.

He pulled back to thrust again, and she locked on to him and came back with him. He began working his hips, trying to come out some so he could thrust, but she moved with him and remained locked right to the root of his penis, their pubic hair intermingled and wet from the penetration and movement.

Soon he was frantic and began moving sideways trying to fake her off. He'd begin a thrust and jerk back suddenly trying to get free, but no matter what he did she stayed right with him, her fingernails digging into his shoulders.

"Goddammit, Gail!" He began gasping and moving more forcefully. It was the most frustrating thing he had ever experienced in his life. He could feel her vagina gripping and tugging at him all the way down to the head of his penis.

He began battering at her until her head was pinned sideways against the head of the bed and she was groaning loudly through clenched teeth. Now and then he'd get maybe an inch to stroke, but she stayed right against him no matter how he tried to get free.

When he knew he was coming, he went crazy, and the pressure built in his head until he thought it would burst. He held his breath, slamming at her until he almost passed out, but he still couldn't get loose.

He wasn't going to be able to stand it, and when the head of his penis swelled just before he came, he threw his head back and yelled as if he were being tortured. When she felt the swelling and heard him yelling, she let go and groaned in completion. As he thrust insanely into her, his torture altered slightly to become the most exquisite pleasure and relief he had ever experienced. When he collapsed atop her, feeling her heart beat against his behind the hard nipples, he finally remembered one of the reasons he'd wanted out of prison so badly.

I'd wash every dish in the fucking world to stay out here with her, he thought just before he was folded in fur and cotton arms and flown on silver wings to a universe of true slumber. When he woke up, she was gone from the bed. He smelled bacon and coffee and heard her and June talking and laughing in the kitchen. He stretched luxuriously, thinking it would be nice to lie here all day anticipating her return tonight. He rolled over to the edge of the bed, put on his shorts, and walked to the bathroom.

When he came back to the bedroom, she brought him a cup of coffee and an ashtray.

"Do you have Richard Avakian's phone number?" he asked her.

"Sure," she said.

"Well, see if you can get hold of him, and tell him I need to see him right away."

She went for the phone, and he began reluctantly putting his clothes on. Tomorrow had gotten here way too fast for him.

16.

On Saturday morning, Officer Jewell called Detective Torres at home and told him about the ruckus at Ferraro's.

"I don't think either one of them will die, but it looked like some heavyweight fighting, and it happened right in that neighborhood. So who knows? Maybe one of them Sandino boys done old Perfecto in," Jewell told him.

"Thanks a lot, Robert. I'll look into it," Torres said. As he hung up the phone he felt pleased that his chewing-out might have had some impact. There was something interesting about this assault, and he decided to check it out. The wise guys didn't usually beat up on each other like that.

He called the county hospital and learned that Freddy had been treated and released and Joey had been moved to Catholic Hospital and placed in intensive care. A doctor checked the log and told Torres that Joey had suffered a hairline skull fracture and was semicomatose.

Dressed in Levi's and sneakers, he drove down to the county building and retrieved Fitz and Jewell's reports of the incident.

By the time he finished reading them, he had a lot more questions than answers. He also had a conviction that he should follow this up.

George Ferraro knew Martin Torres from way back when Torres had worked vice and narcotics. It only mildly surprised him when Torres showed up at his little cubbyhole of an office behind the bar on Saturday morning.

"Hey, George, how's Regina and Sophie?" Torres said as he came into the office.

"They're doing good. What brings you out this way, Martin?" George asked, rising up from his chair behind the desk.

"Keep your seat," Torres said to him as he plopped down in the chair across the desk. "I just wanted to ask you a few questions about that rumble in your dishroom last night."

"Jesus, neither of those boys died, did they?" George asked.

"Nah. I just happened to be the duty officer this weekend, and being those two are from a family we watch pretty close, I'm doing some follow-up, getting in some overtime. You got any idea why these two birds would beat each other up like that?"

"No idea in the world," George replied. "Like I said, they went back there and run my dishwasher out, so no one really knows what happened."

"What about that gunshot?" Torres asked, looking closely at George.

"Beats me. Maybe it was some other kind of noise," George responded.

"Maybe there was someone else involved that had a gun and beat them both up," Torres said.

"Well, I doubt it, but you could ask Joey and Freddy," George replied.

"Come on, George. You know, I'd get the old see-my-lawyer routine. I'm not concerned with charging anyone on this. I'm just curious about what the fuck happened. What about your dishwasher? This Malone guy?"

"What about him?" George shot back.

"Is he here? Maybe he heard more of their argument before they ran him out," Torres said.

"I'm sure he didn't, but he took today off, won't be in until Monday."

"You got his address there?" Torres asked.

George opened the desk drawer, rustled around in it for a moment, and came out with a pink five-by-ten card and laid it on the desk.

"He lives over at the Star Motel, and the motel phone number's on here."

"Let me see that." Torres slid his chair closer, turned the card around, took a notebook from the pocket of his designer sweatshirt, and took down all the information, including the social security number.

On his way around to the Star Motel, he called in for an NCIC computer record check on a Bill Malone. He gave the dispatcher the information he had written down from the card.

Gail heard the bell ring out in the office, and when she went out, Torres was standing there.

"Hi there," he said affably. "You remember me, don't you?"

"Sure do. What can I do for you?" she asked with a friendly smile.

"I'm looking for the guy in 7A, a Bill Malone, and he doesn't answer the door. Does he still live there?" Torres asked.

"He hasn't checked out, but I don't know where he is. Maybe he's at work," Gail replied.

Torres took out a business card.

"Would you give him this and ask him to call me when he comes in? I need to talk to him," Torres said, handing her the card.

"I sure will," she said, taking the card and putting it in a drawer behind the counter.

He was halfway home when the dispatcher called and read him the police record of one William Malone. There were several assaults, all dismissed, close to twenty-five years ago. A conviction on a stolen airplane for which he had served time in a California prison. A robbery charge in

Madera that resulted in a not guilty verdict, and a bank robbery conviction fifteen years ago that resulted in federal prison time. It all sounded like this dishwasher had led a pretty busy life.

Torres had always had the feeling that the woman who owned the motel had not been fully cooperating with his investigation. Oh, she was polite enough, but nothing of any help was ever forthcoming. As he heard Malone's record, he thought he had an idea why she was not helpful.

This guy lived fifty yards from where Perfecto got his and was right on the scene of Freddy and Joey's altercation, or whatever happened at Ferrarro's that night. Torres had a strong hunch he had found his man. Mainly because he didn't believe in coincidences, and all the elements were there, including the man's violent nature.

It didn't make sense that a dishwasher would be involved in all this. But neither did it make sense that a thug like Malone would be working in Fresno as a dishwasher. At this point, Torres couldn't prove anything, but he could damn sure put some pressure on someone. He picked up the two-way and told the dispatcher, "Find out who his parole officer is and get his number for me."

As he turned into his driveway, he was thinking about computers and the progress that had been made in computer technology. They were amazing machines that obviously had been patterned after the human brain. But humans lie to you, jack you off, and run you around and around.

Computers didn't do any of that. They just backed up in a corner, looked the world in the eye, and spit out cold hard facts. Every fucking time.

17.

Richard Avakian sat in the living room on an easy chair. Bill sat across from him on the black leather couch. Gail and June had gone out to the front office so they could talk. Richard watched the fish swimming for a long time and then said, "I don't want to pry, man, and I understand what you're saying, but I still can't figure how you came to be busting Joey's head over there in the dishroom at Ferraro's."

"It looked like they were getting ready to bust my head. So I got down first," Bill told him.

"Okay, we'll just leave that part out," Richard said.

"I don't want to go into it other than to say they came for money they thought I owed that I don't owe and even if I did owe I couldn't pay on my six bucks an hour. What I need to know is what you know about these guys and what I'm up against," Bill said.

Richard studied the fish awhile longer, nodded his head, and began.

"The Sandinos are a local mob family. The head honcho is Small Bob, who runs a Caddy dealership over on Blackstone. His brother is a real cold monkey called Fred the Glove. He runs a sports bar near First and Cedar. The two youngsters you fucked up are the Glove's kids, Fred Junior and Joey. He's also got a daughter named Florence who is a pretty smart cookie. She's going with a cousin of mine right now, a good Armenian boy who is a decent thief. Pete Avakian is his name, and the Glove would have a shit fit if he found out. Those old boys don't like Armenians.

"Their family has been here for like fifty years. Own a

lot of property and could be hooked to the L.A. mob. They own every bookie in town, run a few card games and a couple of classy escort-service whorehouses. Probably fifteen made members and twenty or thirty associates.

"It was a pretty tight show up until a few years ago when Small Bob and Fred's dad died. They're getting weak now, because Small Bob doesn't seem to have the nuts it takes to run a family and Fred is just plain crazy. The other characters around here are beginning to take a bite out of them here and there, and the more they get away with it, the more bites they take.

"See, you got to understand that judges in this county are appointed, not elected, and it's hard to get them in a pocket. So the muscle stuff has to be done with discretion and good judgment. Big Bob used well-chosen examples to keep the fear and respect at a high level. Small Bob thinks like about a half square and makes stupid moves or lets things go that should be dealt with. That family's days are numbered around here.

"The two youngsters you had the scrape with are nuttier than a couple of pet raccoons. They are violent and there's no tellin' what they might do. They deal dope like they think it's legal, and the family has never been into that. They think they're bulletproof because of the family, but the shit they're doing around here is getting out of hand."

"Will the family back their play?" Bill asked.

"That's a good question. If there's dope involved, I'm pretty sure they couldn't even go to Small Bob. About all you've got to worry about is them and Fred the Glove. If their dad gets involved, you got big problems, because like I said, he is one cold monkey."

"Why do they call him the Glove?" Bill asked.

"Two things that I know of," Richard replied. "Years ago he knocked in a sporting goods store and stole all the guns, but he left a glove in the store. He got caught with the other glove still in his coat pocket, and it got him convicted. Done a couple years at Quentin for that.

"A few years after that incident, he stabbed a guy to death over a broad, and I'll be damned if he didn't leave another glove in the apartment where he done it. He got rid of the other glove that time, but they had his initials on them. He beat that case. He loves to hurt people in close with his fists, and he always wears leather gloves. He's still tough as a yard dog, and people around here are scared to death of him."

"I get the idea," Bill said.

"The problem you've got now is this small-town talk. Three people called me this morning before Gail called and told me about the dishwasher at Ferraro's fucking up Joey and Freddy. I didn't know it was you until she called me. That shit about them doing each other didn't go anywhere. Although you might have been better off if it had. They can't let that go, man. If I was you, I'd break camp right now. Just ease on out of town and stay gone. The more this talk gets around on the street, the unhappier they're going to get. Your future don't look bright here in Fresno."

"I'm not leaving," Bill said.

Richard looked at him for a long time, then at the fish awhile, and then back at Bill. The silence got heavy, and they could hear Gail and June talking out in the office.

"I was afraid you were going to say that," Richard finally said.

"Do you think they would hurt Gail or June?" Bill asked.

"Nah, the family's always been careful about avoiding that kind of heat. They don't bother women, although it's rumored that the Glove beat his wife to death. I think that's the main reason Florence hates his ass. But they won't even be thinking about Gail or June. Look here, Malone, I know some people around here who would be willing to move against the Sandinos. I can get you some help, and I'll do what I can myself. You're going to need some help, man."

"I don't want anyone's help. But I do want you to let me know about anything you hear that I should know."

"You got it, brother," Richard said.

"Will this Florence take a message to these guys from me?" Bill asked.

"I'm sure she would."

"I want to tell them that I really don't owe the money. If I did I would pay it. I'll apologize for the misunderstanding, but if they can't accept that, they can call me at Ferraro's and I'll meet them on whatever terms they choose. Can you remember all that?"

"I'll pass it on, but man, be real careful and watch your back," Richard said as he rose and stuck out his hand.

Bill took his hand. "Stay in touch," he said.

"You'll hear from me," Richard told him.

"June is on me to walk up to Roeding Park with her," Gail told him after Richard left.

"Well, let's get our coats and go. I need some exercise anyway," Bill said.

Gail put the Closed sign on the office door and they took off, with Shadow unhappily trailing along behind. Every time June looked back at him, he'd lift his ears and tail.

"Do you think he will stay after the prime rib runs out?" Bill asked June.

"Oh yes, he loves me," June said.

"I do too," Bill said and put his arm around her.

"What about me?" Gail asked.

"Let me check those prime ribs," Bill said and put his other arm around her.

A feeling of sadness settled on Bill as he walked along in the nippy air with his arms around June and Gail. The love he felt for them and the way that part of his life was developing was damn near perfect. But the madness and chaos that seemed to have followed him from the prison gate threatened everything positive in his life.

Now that same cruel luck had put him at odds with a Mickey Mouse Mafia family. There wasn't much use in trying to deal with them or to work things out, because there was no telling what they might do or where they would do it. He would be in much better shape if they had been a real mob family who lived by mob values. At least he would have some legitimate expectation of what they might do next.

This Fred the Glove didn't sound like someone you could talk sense to. The two boys he'd had the run-in with were obviously people who were more concerned with how others perceived them than with what they really were. It was hard to believe they would give that much dope on credit to a degenerate little thug like Salazar. But it was even harder to believe they would expect a total stranger who had a dishwashing job to pay the debt.

Then there were George and Regina, both nice people. Bill didn't want them sucked any deeper into this mess. He decided that when they got back home, he'd call George and tell him he was quitting. If George had to fire him, he'd probably have to explain it all to Regina, and Bill didn't want that to happen any more than George did. Bill resolved to just quit and relieve the little man of that chore. Another thing that surprised him was the added sadness he felt about leaving the machine, the dishroom, and Leona and the other help. The job felt like family to him now.

They entered Roeding Park and were walking along, admiring the big trees and, well-tended lawns and flowers, when they heard a raucous crowd up ahead. Thirty or forty people, men, women, and children, were gathered around. Men were yelling and taunting someone, and Bill heard Bullfrog's distinctive voice: "You just think I won't do it, white folks, put another twenty in there and I'll set the whole thing on fire!"

June pulled loose and began running up ahead.

"Come on, you guys! You got to see this!" she yelled back over her shoulder as Shadow sat down in the street and began barking furiously.

Bill and Gail hurried to catch up to her, and when they reached the crowd they had to push through a few people to see clearly what was going on. It looked like most of the people in the park were there, and more were drifting over to watch.

Bullfrog had on a pair of overalls with the legs rolled up to his knees and a blue denim shirt. A baseball cap with the New York Mets logo was turned sideways on his head, and he was barefoot. He was standing atop an overturned bucket looking defiantly at the crowd. Bill could have sworn he winked at him and Gail. June had made her way right up to the front row.

There was a good-sized pile of glass and broken bottles in front of the bucket. An upside-down bowler hat lay beside the glass. Cabbage Head stood beside the hat holding a one-gallon gas can in his hand. As they looked on, a man came through the crowd with two empty beer bottles, broke them by whacking them together, laid them on the pile, and put a five-dollar bill in the hat.

"Come on, man, are you just talking shit or are you going to jump?" he yelled at Bullfrog.

"I'm jumpin', man, you can bet your bleached-out ass on that. I loves pain, but I shore hate jumpin' for a bunch a' cheapos!" Bullfrog yelled back.

Bullfrog threw his arms back and bent his knees as if to jump, and Bill felt Gail's fingernails dig into his arm. Cabbage Head reached out and grabbed Bullfrog by the elbow.

"Wait a minute, Frog! I ain't lit it on fire yet, and they ain't enough money in that hat. Let's just give 'em back the small change and call the whole thing off," he said and handed Bullfrog an open quart of Tokay wine.

"Oh no you don't. You promised to jump!" a man in the crowd shouted as Bullfrog turned up the bottle and chugged at the wine.

As he wiped his lips on his shirt sleeve, another man walked up with a gallon wine jug and crashed it into the pile of broken glass, trying to break it. It didn't break, and Cabbage Head reached into his back pocket, brought out a large screwdriver, and broke it for him. It looked especially dangerous with big, jagged edges lying atop the already impressive pile. The man dropped a twenty-dollar bill into the hat.

"All right. Light 'er up!" he instructed Cabbage Head.

Cabbage Head took the lid off the gas can and poured it liberally onto the glass. Bill realized that most of the men in the crowd were drunk. Some of the women were trying to pull their eyes away but seemed mesmerized by the pile of glinting broken glass and the forlorn yet defiant little black man perched atop the bucket.

Cabbage Head threw a match onto the gas, and the whoosh of the flames made everyone close jump back. Bullfrog bent his knees and threw his arms back again. Gail's fingernails dug deeply into Bill's arm.

"Oh my God! Can you stop him, Bill?" she asked, and Bill heard another woman nearby moan.

But when he looked over at June, she was grinning from ear to ear and looking at Bullfrog. Cabbage Head was dropping a few more dollars into the hat.

"Hit the hat! C'mon, hit the hat, y'all! We got to help pay his doctor bills. Come on now. Ain't got but a few seconds. Hit the hat!"

A few people nearby dropped more bills and change into the hat. The flames had subsided somewhat when Bullfrog let out an overpowering Geronimo yell, leaped high in the air from the bucket, and came down with both feet rhythmically stomping at the fire and glass.

A woman screamed and turned away. A couple of the men yelled and tore their eyes away. Gail buried her face in Bill's chest as Bullfrog went on yelling and stomping until the fire was out and the glass lay scattered in the road like smoldering gravel.

Before Bullfrog finished, Cabbage Head had emptied the hat into his pockets and put it back on his head. Bullfrog calmly walked over to his shoes and socks, sat down on the grass beside them, and began putting his socks on. Everyone gathered around him, and there wasn't a drop of blood anywhere.

"How did you do that, man? How in the hell did you do it?" a man asked him incredulously.

"Put myself in a voodoo trance," Bullfrog replied, smiling up at the man as he tied his shoe.

"I'll be damned," the man said.

A woman who had had a hard time watching stepped forward. "I can't believe this. I saw it but I can't believe it. Here," she said, handing Bullfrog another ten-dollar bill.

"Thank you, ma'am," Bullfrog replied, then looked at the younger kids who were standing in awe near him.

"Now look here, kids, don't you go trying that. Last man I saw who tried that cut both his feet off. You got to be a real voodoo man to do that. Y'all hear me?" he said forcefully.

The kids all nodded in unison. They were too shocked and delighted to say anything.

Bullfrog got up, waved at June and Bill, took Cabbage Head by the arm, and walked off through the park, with the crowd looking after them.

"That was one hell of a show," Bill said to June when she rejoined him and Gail.

"I saw him do it last year," June said.

"How in the hell does he do it?" Gail asked.

"Beats me. He says it's voodoo," June replied, and they all laughed. Bullfrog resembled a Ringling Brothers clown more than he did a voodoo man.

Bill called George Ferraro from the house and was surprised by the man's attitude. George told him about Torres's visit, but that wasn't really news. What was a surprise was that George told him he could come back to work if he wanted to. Although Bill was pleased with the prospect of returning to his job, he couldn't figure such a change of heart in George, and he told him so.

"Look here, Malone, you know how Regina feels about you, and I've got a lot of respect for you myself. I don't have the heart to tell her what's really going on here. But believe me, I'm not keeping you on from the goodness of my heart, and I'm not doing you a favor, either," George said.

"I didn't think you were," Bill replied.

"Okay, what I'm telling you now is between you and me. I never said it. This won't ever be mentioned. Have I got your word on that?"

"You've got my word," Bill promised. He could hear a note in George's voice that he'd never heard there before.

"Fred the Glove told me not to fire you. He knows what happened. I told him I'd get rid of you, and he said not to do that. Then he asked me to have you work overtime on a banquet or something. I refused to do that, and let me tell you, it scares the shit out of me to refuse that man anything.

"But I stood up to him that much. I told him nothing is going to go down in my place of business and that I'm not going to help anyone do anything to you. The only thing I did was to promise not to lay you off. But if you quit, I got no control over that, so you can quit right now and I'll just tell him you quit, no problem," George said.

"What's he mad about?" Bill asked.

"Jesus Christ, man!" George yelled into the phone. "You put his two kids in the hospital. One of them in a coma, for Christ's sake, and you're asking me what is he mad about? What the fuck do you think he's mad about?"

"I just thought maybe there was something in particular that pushed his button, you know. People get hurt in fights all the time, especially people like his kids. They can't expect to win every fight they get into."

"Evidently Fred told him you blind-sided him," George said. "Hit Joey when he wasn't looking or something like that. He asked me a bunch of questions about you. I told him all I know is on that five-by-ten card, and he now has all that information.

"But I imagine what pushed his button is all the talk about it. I must have had ten calls today from people who've heard the rumors. By Monday the police will know all about it, and that's another thing that worries me. It's some kind of felony to lie to a police officer about a fucking crime. I didn't have time to think that lie out very good."

"No way they could ever prove that. What you told them could actually be what you thought happened, so just stay with that," Bill told him.

"Yeah, I guess you're right. You got some money coming here, Malone, and we planned to give you a Christmas bonus anyway, so why don't you come get it tomorrow? I'll make a special trip down here, say around noon. Then Monday night I'll just call Fred the Glove and tell him you never showed and I don't know where you went, which I won't," George said.

"I'll be in Monday to work. I'm not going anywhere," Bill said.

The phone went dead silent for a long time. But Bill knew George was still on the line, because he could hear bar and kitchen noises and loud intermittent laughter.

"George, you still there?" he finally asked.

"Yeah, I'm here. Would you tell me something, Malone?" George asked.

"Sure," Bill replied.

"Are you crazy, man? I mean, have you got some kind of suicide fantasy or something? Because that's what you're doing here, pal. You're laying your life right out there on the table and saying, 'Come on and get it.' "

"No, George, I don't think I'm crazy, and I know I don't have any suicidal tendencies. I'm just tired of running, and I'm not running anymore from anyone or anything," Bill said.

After another long silence George said to him, "Malone, there's one other thing I need to tell you."

"What's that?" Bill asked.

"I like your style, buddy," George said and hung up the phone.

18.

On that Saturday evening, Small Bob paced back and forth on his screened-in porch at One Zero Way while Fred the Glove sat dejected in a leather easy chair watching him.

"Fred, you know my wife's brother, Louie, now has full ownership of that furniture moving and storage company in Los Angeles that I helped him to buy."

"Yeah, he's doing okay," Fred replied, uneasily watching Bob as he paced the floor.

"I talked to him an hour ago," Bob went on. "Told him Fred Junior and Joey will be coming down there to work for him awhile. I want you to send them there for a year. I don't want to see either of them for at least that long. Is that understood?"

"I'll send them soon as Joey is able to leave, but I still think you're too excited about all this shit," Fred responded.

Bob quit pacing and sat down in his chair across the room from Fred. They looked at each other for a long time. Small Bob wished there were some way he could explain the critical nature of the situation to Fred. But Fred had never been one to grasp the finer points of a concept. Fred was able in a lot of ways, and his ferocious nature had been good for the family image, but his intellect was shaky.

"Our family is falling apart, Fred. We may as well admit it. You and I just can't run it like the old folks did."

"That's bullshit!" Fred roared, and Bob held up his hand to stay him.

"Hear me out, Fred. Now take those boys, for instance. Right after they got hurt I thought it was over some bookmaking that they take care of, or they were supposedly taking care of. I talk all night with some of our bookies and I find out why our take is down so bad. The boys been neglecting that and selling dope on their own. They got hurt over a fuckin' dope deal, and the guy did it is a fuckin' dishwasher at Ferraro's. A bona fide fuckin' dishwasher!

"They been letting sports collections go and collecting their own dope money, Fred. So now they got some of our bet runners selling dope. Our bookies are winning all kinds of money on paper, but they're going broke anyway because they pay every winner and can't collect from the losers. The boys ain't got time.

"They make so much off the dope that they can make up some of the gambling loss so we don't get the idea. But what they've done is ruined our whole operation. Deadbeats are going from one bookie to the next and taking potshots at us. Some of our bookies see what's going on and they're betting themselves and paying themselves and giving us a slip saying 'owed' if they lose. It's a fuckin' mess, Fred. If they wasn't your kids, I'd whack both the fuckers."

"Are you sure of this?" Fred asked. Bob could see pain in his brother and knew he must really be bothered. It was seldom that Fred showed any emotion at all.

"Yeah, I'm sure, Fred," Bob sighed. "But a fuckin' dishwasher putting them down? People are talking about that, Fred. I mean, we are the talk of the town. That's another thing I don't understand—I hear Fred Junior is running his mouth outside the family about that. I mean, really flapping his jaws. You got any idea why he's doing that?"

"I'll talk to him," Fred promised as he got up. Bob could see that his brother had heard enough bad news. It would be dangerous even for him to say much more.

* * *

"The fucking little hoodlum bastards," Bob mumbled to himself as he went in to bed.

But sleep wouldn't come. He lay there most of the night tossing and fighting his pillow. Bob understood in his own mind that the Sandino family was finished in Fresno. His first thought was to try to downgrade their operations and let the family die by attrition. But while that scheme would work in a legal operation, it wouldn't do here. He was becoming convinced that the only way was to admit defeat, disband the family, and pull out. There wasn't much hope of making Fred the Glove see the logic in that.

The trouble between the Glove's kids and the dishwasher was unfortunate, but it was clear that the problem was the direct result of a dope deal. About half the family were now dealing in drugs, and there was no way to stop it short of a massive internal bloodletting. The profits were enormous, but so was the heat, and the love of drug profits wasn't their only problem.

Local pimps who had been successful running girls to labor camps were now opening motels and massage parlors. Some of them right next to Sandino-owned escort services. Their reply lately when told they were on Sandino turf had been "Fuck you! We operate where we please."

That attitude, plus the problems with the bookies and drug dealing, was killing the family. People didn't respect them anymore. He remembered old Giuseppe saying that you had to hurt someone regularly in order to keep respect at a high level. The Glove did hurt a lot of people, but his violence could just as well be over a woman or booze as family business.

It was obvious now that he would have to preside over too much killing and bloodshed to whip the family back into shape. Bob knew he didn't have the stomach and maybe not even the will to do it. He could turn it all over to the Glove, but that would more than likely be a royal mess. Toward morning he fell asleep not having decided much of anything.

19.

Ray Harrelson from vice and narcotics had brunch on Sunday with Martin Torres and his family. After the meal in the dining room the two walked out onto Torres's redwood deck with their coffee and Harrelson told Torres what everyone else in town seemed to know already.

"It looks like the dishwasher over at Ferraro's, a guy named Bill Malone, is the one who beat Perfecto Salazar to death," Harrelson said.

"You're way ahead of me there, Ray," Torres said, shaking his head.

The big Swede leaned back in a deck chair, crossed his legs, and fished a pack of Camels from his corduroy jacket pocket. Torres had a lot of respect for him as a detective. His ability to run a network of reliable stool pigeons was legendary. Especially these days when it was so hard to separate bullshit from hard facts. The drug war had placed some sophisticated liars among the ranks of informers.

"I don't have any proof, of course, but according to a couple of my best people, it came from Fred Sandino's own mouth," Harrelson said.

"You mean Fred the Glove?" Torres asked, sitting up in his chair.

"No, I mean young Fred. The one who had his arm broken by that guy Malone Friday evening over at Ferraro's," Harrelson said.

"Damn, Wayne. You're ahead of me in two spots now. I thought Fred and Joey beat each other up over there on Friday," Torres said.

"I doubt if you ever really believed that, Martin, although

I heard the same story. But Fred wasn't out of the hospital an hour before he was telling people that this guy Malone sneaked on Joey with an iron skillet and broke his elbow with it when he went for his piece."

"You don't say?" Torres remarked. He had already figured out pretty much the same thing but preferred to act dumb and find out everything Harrelson knew.

"Yeah, but the funny part of it is Fred saying that he and Joey went there to talk with Malone about why he had beaten their friend Perfecto to death. That doesn't make any sense, because neither of those assholes cares much about Mexicans. Especially lowrider Mexicans like Perfecto Salazar."

"Could be Perfecto was selling dope for them," Torres surmised.

"Now that could very well be," Harrelson said, taking a deep drag of his Camel and letting the smoke idle out his nostrils. It was all Torres could do to keep from wincing. He hated cigarettes.

"But what I really mean by funny is him telling that to everyone. This kid has been closemouthed in the past, and here he is talking to all these honky-tonk heroes and any would-be gangster in bars he frequents. It's like he knows this talk is going to get back to us. It's like he wants it to get back to us. He's dry-snitching on this Malone guy is what he's doing."

"Maybe he's in shock," Torres said.

"I don't doubt that a bit. That was a very nasty broken elbow. Compound fracture. He's no doubt taking some strong pain medicine, but still . . ."

"What do you think? Do you believe him?" Torres asked.

"Well, yes I do. I'm not sure why, but his own admission that he and Joey got fucked up by an old dishwasher goes a long way toward convincing me the rest of it is true. But I'm not working the case. Do you know anything about this Malone?" Harrelson asked.

"Yes, I ran a make on him. Old dishwasher don't fit. Old

thug would fit better, but he's not that old. Early forties. He just did fourteen for the feds on a bank robbery and paroled back here to Fresno.

"He did time before on a weed-smuggling beef. Lots of suspicion on his record, including armed robbery—only one conviction on that. He did a small jolt in Folsom prison over a stolen airplane. I'm sure you remember the time when the feds raided Big Ed Arkin up in the hills and found all those scofflaws tied up in a pile."

"Goddam, that Malone! Hell yes, I do remember that name! Is this the same guy?" Harrelson asked as a look of surprise crossed his face.

"The one and only." Torres smiled at him.

"I'll be damned. Let's bring him in for questioning, Martin. He won't tell us anything, but I want a good look at that fucker. That story is still told by cops around here as if it happened last week."

"Yep, he sure made their job easy that morning," Torres laughed. "But I think he skipped. He checked out of his room at the Star Motel."

"He was living there then?" Harrelson asked.

"Yes, he was," Torres replied.

"Then that's it. You've got your man," Harrelson said.

"Well, we may know he did it, but I don't see old Fred Junior on the witness stand. In fact, he'd deny he ever said it. I don't see a lick of proof anywhere. What was really unfortunate is that it was first reported as a routine assault. By the time Perfecto died, the crime-scene evidence was destroyed. His wife picked up his car and had been driving it for over two weeks when he died. She had had the fucking thing vacuumed and washed and the seat covers changed," Torres said with disgust.

"Are you sure he skipped?" Harrelson asked.

"Not a hundred percent, but it looks that way," Torres replied.

"It sure would be interesting if he hadn't. There's no way that family could let that one go, what with all this talk about it. These country boys would be making cowboy boots out of their nut sacks," Harrelson ventured.

"You know, you may have hit it right there, Wayne. Fred might have done all that talking to make sure Malone would run or go to jail. He probably figured he or Joey would be told to take the guy out, and after that one run-in he wanted no part of Malone," Torres theorized.

"Yeah, this fucking new breed does think like that. Dry-snitching is part of their game. They don't make gangsters like they used to," Harrelson said with a touch of nostalgia entering his voice.

"They don't make anything like they used to," Torres retorted.

The weekend had been one of the worst Small Bob could remember in his life. His phone had been ringing since Friday night with reports on the aftermath of Freddy and Joey's fight at Ferraro's. His people were telling him horror stories about Freddy. He was running his mouth everywhere he went, and Bob had people out looking for him and just barely missing him all weekend.

It was Monday afternoon when one of the boys found him at his girlfriend's house and drove him home. Small Bob walked into the Glove's living room to find Freddy sitting in a recliner, arm in a cast, head hanging dejectedly, with a monumentally mad Fred the Glove standing over him looking as if he might kill him any second.

All weekend Bob had been telling Fred what the boy had been doing, and all weekend the Glove had been trying not to believe what he heard. He had to hear it all from Bob, because the rest of their crew had been afraid to tell the Glove that kind of news about his own son.

When Bob walked into the dim living room dominated by a giant TV screen, a mere glance at the Glove's face told him that somehow his brother had finally gotten the message.

"He admits it! He fuckin' admitted it!" the Glove roared

when Small Bob came in. Every time he yelled, Fred Junior's head ducked between his shoulders like a turtle's. He kept his head down as if he was studying his crotch.

"Take it easy, Fred," Bob said, taking Fred by the arm.

"Easy, my ass!" Fred roared, jerking his arm loose. "The little bastard admits it!" he yelled again.

Bob took his arm again and put his other arm around the Glove's shoulder, turning him toward the door.

"Listen, brother, you've got every right to be mad, but we've both been up all weekend. Go have a smoke or something and let me talk to Freddy. After I do that, we'll figure what needs to be done. You're too mad right now to think. You know how you get." As Bob droned on soothingly, the Glove allowed himself to be steered out toward the kitchen.

Bob had always been the only one who could handle the Glove. He would listen to Bob when he wouldn't even listen to their own father. Bob tried to act calm, but right now he figured he felt exactly like the Glove did inside. He felt like he could kill the fucking little bastard.

He was also thinking of how typical this scene was of the Glove's character. It was obvious that the rage he displayed now was brought on more by the fact that Freddy had admitted what he had done than by the fact that he had done it. When the Glove walked into the kitchen, Bob slid the door shut behind him.

"Freddy?" he said, turning back toward the dejected youngster in the recliner. Freddy raised his head slowly to look at Bob, and Bob was shocked to see tears running down his face along with snot leaking from his nose into his mustache. He was about two shades paler than Bob had ever seen him.

"I'm, I'm sorry, Uncle Bob," he stammered and dropped his head back toward his lap.

Bob fished a handkerchief out of his back pocket, shook it, and dropped it on Freddy's good arm. "Wipe yourself off, Freddy and tell me what's going on with you. Why have you been going around all over town saying all this stuff?"

Bob asked, trying to keep the exasperation he felt out of his voice.

Freddy wiped his face with a handkerchief and looked at the wall for a long time before looking up at Bob. "I'm not real sure why I done it, I wasn't thinking. Well, I was thinking, but thinking wrongly about some of it. To tell you the honest truth, that guy scared the shit out of me, and I've never been scared that bad before, not even by Dad."

"But the talk, Freddy. We can straighten almost anything out but the fucking talking you did. That's what I'm talking about. Why did you say all that? There's no way to unsay it." Bob kept the tone of his voice as gentle as possible. The kid was obviously still scared to death.

Freddy raised his head again and looked Bob directly in the eyes for a long time while mopping at his face with the handkerchief before he replied.

"I'll tell you the truth, Uncle Bob. You'll have to tell Dad, because I don't know how to say it to him. He will probably kill me."

"Nobody will kill you, Freddy. You got my word on that. You're part of our family, son," Bob assured him.

"Well, that's just it. I'm not part of the family as of right now. Of what is not legal about our business, anyway. I just realized I'm not cut out for this, and I should have known it a long time ago. I've been going around pushing people and acting tough all my life. But I'm not tough. That dishwasher woke me up to that real quick. I don't have the heart for this shit. People have let me push them around and took my shit because of Dad and our family, so I got to thinking I'm tough. But I'm far from it, and I should have known that."

"But the talk, Fred. You knew better than that!"

"Well, I'm coming to that, Uncle Bob," Fred said, lowering his eyes again.

"That broken elbow hurt worse than anything that ever happened to me. It took the doctors three hours to set it, and they wanted me to stay in the hospital. But I was still in pain, and the shots they gave me didn't help much. So I checked out and went to my girl's apartment. I had some dope there and stuck some of it in my nose to kill the pain. It worked pretty good, even though I damned near overdosed myself. I went to some after-hours clubs Friday night and got to talking to some people who laughed about the arm, but I didn't say too much that night.

"Saturday around noon I was still higher than a kite and I went over to Sparky's bar. That's where my fear took over. I figured Joey and I would probably have to hit the dishwasher. You know how Joey is. I thought if I let out some of the information, he would be arrested, so I started talking about what happened. I didn't mean to tell it all, especially about the Mexican, but people kept prying, asking questions, and I kept getting in deeper and deeper.

"The more I talked, I figured if he don't get arrested it would be common knowledge, so me and Joey couldn't do anything to him. I figured Dad would bring someone in from L.A. or San Francisco to do the job. After I came down I felt bad about what I done. I wish I could undo it now. No matter how bad I'm scared, the guy didn't have that coming, and our family never deserved the heat I put on us. So I'm sorry. I'm very sorry, Uncle Bob," he said dejectedly, putting his head down and sobbing.

"Freddy, did you and Joey have that Mexican dealing heroin for you?"

Freddy just nodded his head as he kept on sobbing. Bob stood there listening to him trying to choke back his sobs and watching him use the handkerchief to try to stem the flow of tears.

Bob wasn't surprised at what he was hearing. He'd known other men, dedicated thugs, who'd turned chickenshit the first time they experienced real pain. At least Freddy hadn't lied to him, and Bob couldn't think of a more difficult admission than the one the kid had just made. This boy might be even tougher than he thought he was. After being raised by a maniac and a terrorized, powerless woman, the kid probably knew very little about himself.

"Freddy, is your dad in on this dope business with you and Joey?" Bob asked, lowering his voice until Freddy could barely hear him.

Freddy's sobs stopped abruptly, and he met Bob's look directly. The color was coming back to his face.

"I wouldn't tell you if he was," Freddy replied.

"I figured that. So how about not telling him that I asked?" Bob said.

"I won't tell him," Fred replied.

"What do you think about learning the furniture moving and storage business like my brother-in-law Louie does in Los Angeles? If you go from the ground up and get it down, I'll help you open one down here somewhere," Bob said.

"I'd like that, Uncle Bob. I don't want to be a wise guy anymore. I know now that I'm not cut out for it. The furniture business sounds good to me," Freddy replied.

"Joey will be going down there for a while also. Now, he's going to get itchy and want to come back in a few weeks. But if you want to learn the business, you hang with it and stay there. Never mind what Joey does, and don't let him talk you into anything."

"I won't. I'm done with this," Freddy replied, and Bob could hear the relief in his voice.

"Well, you clean yourself up and go on up and see Joey. He came out of that coma this morning. He'll be wanting to see you," Bob said as he started for the kitchen. Then he thought about something and turned back.

"Freddy?"

"What is it?" Freddy asked.

"Don't ever put any more of that shit in your nose unless you got another broken elbow," Bob told him.

"I won't, Uncle Bob. I don't know how to thank you enough for trying to understand," Freddy said.

"You can thank me by making us some money in the furniture business," Bob said as he went out to the kitchen, where the Glove was sitting morosely over a cup of cold coffee.

Although Bob knew exactly what kind of insight the kid had gained about himself, he had no intention of trying to explain it to his brother. There was just no way to explain it to the Glove. He would view it as extreme weakness and probably beat the boy to a pulp.

"Fred, I'm sending the boys to L.A. until this thing blows over. Freddy got drunk and full of painkillers and ran his mouth. All we can do now is hope things die down and the cops don't get the whole story. But even if they do, it won't matter to us all that much. We'll just lay low and see what happens," he said.

The Glove looked up from his coffee, and Bob didn't care for what lurked behind his bloodshot eyeballs.

"Yeah, send them off for a while, and I may never let that fuckin' Freddy come back. I'll have to think about it, but right now I don't want him in the fuckin' house with me," the Glove replied.

"Well, that's fine. He can stay down there with Louie awhile, and we'll see what needs to be done here. But we got to get some grip on these bookies we got working. Their books are really getting messed up bad. Our take is down fifty percent and getting worse every week. We got problems, Fred. There's a lot of disrespect involved, and we got to deal with that somehow, and quick," Bob told him.

"I'm taking that dishwasher out of the box. That should get their attention," Fred said, and Bob noticed his big hands tighten around the coffee mug.

"I don't see how we can do that, brother. By now everyone in town, including the cops, knows all about what happened at Ferraro's. Everyone will know our family had something to do with it. Besides that, I don't see where we gain any respect by killing a fuckin' dishwasher in a restaurant. There's no percentage in it. I was thinking about it myself until I heard Freddy put it all out in the streets," Bob argued.

"You ain't lookin' at this right. In the first place, the guy whipped my kids like they was a couple of bitches or something. That makes it personal, and I've got to do something to him. You keep saying 'we,' but this is my deal. If he stays around I'm taking him out.

"Everyone knowing about it, well, that's good. Makes it even better. There won't be any question about why it happened. They will think twice before they fuck with us again. Far as the cops go, they know we been responsible for other shit they can't prove. This will die down just like everything else. Be some heat for a while, but it'll blow over," the Glove said.

Bob had to agree that some of Fred's logic made sense. He also knew that something drastic was needed to get their people back on the right track. The dishwasher would probably be gone anyway when he found out whose kids he beat up. Or the police could have him in jail tomorrow. He decided reluctantly to cosign the Glove.

"Go ahead, Fred. But be extra careful, because the cops are going to be watching this guy and probably watching us as well," he admonished.

"I know all that. I'll pick my spot real good," Fred replied.

"I'll bring Doug up from Visalia for some backup," Bob said, speaking of a tough, capable man who ran a card room in Visalia for the Sandinos.

"No, don't do that. I want this one all to myself," Fred replied, looking deep into Bob's eyes and holding the gaze for a long while.

Bob had never been one to concern himself about a stranger's destiny. But as he looked at the rage burning around the edges of his brother's eyeballs, he found himself feeling sorry for the dishwasher at Ferraro's.

20.

Regina and Leona followed him back to the dishroom when he showed up for work Monday afternoon. Regina, obviously relieved to see him back at work, kept chattering as Leona patiently waited for a chance to get him alone.

"I was worried you wouldn't come back to work," Regina said. "I don't know why these men picked our dishroom to fight in, but that sort of thing just never happens here. I'm sure it won't happen again." She was obviously worried that Bill might quit. As he listened to her he found himself wishing that his own troubles were as inconsequential as Regina's.

"They probably got so mad they couldn't wait. But it's no problem. I'll be around awhile," Bill soothed her and kept glancing at Leona, who waited her turn. When Regina finally left, Bill puttered around getting the machine ready as Leona spoke.

"Those are some real bad men, D.W.," she told him.

"Is George in with them?" he asked her.

"Nah, he likes to talk that gangster talk and chew them stogies, but George is just a business and family man at heart," she replied.

"What did you do with that gun?" he asked.

"I gave it back to George," she replied.

She kept standing there as he got the machine ready to go. He began loading it with the day's leftover dishes, trying not to look at her, but he finally looked up from what he was doing and saw those big liquid brown eyes were locked onto his face like radar. Leona was smiling.

"You having a hard time telling me something?" she asked softly.

"Well, sort of. I found a woman that I care a lot about," he replied.

"I figured that out, D.W., and it's okay. Don't nothin' last forever. I thought you needed something and I needed the same thing and I will always be glad we got it," she said.

Bill glanced over at the door to make sure no one was looking and folded her in his arms, drawing her tightly to him.

"Thank you, sweetheart. I'll always be glad of that myself," he whispered into her warm neck.

"Why won't you draw up your money and leave, D.W.," she said as she pushed back from him. "You ain't got nothin' holding you in this town, man, and I'm serious—them are some real bad people. They're dangerous and will do something to you," she told him anxiously.

"Life is dangerous. There's all kinds of germs waiting out there to kill me."

He felt better when the machine was running and the busboy began picking up clean dishes. There was something about the sound of the big machine performing all its functions that soothed him and put his mind in a space that was near meditation.

For a lot of years now, he'd lived a fantasy of life outside the walls in his mind while his body sweated and toiled over a dishwashing machine. But the life he was now living outside wasn't at all what he had envisioned. His dreams had left out madness and violence.

Yet finding Gail and June was near the best of his prison fantasizing. A ready-made family with nothing but love on their side of the equation. He felt blessed and fortunate about them, but he could never build on that dream until something was done about the Sandinos.

It was astonishing to him that Tough Tony was willing to give Gail and June up so easily while Bill valued them as highly as anything he could think of. When he thought about that, another element reached into his mind, plugged in, and illuminated a dark corner of his being. Something he'd read or heard at some time or another that rang very true.

Nothing that a person values highly ever comes easy, and one must be willing to pay whatever price is demanded. Loving someone often exacts the most exorbitant remittance that nature can arrange.

The thought made him feel better. He could see that dealing with the Sandinos was an obstacle to picking up a claim check on the life he wanted and the love he wanted to share it with.

In a way, there seemed to be some justice in the proposition. He'd never paid any taxes to the society he now wished to be a part of, or worked to earn himself a peaceful corner in that world. It looked like fate was going to make him wash his hands before coming to dinner. Or make him die trying.

Convicts called a situation like that "paying your dues," and Bill realized that there was nothing left but to pick up the tab. Thinking all this cleared his mind of lingering thoughts of moving on or maybe asking Gail and June to go away with him. There was really nothing to do but to end his problems with the Sandino family once and for all.

Along with these thoughts came another certainty about the reality of his situation. He remembered a day on the yard in the first prison he had ever served time in. An old convict friend of his had had an argument with several men who were members of a deadly prison gang. After the argument ended and the men walked away, Bill had said to his friend, "Don't you think you had better start watching your back?"

His buddy looked at him for a long time and said, "No, I'm not going to watch my back. There's really no reason to do that. If a fool decides to stab you in the back, he's going to do it anyway, whether you're watching or not. If he's patient, dedicated, and determined, he'll just stalk you until you aren't looking. You can't look over your shoulder all the time.

"All you can hope," he went on, "is that he says something or mentions it to someone and it gets back to you what he intends to do. If that happens, you got to go take him out before he gets his shot at you. But as far as watching your back, forget it. No use worrying about anything you have no control over."

Bill realized for sure that to just keep working here made him a sitting duck for whatever they dreamed up. Beating those two up was a mistake in hindsight, but the harm was done. He decided to try to focus on the family and hit them hard enough to get them off his case.

"You got a phone call back in George's office, D.W.," Leona yelled over the steady throb of the machine.

Bill looked up, startled out of his reverie, to see her there grinning with a tray in her hand that held a half-gallon pitcher of beer and a frosted glass.

"Bringing the old nazi a beer and a message, huh?" he said, smiling at her as he turned off the machine.

She set the tray down on the conveyor belt and as she turned to leave said to him, "I know for sure you ain't no nazi, D.W. They all had little bitty short dicks."

He laughed as he followed her through the dishroom door. He'd been worried about how she was going to take the news about Gail, but she'd taken it like a champ. Leona was a friend he could keep always.

"Bill Malone," he said into the phone and winced as Frances Logan's voice bit his ear.

"Goddam you, Bill. I'm not dead yet, at least I don't think I am. Why in hell haven't you been up here to see me?" she demanded.

"Ah, Frances, it's good to hear your voice. I've planned to come, but things keep going haywire. Hang on a while more and I'll explain it all when I see you," he replied, trying to soothe her with the tone of his voice.

"Are you still at that Star Motel?" she asked.

"Yeah," he replied.

"Well, you know, I'm getting hard of hearing and it's hard to talk on the phone, so I'm driving down there. I'll see you in a few days," she said.

"Wait a minute, Frances," he said urgently, trying to get her attention. He certainly didn't want her coming now, of all times.

"I'll see you in a few days, sweetheart. Bye," she replied, and the line went dead.

He knew there was no use calling her back and trying to reason with her. If she had decided to come, there wouldn't be any changing her mind. But his heart did begin to beat faster with the thought of seeing her again. He noticed the spring back in his step on his way back to the dishroom. He was getting a feeling that somehow things were going to work out fine in the end. The old American dream.

On Tuesday morning, Martin Torres sat in Campbell's office in the federal building. The conversation had not gone the way he had assumed it would.

"Mr. Torres, I understand your concern," Campbell was saying. "But I hope you can understand my position. I just can't violate a man's parole because you think he may have done something. If you bring me some proof, then I can make a recommendation based on that. But right now my hands are pretty well tied."

"He's already beaten one man to death and put a couple more in the hospital. The last two being local mob people. Now he's either going to get killed or wind up killing someone else. He'd be safer in jail. You'd be doing him a favor by violating him. I'm sure he's moved. Can't you violate him for changing his address without asking permission?" Torres asked, his voice beginning to show his frustration.

"I'll check that out. But it's such a minor thing, I doubt I'd violate him even if he did. I'm just not convinced that he did all the stuff you think he's done. It just isn't his style."

Torres looked the big man over a bit more carefully. There was more recalcitrance in Campbell than he normally met in federal officials. In the past when he wanted a parolee off the street, all he'd had to do was to confide his suspicions to the parole agent and they'd find some pretext or other on which to violate the man. But Campbell wouldn't even entertain the notion.

"I may have to talk with your supervisor, because I feel this is an extremely dangerous situation. Not only to Malone but to the citizens of this community as well," Torres informed him.

Campbell leaned back in his chair and spread his hands wide apart.

"Hey, go ahead. He's right next door. But you're wasting your time. He would just refer you back to me. This is civil service, and we don't pull rank around here. Politicians do that kind of stuff, but we don't.

"Look, Torres," Campbell continued. "I'm not hard-nosing you. If you can get some proof, an ID by one of the victims, something like that, I'll have him headed back on the first bus rolling. But the man just did fourteen years, and I'm not taking his freedom back after a couple months because of something you think he did." The big man emphasized the word "think" so that it sounded like "stink."

"If I can find him, I may run him in for a few days on suspicion," Torres said.

Campbell picked up the phone and dialed Gail's number at the Star Motel. She answered on the second ring.

"Gail, this is Campbell. Has Malone moved out?" he asked her.

"No, he hasn't. He's moved in with June and me, but he'd rather no one know about it right now," she replied.

"Is he still working over at Ferraro's?" Campbell asked.

"Yes, he hasn't missed a day. He'll be going in at four today. Is something the matter? Would you like to speak with him? I can wake him up," she replied.

"No. That's okay. Just checking. Tell him I may be out there the end of the week," Campbell told her.

"I'll tell him," she said.

"He's still there," Campbell informed Torres after he hung up the phone. "Hasn't moved and is still on the same job." He didn't see any reason to tell Torres that Malone had moved in with Gail and June. He made a mental note to find out what Tough Tony's thinking might be on that issue.

After Torres left, Campbell walked next door and explained the situation to his supervisor, who viewed things pretty much the same way Campbell did.

"I don't see yet where any citizens are in danger," his boss said, putting an emphasis on "citizens."

"I don't either. Even if he's right, it's just a bunch of thugs at each other's throat," Campbell replied.

"Well, don't get in bed with the guy, because we may have to send him back," his boss said as he left the office.

"I won't," Campbell told him while wondering to himself if he wasn't there already. Malone was an interesting individual, and Campbell found himself wondering how in the hell he'd gotten himself mixed up in that kind of a mess after only a couple months on the street.

21.

Bill and Gail couldn't keep their eyes or hands off each other. There were times when he'd stand in the kitchen doorway for long minutes watching her wash dishes, putter around cutting vegetables or stacking groceries on shelves. If she noticed him watching, she would usually just smile self-consciously and continue whatever she was doing.

Then she would watch him as he learned the routine of feeding the fish or just sat reading the paper. Their lovemaking was still so intense and physical that it hadn't come near to being just comfortable and intimate. Gail still found ways to make their loving more like a contest than a mutual conquest, but her inventiveness affected him like an exciting promise.

Still, as lovers they stood back from each other warily watching as if trying to learn what was to be expected or required in the long run.

June watched them both with ever greater intensity. She had become more quiet and withdrawn, and they could almost see shattered dreams written across her face. The plans she had made for herself that included Tony and Gail were lost. Her world was being shaken down and reordered, and it wasn't easy for her to live with. Her jealousy at the beginning when Bill moved in was obvious, but that seemed to disappear after a few days.

Gail understood what was going on with June a lot better than Bill did, and she was glad that Bill had a heavy factor in his favor. June loved him to death, which was a whole lot more than many stepfathers had going for them. It didn't stop her from worrying about how these profound changes in their lives would affect June, but it lessened her fears about June missing Tony.

Gail had always known Tough Tony would never be a conventional dad, and she now thanked God she had been sensible enough to have only one child by him. He really did love June but was never around long enough to get the point across very well. He was like a tomcat who just might pause to lick a kitten or two before he went chasing a full moon until it became a sliver in the purple night.

Bill was almost uncanny in his intuition about June's feelings, and Gail felt that as another unexpected bonus. He sort of danced around her emotions and tried to catch her on the upswing, never trying to interject himself on her sadness or to force a mood swing. She knew it was difficult for him to adjust.

Sometime Tuesday, she heard June sobbing on her bed in her room, and fifteen minutes later she was outside shooting marbles on the lawn with Bill, giggling because there would be a struggle with Shadow after every shot to keep him from eating the marbles.

But the wave of exhilaration that she and June and Bill had caught could just as easily roll back like a wave from a battered shore. For now they enjoyed loving, but both of them knew something was going to happen.

She sensed that Bill didn't want to talk about it. His eyes that caressed her almost as palpably as his hands asked her to trust him and believe in his capability to love her regardless of what lurked beyond their control. She was glad to do it. That was the only kind of man she had ever wanted to love.

Richard came back Thursday around noon while they were having Thanksgiving dinner and told Bill that Florence said Freddy and Joey had left for Los Angeles and she believed that the family wouldn't get involved in the problem. But the Glove was very much involved. At least that's what she had told Pete.

"So it looks like it's just down to you and him, which I still don't think is very good news for you," Richard said.

"That's how I hoped it would turn out, but it still seems to me that if I deal with him, I've got this Small Bob and all these other monkeys in the family to contend with," Bill replied.

"Maybe so, but if you can handle the Glove, I think they may call a truce with you," Richard told him.

"We'll see," Bill said as Richard left. He told Gail that he was really grateful that she had introduced him to this man.

"I just wanted you to have a few clothes," she replied, and kissed him until he felt crazy.

Bill left right after Richard and returned around two o'clock on a new ten-speed bicycle. Gail had been trying to talk him into getting a driver's license, but he had told her he wasn't ready yet. She figured the bicycle was just his next stage of transportation. She loved the way he looked in spandex shorts and a long-sleeved T-shirt.

He took off on the bike and began learning the gears while riding over the Clinton Street overpass. It felt good to be riding again. Before he reached Zero Way, he stopped and put on a leather biking cap with a chin strap that he had bought along with the bicycle. It covered his facial features somewhat. If Fred Junior or Joey did happen to be around, he doubted they would recognize him.

He turned into Zero Way and saw an old man kneeling down in a flower bed near the first house. He wore a wide-brimmed straw hat and walking shorts even though the day was overcast and cool. He went right on with his digging and never seemed to notice Bill passing silently behind him. A brand-new red Mustang convertible sat in the driveway of the first home.

Bill pedaled around the cul-de-sac slowly. The garage was closed at the second house, and a black Lincoln Town Car was parked in the drive of the last. He halfway expected the license plate to read GOOMBAH or something similar, but both the Mustang and the Lincoln had regular, nonvanity plates. He made a mental note of the first three digits on each as he sailed by the Lincoln and back onto Van Ness Avenue.

On the ride home he digested what he knew about where his adversaries lived. All the houses were wired with regular ADT alarms and were sited in such a way that it was very difficult to get behind one without being in plain view from the one next door. Impossible if they owned a dog, even a little lapdog.

The houses were no place to stage an ambush, if it came to that. Tomorrow he would ride out to the Glove's bar and look things over. The bar would probably be the best place for any action, and it would be appropriate, because it was the Glove he was concerned about anyway. The man needed to be watched closely, and Bill didn't even know what he looked like yet.

A feeling of unease came over him before he went to work and persisted against all his efforts to think of something positive. But he felt naked and defenseless as he worked the big machine. If they chose to be bold enough, they could just walk back here and blow him away. The only protection he had was the people around who would witness such an event. But a ski mask would eliminate most of that risk. No matter how he tried, he couldn't shake the feeling until he looked up and saw Bullfrog standing hesitantly at the end of the machine.

"Hey, Bullfrog, did you come for the meat early?" Bill asked, glancing at the full sack of meat scraps on top of the machine.

"Nosuh," Bullfrog replied, and looked down at his feet. There didn't seem to be much of the usual joy about the man, and Bill became alarmed.

"Is June okay?" he asked.

"Yessuh, I expect so, but that's not why I come. There's a man lying out back here in the field and he got a rifle or shotgun of some kind. Me and Cabbage don't believe he huntin' quail and don't think he huntin' us. He just layin' out there, and we thought you might want to know," Bullfrog replied.

"How long has he been out there?" Bill asked as his heart began to thump at his breastbone.

"He jes' got there 'bout fifteen minutes ago and he jes' layin' out there right in back of the café," Bullfrog said.

"Did you come in the front door?" Bill asked, picking up the sack and handing it to Bullfrog.

"Yessuh," Bullfrog answered.

"Go back out the front and don't let him see you. He might mistake you for someone, and I really appreciate your telling me about it," Bill said.

"Nosuh, he won't see me. I blends right in with the dark," Bullfrog chuckled, taking the sack and ambling toward the door.

Bill glanced at the clock as Bullfrog went out. It would be quitting time in a little over an hour, and he had the strangest urge for a moment to just walk out the back door and go home as he usually did. That would be one way to maybe get a look at Fred the Glove. It was much more likely, though, that he'd never know what hit him. He finished cleaning the machine and left one hour early, going out the front door as Bullfrog had and waving to Leona, who was behind the register.

When he went out the door he broke into a jog up toward Roeding Park in the cold night. As he ran along he wondered how Fred the Glove knew the way he went home every night. It was scary to think he'd been watched without knowing about it. Especially these days when he watched his back trail very carefully. He had relaxed his vigilance somewhat because it was Thanksgiving. Fred the Glove had probably picked tonight for that very reason. Bill vowed to not ever let his guard down again. He knew he was lucky it wasn't too late.

After two blocks he turned and jogged over to motel row and back toward the Star. There was a Lincoln Town Car in the parking lot, and the license plate told him he had seen it before. By the time he reached the office he was walking very softly and all his senses were alert.

He went around it and squatted down by the back door of the building. He sat there scanning the dark field, but he couldn't see a thing. He wished it were summertime so he could think about setting the field on fire. He also wished that June hadn't made a house dog out of Shadow, because he'd be out here barking his ass off right now. If he had a gun it'd be easy to catch the Glove now, but he didn't and until now had never even thought about one.

This Fred the Glove must really be stupid or have more guts than John Dillinger. Lying in ambush for someone is one thing, but parking your own car not fifty feet from the intended victim's door is another. Bill thought that maybe the idiot didn't even know he lived here.

He eased over to the garage next to the office, where Gail kept her Bug parked. The garage door creaked as it opened, causing the hair on the back of his neck to stand up. He was going to have to make some noise, but the Glove should be concentrating on his task to the point where he wouldn't be distracted by or even concerned with extraneous noise. Especially now that quitting time was drawing near. He made a mental note to try to find out how the Glove knew his working hours, but it was probably just an easy guess. A shiver went down his spine at the thought that the Glove had been out there last night casing things out. It was all too close for comfort.

He turned the light on and was relieved to see two spark plugs on the workbench among the assorted tools and motorcycle parts. The bench looked as if Tough Tony had been in the middle of a repair job when he went off to jail. He put on a pair of greasy work gloves, pulled a heavy hammer from the bench, and placed one of the spark plugs atop an iron vise. It only took two blows from the hammer to break the spark plug into small pebblelike pieces.

He couldn't locate any gas, so he set the lawn mower up

on the bench and siphoned about a half gallon into an old rusty parts can. As it drained, he tore a sheet that Gail had used to cover an old desk into strips, tied them together, and dropped them into the gas can to soak. He then opened a quart of oil and poured it into the gasoline.

In a perverse way, he was enjoying these preparations. He couldn't go in and go to sleep with the Glove lying not fifty yards from him, and he wanted to give the man some food for thought. At least let him know this was going to be much more difficult than shooting a big fish in a small barrel.

The Lincoln had shatterproof windows. There was no doubt about that. Bill could hit them ten times with a hammer, and no matter how much force he used, they wouldn't break. But one little dime-sized piece of the spark plug would bring the whole window out. It was an amazing fact he had learned from a thief in Portland. It had also eased his curiosity about the patches of shattered glass he saw regularly near curbs around the city. If the thief saw a purse strap sticking out from under a seat, the window was coming out. The man swore the spark plug projectiles also worked on bulletproof windows, but Bill had never had occasion to try that out.

He stirred the oil into the gas with a stick and scraped off clumps of grease from parts and shook them into the mixture, along with some broken pieces of Styrofoam he found in the garage. He wanted this fire to burn especially hot, and the Styrofoam would create a napalm effect when mixed with gasoline and oil. He turned the garage light off after putting the mower back in its place on the floor and shut the door securely when he went out, can and spark plug bits in hand.

He checked his light after he set the can down by the Glove's car. There was a bit more light out here than he wanted, but nothing was ever perfect. He walked over to the office naturally, trying not to look sneaky, unlocked the door with his key, and left it partially open for a quick entry. There were only two lights on in rooms, and they were on the far side of the V-shaped driveway. Right now was as good a time as any.

He stood about ten feet from the passenger-side door of the Lincoln and hoped his aim was still good. If he could hit even near the center of the window, it would be a good shot.

He wound up like a major-league pitcher and released the piece of plug like a fastball. He was maybe eight inches off target, but the window shattered into shards of glittering glass, some no bigger than BBs. His heart thumped as he grabbed the can, reached in, and carefully poured it around. Most of it went onto the front seat, floorboard, and dash.

As he poured he saw a light come on and was relieved to see that it was in the pimp's room. The breaking car window had made some noise, and it was a sound that no one with a car likes to hear.

He left the can on the seat, then played out the gas-soaked line he had made of the sheet, trying not to get any gas on his clothes. Another light popped on in a room, and he decided he had to move. He threw the gloves into the car, then lit the end of the line with his lighter and ran for the office. He heard a *whomp* and saw the Glove's car turn to a fireball just as he closed the door.

He stood there for a minute watching the flames play on the window until he heard a door bang shut, running feet, and someone yelling. "Call the fire department, for God's sake!" a panicky woman's voice was saying. "Is there anyone in there?"

As he went on in, he met Gail and June, both stumbling groggily in their nightclothes toward the office.

"What's happening, Bill?" Gail asked, and he could hear the panic in her voice also.

"It's okay," he told her. "Just go on out in the office and call the fire department. There's a car on fire in your parking area. I need to grab a quick shower." He didn't want to smell like gas if the police came. Arson is a serious crime even if it's just burning up a car.

"Dial 911 also and then come on back to the shower," he said over his shoulder as Gail and June went out into the office.

He was soaping up when Gail came into the bathroom. She was nervous and her features were strained with tension. He explained to her as gently as he could while showering that the Glove had tried to ambush him and he'd burned up his car.

"When the police get here," he told her, "tell them you heard glass breaking and got up in time to see a man run around the office out into the field just as the fire broke out. Say you didn't get a good look at him."

"That car's completely ruined," she said before she went back to the office.

"Maybe he won't park around here anymore," he replied. One thing was for sure—he was going to have to get a look at Fred the Glove soon. He didn't even know what the man looked like. It would be nice if he was still out in the field, rifle in hand, when the police went out there looking for the arsonist.

On Friday, the charred hulk of the Lincoln was removed by a tow truck. Bill and June cleaned up the glass and hosed down the ashes. If nothing else was accomplished by the burning, Fred the Glove had to realize now that Bill was aware of him.

22.

Bill was gone on his bicycle when Frances Logan rolled in on Saturday morning. Gail was expecting her, but "rolled in" was indeed the way she came. Even Shadow was intimidated by her. She gave him a look that said, "You'd better not bark at me." And he didn't.

Gail couldn't determine her age. She was a tall woman somewhere around sixty, if one could see beneath the face-lifts. She was slim, with long, thick black hair threaded with gray, but the gray looked more like silver. She had the most startling blue eyes Gail had ever seen, and her disposition seemed warm but commanding. She carried a purse as large as a suitcase and hadn't been in their living room more than five minutes before she was calling June and Gail "honey."

She wore big silver hoop earrings, and she still looked good in designer jeans that were complemented by a long-sleeved bolero jacket. Underneath the jacket was a dove-gray raw-silk T-shirt. Her shoes were black-and-silver pumps that matched her huge purse.

Every finger except her thumbs had a ring, and some had two. They were extremely beautiful rings and obviously not costume jewelry. Gail was thinking while looking at them that many women yearn for just one ring like the ones Frances wore. June was totally in awe of her, and Gail was amused to notice that for once she was at a loss for words.

When she asked about renting a room, Gail asked her to come back and have some coffee or breakfast with them first.

Frances took a long hard look at Gail. She scanned her up and down from hair to bare toes, and Gail unabashedly accepted the scrutiny. She knew the woman had intuited that Bill was her lover just by the invitation into her home. This old girl would be awfully hard to fool.

Frances went like a dervish through the house oohing and aahing over the fish and the black-and-silver furniture.

"My God, honey, this all matches the clothes I'm wearing. It's so beautiful it makes me look tacky," she laughingly exclaimed.

"I don't believe you could look tacky if you tried," Gail said.

"You look so nice you make my rare fish look tacky," June chimed in.

"Oh, you dear sweethearts," Frances said, putting her hand on June's head. "I think we're going to get on just fine.

"So tell me, has my Billy boy moved over here with the manager, then?" she asked in such a straightforward way that Gail was startled. She tried to be as straight with her answer.

"He sure has, and he is making June and me very happy." As she spoke, she smiled and put her hand next to Frances's on June's head. June was looking down at her feet, obviously embarrassed.

"But my goodness, how is he supporting you two and all this," she asked, waving her hand expansively, "on a dishwasher's job?"

"June and I own the joint." Gail grinned at her.

"Oh I see—why, that sly old devil," Frances laughed, and went on surveying the house, which obviously met with her satisfaction. After she sat back on the couch, Gail made coffee and put together a tray of sweets while June sat on the rug, arm around Shadow, watching Frances as if she were a mirage.

They all laughed when the next words June said to her were, "Frances, do you know how to shoot marbles?"

"I gave that up a long time ago, honey. A lady's legs

don't look their best with the kneecaps showing through the skin."

Then Frances reached for her purse, which was beside her on the floor, and went rummaging in it, trying to make her way closer to the bottom. As she went along, she stacked things on the coffee table. Wallet, key chain, whiskey flask, box of Kleenex, jewelry case, compact, address book, nail polish, and a variety of other items. June was mesmerized by all these goodies, but Gail was interested herself.

"Ah, here it is," Frances said, as she pulled a folded leather-bound game board from her purse. "Do you know how to play backgammon, honey?" she asked June as she unsnapped the board and made room on the coffee table by piling everything back into her purse.

"I've never even seen one of these," June said. She came up on her knees across from Frances and stared intently at the board as Frances arranged the pieces and dropped the dice into a small leather cup.

"Well, I'm going to get you well acquainted with it, if your mom doesn't mind," Frances replied, looking over at Gail.

"Oh Lord, I don't mind, but she will probably make a good player. Her dad used to play it all night long," Gail said.

"Well, here we go," Frances said. She rolled the dice from the cup out onto the board and showed June how to move the pieces.

June caught on pretty quick, and soon they were engrossed in the game. Gail watched for a while, then went into the kitchen, where she began making clam sauce and angel-hair pasta for lunch.

She was very worried about Bill, but so far he seemed to know how to take care of himself. He also seemed to be lucky. The police appeared to believe exactly what she told them while they were writing up their reports on the Glove's car.

When Bill came in, Frances jumped up, and they hugged fiercely, Bill swinging her around the room. He put her down and they stood at arm's length and studied each other, then he hugged her again for a long time.

"It's been such a long, long time," she told him.

"Well, Frances, you've not got a bit older," he said.

"I'm not getting any older until you grow up," she replied, looking deep into his eyes.

Gail told them lunch was ready, and Frances told June they could leave the board right there and finish the game after they ate. June walked Shadow to the door and put him out to keep him from eating all the checkers.

Bill looked over at Gail and smiled. It was the first time June had been willing to put Shadow out without a fight, and they were both relieved.

Gail was glad she had cooked a lot of food. She and Bill ate moderately, but Frances and June ate like a couple of lumberjacks. The grown-ups drank a bottle of white wine among them with some help from June whenever any of them turned away for a moment. Gail was hesitant to start a long conversation with Frances, because June would drink the woman's wine the moment she looked Gail's way. It was a habit Gail had long since given up on breaking June from.

She didn't think it was that June liked the wine or beer all that much. She just loved the idea of taking it when they weren't looking.

After lunch, Frances and June finished the game, with June getting beaten unmercifully.

"If this was a fight, someone would stop it," Frances told her.

Bill and Frances decided to go for a ride in Frances's car so they could talk while Gail washed the dishes and June took a nap. The wine and pasta had taken a toll on her.

"That girl could become an alcoholic, if you all don't watch her," Frances said, as she tooled her plush two-year-old Coupe de Ville out of the motel parking lot.

"No, she just gets a kick out of stealing people's booze, and it will wear off before she's twenty-one."

"Better keep an eye on her just the same," Frances cautioned. Then she added, "Speaking of stealing, you've got over a hundred thousand dollars up there that I haven't stolen from you, and you can have it anytime you need it, you know."

"Jesus! Have I got that much?" he asked incredulously.

"Money doubles in about nine years at eight percent, and I've kept the forty thousand you left me in decent accounts, so you've got a little nest egg there, Billy boy. Taxes all paid and everything."

He grinned at the "Billy boy." It still made him feel wonderful to hear her call him that, but he didn't want her to know it. She might overuse it trying to please him. Frances had been trying to please him ever since his father had been murdered in prison. She had redoubled those efforts when his mother died, and he felt very fortunate to have had her love all his life.

She turned the big Caddy into Roeding Park and cut the motor near a grassy knoll where people lay around drinking beer and throwing Frisbees for their dogs. They sat watching for a while, enjoying the nearness of each other. She turned those blue eyes on him, and he could feel them touching him without returning her gaze. After what seemed a long time she asked softly, "Bill, are you back on that shit?"

The question really bounced him. The loss of his father had instilled a pain in him that was like a brick burning in his gut. From the time he was sixteen until he was twenty-one, he'd been a heroin addict, roaming the streets of Portland and Seattle. He'd done some really stupid things during those years, and the only time he'd go home to see Frances or his mom would be to ask them for money. They never failed to give him some, though they knew what it was for.

What they didn't know was that the heroin was all that

could ease the hurt and give him at least a few hours of relief from a burning emotional pain that threatened to destroy him and anyone who stayed around him very long.

He'd finally quit when he was twenty-one. Quit on his own—cold turkey—with no drug program or anything. He'd never felt the need for it since. In fact, there was nothing much he hated worse in this world than heroin. Half his young junkie friends had died of overdoses. Some that he had run with as a youth now limped around because of bacteria-tainted drugs that had infected hip sockets and spines and literally eaten their bones out.

One man he knew had shot too deep into an artery and lost four fingers on his left hand. Bill was lucky that he'd woken up one day and seen how ugly the whole scene was. He had never used or wanted any since.

The only plus he'd brought away from those years was that they had taught him to fight like a wolverine. In those days in cities like Portland and Seattle, there wasn't much heroin or money, and a lot of dope fiends were after what little there was. The Northwest was too far from the Mexican border and New York waterfronts, where the dope came in, and towns like Los Angeles and New York consumed most of it. What reached Portland and Seattle was seriously fought over.

He'd been lured into many alleys and tenement rooms by people intent on getting his dope or his money. He'd fought off grown men armed with knives, guns, boards, and bricks. By the time he was twenty-one, if they knew who he was, they seldom tried it. Fighting was something he'd had a knack for.

"No, Frances. I'm not back on it, haven't used since I was twenty-one, and I'll never use it again."

"Well, I'm sorry I asked. I just couldn't figure any other reason you wouldn't come see me." Her voice began to choke up as she said this, and he reached over and took her in his arms.

"Frances, you're still my main woman. Always have been,

always will be, and I'll always love you," he said, rubbing her back with both hands.

"Well, what's the matter, then? Why won't you come home?" she asked, her voice still breaking.

"Well, for one thing, I have a dishwashing job that I like and I'm in love with those two women you met. But there's something else besides that I'm having a hard time dealing with," he replied, letting go of her and settling back in the leather seat.

She smoked Winston 100s, and they both lit up and sat there smoking while watching the people. She put hers out in the ashtray, looked over at him and said, "Tell me about this something else you're having a hard time dealing with."

He told Frances everything. Even the part about June. He left nothing out. He was talking to someone he trusted, and it felt good to get it all said.

"How can I help?" she asked after a long silence.

"Just visit awhile. Let me know you still love me, then go on home and I'll call when it's all over," he told her.

"I don't think I could stand waiting up there and not knowing what's happening to you, Bill. I've got an old customer here who's in love with me. He owns a packing shed over by Clovis somewhere. I'll get a room at the motel for a week, then I'll move over to his place and stay with him until this all gets settled. No use having to pay rent," she said.

"My God, Frances. Are you still in business?" he laughed.

"A girl's got to make a living, honey." She smiled as she held up one hand and looked at her rings.

I'll be damned, he thought. He didn't see any need to tell her it would all be settled very soon.

"I would insist that you come home with me right now, but you're just too much like your crazy fucking father. If anyone ever bit him, he'd bite back and lock on like a pit bull. He'd keep his hold until they let go or he'd just stay there and starve to death with the son of a bitch. You're just like him, Bill."

"Not really, Frances. I've never been able to be a pimp."

"Don't tell me you're a jealous man now, Billy boy," she said and fixed him with that blue-eyed stare.

"Well, let's just say I couldn't stand to hear those bedsprings squeaking," he replied, and they both began laughing so hysterically that the people on the lawn began looking their way.

"I wonder what all those people would think if they could hear this conversation," she said, starting the Caddy.

"Probably think we're crazy," he said.

As they drove back toward the motel, Frances asked, "What about this Small Bob guy who runs this so-called mob around here? What's he about? I know all the mob around Portland, and I've never even heard them mention any friends in Fresno."

"All I know about him is he runs a Cadillac dealership over on Blackstone. I don't think they're connected anywhere. It's more or less a local tip, from what I understand."

"Sort of a shade-tree Mafia, huh?" she ventured.

"Yes, I think that would about describe it, but I don't think even they are sure who is running it," he said.

"I don't know what you plan to do, Billy, but goddammit, be careful whatever you do, and I'll be around to help with the lawyer or bail money or whatever. Just keep yourself alive and we'll sort all the rest out somehow. You know I'm in your corner, and it pisses me off that you never called me when all this shit started."

"I didn't want you worrying, Frances. Worrying gets hard on a woman your age."

"You've got that wrong, buddy. It's little smart-alecky bank robbers that get hard on a woman my age," she said as she pulled into the motel lot and turned off the ignition.

They spent most of the rest of the day arguing about Frances taking a room. Gail and Bill wanted her to stay with them, but all Frances would say was, "I need my privacy, honey."

She wound up in the end room where the two drug addicts had once stayed. After they all had helped move her in, she came back to the house and continued her backgammon game with June while Bill and Gail drove to a nearby country-and-western bar for some beer and music. By the time they returned, June was holding her own in the game and Bill heard Frances say, "You little hussy. Have you been studying a backgammon book?"

Bill and Gail closed the bedroom door and began undressing each other. Every time she unbuttoned a button, she licked and kissed the place on his chest or stomach where the button had been. By the time she began fumbling at his belt, he was shuddering and shaking like a palsied old man. The feeling of her lips and tongue stayed with him long after the lovemaking was over. These most intimate caresses were real now, feelings that a convict could not even imagine after a few years of concrete and iron.

Sunday morning he woke up early, donned his spandex shorts, and was riding hard by eight. There was an overpass nearby that he liked to ride over. Going up this side was a bitch, but it was a real thrill to open up the ten-speed on the down side with the wind blowing in his hair. He really liked what bicycling was doing for his leg muscles.

Bill had always been very attentive to his legs and made sure they got a better workout than any other part of his body. He'd never looked at an animal or a man with bad legs without feeling a lot of pity. A creature with bad legs had to battle gravity fiercely for every inch in any direction it wanted to go. Someone who had admired Bill's talent for street fighting had once asked him how he won so many fights.

"That's easy. I take their legs out from under them," Bill replied.

He rode around the Glove's bar four times, stopping and looking at all the entrances and exits and how the parking lots were laid out. The bar was at the end of a shopping mall that was almost as well lit at night as it was during the day. He figured the bar must open at six o'clock every morning, which was the legal hour in California to begin selling booze. It was open now at nine o'clock on a Sunday morning. A serious drinking man's bar. When he entered there were two men drinking bottled beer at the end of the bar. Behind the bar was a raven-haired beauty wearing tight jeans, an old Che Guevera T-shirt, and open-toed sandals. She still managed to look like pure class. She was braless, and when she moved, the T-shirt shook and quivered like pudding. She gave Bill a smile with his beer that threatened to suck him right into her mouth.

One of the men at the end of the bar yelled, "Hey, Florence!" It didn't surprise Bill that this was the Glove's daughter. She kept rolling her eyes toward a young man who was playing pool, and Bill saw them exchanging glances. It was obvious that they only had eyes for each other. The man had brown hair cut short and neat with a reddish tint to it. He wore an expensive sport shirt out over a pair of Levi's and black lizard-skin cowboy boots. He was built slim, looked agile, and was a very good pool player. Bill wondered if this might be the Pete Avakian that Richard had mentioned.

When Florence brought him his second beer he asked her, "Are all the bars in Fresno this busy on a Sunday morning?"

"You ask most of these nuts in here, they will tell you it's late Saturday night, not early Sunday morning," she said with a big grin.

She seemed friendly, but before Bill could add anything to their conversation, a big man stepped into the back-bar well from a storage room and yelled, "Hey, Flo, bring that tally sheet back here and help me a minute!"

Florence finished making Bill's change and turned silently to get the tally sheet while Bill studied the big man. He looked like the devil himself, but his cupid-bow mouth was exactly like Florence's. Bill knew he had finally laid eyes on the Glove, and cold chills raked up and down his spine. The man looked as mean as his reputation made him out to be. When their eyes met, Bill understood that those eyes were probably the last thing some unfortunate souls had looked at before they died.

His features were so pronounced he reminded Bill of a child with Down's syndrome. The heavy eyelids under bushy black brows hooded his eyes like a buzzard's. The harsh aspects of his big head and face seemed to mock the dainty mouth. Lips that Bill now ached to drive his fist into all the way up to the elbow.

Dark, curly hair shot with gray framed his countenance. The ears were large and long and lay flat against the skull. Bill figured the man was a couple inches taller and had him by fifty pounds or so. He felt like asking him if he'd been lying out in any fields lately, but today wasn't the time. He wondered what kind of car he was driving now.

23.

In the early afternoon, Frances and June pulled out of the motel parking lot in Frances's Cadillac.

"If you're going to hang out with me, you've got to stop drinking alcohol, girl. I hate drunks," was the first thing Frances said to her after they got in the car.

"That's okay. I don't like it that much anyway," June replied.

"Well, you cut it out, at least until you're old enough to buy it."

"Okay," June responded cheerfully.

"Look here, honey. I have somewhere I need to go for about an hour. So I want to drop you off someplace until I get back. How about an early movie?"

"Sounds good to me," June replied.

"We'll go buy us a nice dinner after I pick you up," Frances told her. Then she added, "I'm going to give you some extra money so if I get hung up or anything, you can call a taxi to take you home. If I'm not back by the time the movie is over, you get a cab home. Okay?"

"Sure, that's fine," June replied, but she gazed at Frances speculatively.

June chose a Clint Eastwood movie that was playing at the Mall Cinema. After Frances walked her in and bought her ticket, June finally got up her nerve to ask where she was going.

"I'll forgive you for being curious, honey," Frances answered, handing June a fifty-dollar bill. "That's for the taxi if you need it, love, and some popcorn, of course." She walked out hoping June wouldn't need the taxi.

* * *

Blackstone Avenue is a flat street that runs north and south through Fresno and eventually turns into Highway 41 going to Yosemite National Park. Motels with names lifted from Florida beaches line both sides of the street, along with small and large car lots, parts stores, fast-food joints, and gas stations.

Frances drove along marveling at how tacky the whole town looked. She couldn't imagine why someone would want to live here unless they needed the work that came with the fertile orchards and fields of the San Joaquin Valley. She saw a sign that said "Cosmopolitan Cadillac" and pulled the big Caddy in, parking as close to the showroom floor as possible.

She was dressed in designer jeans, high heels, and a jacket she had paid a seamstress five hundred dollars to make by hand. It was purple-and-white-wool, worn over a white silk T-shirt. Her long black hair hung down her back, and she knew she looked elegant enough to make a grand entrance, but a salesman opened her car door for her as soon as she came to a stop.

"Can I help you, ma'am?" he asked and flashed her a huge carnivorous smile.

"I came to buy a new car, but I want to talk to Mr. Sandino, the owner, before I buy it," she said.

"Well, he's busy right now, ma'am, but I'm the sales manager here. My name is Glen and I'll get you anything you need."

"I'll come back when he's not busy," Frances said, trying to pull the door from his lingering grasp.

"Wait a minute! Wait a minute! I think he just got free," the man exclaimed as she inserted the key into the ignition.

Frances put the keys back into her huge purse and got out of the car.

"Well, take me to him, honey," she said as Glen turned back toward the showroom.

She followed him through the showroom, where salesmen were steering people around gleaming Caddies on pedestals. When they reached an office at the back, Glen stopped at the door and said, "Wait here just a moment, please."

He went in, and when he opened the door, Frances had a brief glimpse of a man behind a desk with two plush chairs across from him. She figured Glen was telling Small Bob to be sure to send her to him when they finished talking. He would be wanting his commission. Small Bob must have agreed quickly, because the man came back smiling. He held the door for her and said, "Go right in, ma'am. Mr. Sandino will see you, and I'll be here when you finish."

"Thank you," she said, and went in.

Small Bob was immediately around the desk with his hand out.

"Robert Sandino, at your service, miss," he said, smiling.

"Bonnie Parker," she replied, taking the hand and looking him over carefully. When she let her hand slide from his, he waved her to an easy chair in front of his desk and walked around behind it. She sat down and put her purse on the floor beside her.

"I'll come right to the point, Mr. Sandino. I came to buy a new car today. I bought my last Cadillac in Seattle and had some very bad experiences with their service department. What caused most of my problems was a lying salesman. That's why I asked for you. If I'm to be lied to, I want it from the boss himself."

"I'll certainly never lie to you, and our service department is one of the best in the country. We win awards here for excellence in customer service." As he talked he spread his hands wide apart, palms up, as if in supplication to the very gods of honesty and integrity.

"Well, I'm glad of that," she replied. "So let's get down to specifics."

She told him she wanted a new Coupe de Ville, and they began talking the details of color, extras, and options. She reached into her purse, withdrew a bottle of vintage red zinfandel she'd picked up in San Francisco on the way down, and put it on his desk.

"Can we drink to excellence in customer service?" she asked coyly, flashing her best smile.

"Oh, hell yes!" he said, rising from his chair and getting two glasses and a corkscrew from a cabinet on the wall.

They drank the bottle, and not to be outdone, he went to a small room off the office and came back with a bottle of very fine dago red. The relationship was heating up very nicely by the time his bottle was gone. She was saying things like "How about beige alligator-skin hubcaps?"

"Oh, definitely," he would reply, and they'd begin laughing like youngsters. It was obvious he was taken with her, and she decided the time was right for the business she had come for.

She put on the smile again, stood up, and walked around the desk. Small Bob watched her come toward him as if mesmerized. A small quizzical smile jerked to his lips as if he were thinking, What now?

She picked up the empty bottle of dago red by the neck as his eyes lazily followed her movements. She was around the corner of the desk and standing right over him.

"This was very good wine, Bob," she said softly and swung the bottle as hard as she could into his left eyebrow. The force of the blow shattered the bottle, and glass flew everywhere as his head snapped back.

She was left holding the neck and jagged ends where the bottle had broken. She reversed her grip as he began to topple sideways from his chair and drove the jagged bottle edge into the top of his head, breaking off more glass so that she only had the neck left in her hand.

He hit the floor, blood pouring from his eyebrow and head. He was out cold. She was grateful that the office was well enclosed, because the bottle had made a loud popping sound when it broke on his head. She walked around to her purse, withdrew a pearl-handled 9mm pistol, and took the safety off.

She walked back to the chair he had fallen from, rolled it around near his head, and sat down to wait with the pistol in her hand. It was only a minute or two before his eyelids began fluttering. She leaned down, and when his eyes popped open, she stuck the barrel of the gun into his partly open mouth.

"Bite it, Bob. Bite down on it," she told him softly.

His left eye was full of blood from the gash on his eyebrow, but the right eye was an open terrified orb that reminded her of a jerky marble. He followed her instructions and bit down on the barrel with his teeth. He had beautiful white teeth.

"Bite it harder, Bob," she ordered, more forcefully this time.

He bit down harder, and with a sudden motion she jerked the gun barrel out of his mouth. The gun sight on the end of the barrel brought two of his front teeth out of his head when it came.

"Argggh," he exclaimed, and flopped onto his side, bringing both hands to his mouth and feeling the hole where his teeth had been. She put the end of the gun barrel into the hollow behind his right ear and used just enough pressure to let him know it was there.

"Why are you doing thish to me?" he mumbled in a pitiful voice through broken teeth. By now his intercom was buzzing insistently and the desk phone was ringing. She decided she had better get her speech made and break camp.

"It's about a dishwasher, Bob. A dishwasher over at Ferraro's named Bill Malone. I'm sure you know who I'm talking about, Bob." She prodded behind his ear as she spoke, and Bob acknowledged with a nod.

"Your family is after him, Bob, and I'm here to tell you that if anyone harms one hair on his head, I'll come back here and kill you and every motherfucker in this building. Do you understand me, Bob?" She jabbed behind his ear again.

He nodded in acknowledgment. By now there was a big pool of blood beneath his head.

"I'm out of here now, Bob. If you report this, I'll say you tried to rape me back here and take my chances in court." She put the gun back in her purse, picked it up, and started for the door. "Don't open this door for three minutes," she instructed him. She went out, shutting the door behind her.

"Hey, are we ready to roll?" Glen asked with a big smile as soon as she came out the door.

"No, dear. We had a disagreement," she replied, and kept on walking. Halfway across the showroom floor, she shifted her purse and put one hand inside it on the gun, but no one even glanced her way. At the door she looked back. Glen was still standing about where she'd left him but was now turned toward Bob's office door.

When she got to her car and opened it, she looked into the showroom again. Bob's office door was open and people were running toward it across the floor. She started the Caddy, backed up, and drove slowly onto Blackstone Avenue, heading in the direction of the movie theater where she'd left June.

As she slid into the seat next to the young girl, Clint Eastwood was emerging from a saloon, and the scene looked as if he'd killed everyone in it. He was saying to the darkness, "If anyone shoots at me and misses, I'll come back and kill everyone in your family." The movie ended shortly after that speech.

Frances left the motel on Monday morning, telling Bill and Gail she would be in touch. Bill thought it a little odd, but he had plenty to think about besides Frances.

24.

Ray Harrelson called Martin Torres around noon on Monday.

"Did you hear about what happened to Small Bob?" he asked.

"Yeah, I heard. I just talked to one of the doctors who worked on him. Took about forty-nine stitches in his head and eyebrow. The doctor said it looked like someone yanked out two of his front teeth with pliers. This stuff is getting interesting. Do you think the dishwasher did it?"

"It's more interesting than you think," Harrelson replied.

"What do you mean?" Torres asked.

"A woman did it," Harrelson told him.

"A what?" Torres exclaimed.

"A woman. A good-looking old broad walked back into Bob's office, cool as you please, and busted his fuckin' head. I got it from two of the salesmen there."

"Well, I'll be damned. That beats anything I've ever heard," Torres said.

"Yeah, me too, but it's true. What do you plan on doing about this guy Malone?"

"I can't make a case on him yet, but I talked with the D.A. and I'm picking him up tonight. Maybe I'll get him or someone to talk."

"Well, good luck," Harrelson said, and hung up the phone.

Torres had already heard about the woman doing Small Bob. But he liked to play it dumb with Harrelson. Ray would talk and talk if he thought his information was impressive, and often it was. It was time to pick Malone up, evidence or not. There was just too much going on between him and the Sandinos. The incineration of the Glove's car up in the motel lot had to be bad news for someone. His main hope was that if nothing else, he could convince Malone that he needed protection.

He'd been debating himself all day about where to pick up the dishwasher. If he got him at home, maybe he could lean on the two women for information. But if the Sandinos thought they were talking, they could be dragged into whatever was going on and put in jeopardy. Torres didn't want to chance that. He decided to pick Malone up at the café. It would be nice if he could find out what the hell was going on out there. Who in the world was the woman who had beaten up Small Bob? This was the most bizarre case he had ever worked.

He met Fitz and Jewell in the parking lot of Ferraro's at ten o'clock. They left the prowl car and followed him inside. Two cooks were breaking down the serving line while Leona stood talking with Regina at the cash register. Other than one lingering couple, the eating section was empty. He walked straight to the dishroom with the two patrolmen following as backup. No one said anything.

Malone looked up from a grease trap he'd been cleaning when they entered and didn't say a word as they surrounded him. Jewell and Fitz were tensed up and had their thumbs hooked into their belts near their holstered guns. Torres had instructed them not to throw down on Malone unless it was absolutely necessary. You never could tell what one of these old jailbirds might do if he got too excited. This one just stared as Torres produced his shield.

"Are you William Malone?" he asked.

The dishwasher nodded by way of reply, and Torres thought he didn't look much like a gangster standing there in a pair of rubber boots and a rubber apron.

"Martin Torres, homicide division in the Fresno County sheriff's office. You're under arrest for the murder of Perfecto Salazar and being an ex-convict in possession of a firearm." He had decided to add the second charge in the hope that the dishwasher would think someone who had been involved in the dishroom scuffle had talked. "You have a right to remain silent. You have a right to an attorney. Anything you say may be used against you in a court of law," he went on. The dishwasher gazed steadily back at him, making no reply whatsoever.

Fitz spread-eagled him on the side of the dish machine, patted him down for a weapon, and cuffed his hands behind his back. Following Torres, they walked single-file back out into the restaurant.

"Call Gail," Torres heard Malone say when they approached the cash register. He looked back and saw that he was talking to Leona.

"I'll go on over there myself, D.W.," Leona replied, and Torres stopped near Regina.

"Hey, we're in no hurry here. If you want to tell her to do anything for you, go ahead," he said as affably as he could manage. He was hoping the dishwasher would tell Leona a name or two he could check out. There were too many unknown players in this game.

"What are you arresting Mr. Malone for?" Regina asked with genuine concern in her voice.

"First-degree murder," he told her.

"Oh my God!" she exclaimed and looked at Bill as if she were seeing him for the first time.

"That's a bunch of bullshit, Regina," Leona cut in, looking hard at Torres. "D.W. ain't killed nothin' an' they know it."

Leona followed them on out into the parking area. Torres had decided to ride along in the prowl car and return later for his own. He still held a glimmer of hope that Malone would say something he could get his teeth into. Just before they reached the car, Leona said to Jewell, "You all better not rough him up, big boy. I mean, if you harm one hair on his head I'm gonna tell your wife about some a' those extra-long coffee breaks you took with me here last year."

"Goddammit, Leona," Jewell exploded, but Torres noticed that he kept his gaze locked on the ground they were walking on.

"I mean it, man. You better hold his arm like he's an old woman, because if he stumbles and gets a little knot on his head, you got big domestic problems," she added as they put Malone in the backseat and Torres climbed in beside him.

"How long have you been with us in Fresno now, Malone?" Torres asked as they drove off. He was hoping to get a conversation started, but the dishwasher didn't reply, just kept staring straight ahead.

"You know, you're going to wind up riding everything. The murder of Salazar, the gun, assault, arson, the whole ball of wax. With your record, you're not going to look good in front of a jury. If you want to cooperate and give me some info on the Sandino family, I'll help you all I can." Malone still didn't reply.

"Okay, if you're going to be a hard-ass, then you can do the hard time," Torres told him.

They drove into the parking area in the basement of the Fresno county jail. He had intended to pull Malone into a room for questioning when they got to the jail, but it was obvious that would be futile. The man wouldn't even acknowledge his questions, much less answer any of them.

They went up to the booking desk in an elevator, and while Torres talked with the booking officer, Fitz and Jewell walked Malone to a holding cell and began removing his handcuffs. Jewell looked over at Fitz and said in a voice low enough that Torres and the booking officer wouldn't hear, "Tar baby, he don't say nothin'."

When Fitz got the cuffs off, he patted Bill on the back and said in an even lower voice, "Hang in there, bud. You'll be okay."

Bill was stunned and stared after them as they got back on the elevator with Torres. It was the first time in his life he had heard encouraging words from cops who were arresting him. But nothing else made much sense about the madness he was involved in now. It didn't surprise him that he was back in jail, but worrying wouldn't help anything. All he could do now was see what they had and deal with it.

After he was booked in and issued bedclothes and a pair of red jail coveralls, he was allowed to make a phone call at a pay phone on the wall. Gail picked up on the first ring.

"Bill, are you okay?" she asked breathlessly.

"Other than being in jail on a murder charge, I'm fine," he told her.

"You're not in there on a murder charge," she replied. "I've talked to a lawyer already. I got lucky because one of Tony's old lawyers, Jimmy Morra from San Francisco, is down here in Fresno on a dope case. He called over there and he says you're booked on suspicion of murder."

"What's the difference?" he asked.

"Suspicion means they probably don't have enough yet to charge you. They're going to try to hold you three days, but he's filing habeas corpus first thing tomorrow, and with any luck, you'll be out by tomorrow night."

Bill felt better. He hadn't noticed suspicion on his booking slip, but it was all numbers anyway. He had heard a lot about Jimmy Morra. The man was probably the best criminal lawyer in California.

"Someone's at the door," Gail said, and put the phone down. She was back in a moment.

"It's that detective, Torres," she told him.

"If he tries to lean on you and June, call that lawyer," he advised her.

"We'll be fine, and don't forget we love you and we're on your side."

"I won't forget. Tell June I'll talk to her tomorrow," he told her and hung up. A deputy led him to his tank and opened the door to a sixman cell. There was one empty top bunk. The tanks were locked down for the night and most of the prisoners were asleep.

"What did they get you for?" the man on the lower bunk asked Bill as he made up his bed.

"Your guess is as good as mine," he replied, and lay down to toss and turn a long time before he finally drifted off to sleep. He wanted a cigarette badly, but this was obviously a no-smoking jail.

Early Tuesday morning, Torres sat across the desk from Campbell in his office at the federal building. The visit with Gail had not gone well, and he was desperately trying to keep Malone in jail. He had hoped that a search of the man's quarters would turn up something incriminating: a gun, drugs—anything.

"So what are you going to do?" Gail had asked him. "Put him in jail for having a gun and then hope you'll find one in his room?" And then she had shown him the door without allowing him to search anything. He could have sworn he heard the young girl call him an asshole as she held the door for him on his way out. All of this was especially galling because he didn't have enough evidence to obtain a search warrant.

"I want you to put a parole hold on him, so I can hold him a while longer. Give me some time to dig up a little hard evidence. Everything I have on him now is circumstantial and theoretical, but I know he is guilty as hell," he said to the big man across the desk.

"It isn't that easy, Mr. Torres," Campbell explained. "I have to file a report to the parole commission requesting a violation warrant and list any specific violations that I believe have occurred. That takes some time."

"I know that's the normal procedure, but you also have the discretion to place a hold in an emergency, and I need some help on this. I had a call first thing this morning from that fucking lawyer Jimmy Morra. I don't know how Malone hooked up with him so fast. But this guy's a monster in court. He'll have him back on the street by tomorrow, and I need more time."

"That's one of the problems here, Mr. Torres. You're not even sure that with more time you'll be able to dig up anything. You're right about my having discretion, but I don't use it lightly. I don't enjoy having the power to take someone's freedom away, and I won't do it unless I know positively he's a danger to the community."

Campbell had already made up his mind not to go along with Torres on this. Torres did make a compelling argument that Malone was breaking arms and burning up cars. But the hump Campbell couldn't get over was that every incident had taken place either where Malone lived or where he worked. So it looked to him as if someone was after Malone, instead of the other way around.

Campbell knew the convict code well enough to know that if that was the case, Malone would not go to the police for help. He hoped he wasn't making a mistake. Jail could be the safest place for Malone, if people were after him.

"I can't do it until you bring me some evidence, Torres. I'm sorry, but that's it," he said.

Torres noticed that Campbell had dropped the "Mr." He understood there was no use arguing anymore. He picked up his hat and put it on.

"We're both going to feel pretty bad if he kills someone else," he mumbled as he rose to go.

"Let's hope he doesn't get himself killed also," Campbell replied.

As Campbell and Torres talked, Bill was sitting in an attorney-client booth waiting for Jimmy Morra. He'd awakened to the sound of cell doors clanking open and men yelling "Chow!" as they dressed and ran for the door to line up for the trip down to the jail dining room. He noticed that it was still dark outside. A jail breakfast of mush and coffee was the last thing he wanted, so he tried to go back to sleep. The next thing he knew it was daylight and a jailer was yelling into the tank, "Malone! Attorney visit!" He put on his coveralls and followed the deputy to the attorney visiting booths.

It was a small well-lit room with one chair facing another chair through a glass partition. The glass had a grille that you could talk with your attorney through. The door opened on the other side, and Morra entered, briefcase in hand, and sat down opposite him.

"I'm Jimmy Morra, and Gail has asked me to help you get out of here," he said, with a smile. Bill caught a glimpse of a gold tooth on one incisor.

Bill was surprised there was nothing ostentatious about the man other than a gold tooth. He didn't even have on a fancy ring. What was left of his long gray hair was tied back loosely into a ponytail. His suitcoat had been torn and patched in a couple places, and his tie was frizzy from wear. But his clothes looked good on his tall slender frame. He was blessed with a chiseled face and profile that would go well on a coin.

"I couldn't spring you by tonight, but you'll walk at eight o'clock tomorrow, if they don't find some hard evidence and charge you by then. I don't think you'll get a parole hold or it would have been filed already," he said.

"I don't know how to thank you," Bill told him.

"No problem. Tough Tony and his family are friends of mine. I'm glad to help out. From the little I've heard, you haven't had an easy time out here in the free world so far."

"I think it will get better," Bill replied.

"Well, here's my card if it doesn't. I'm due in court in five minutes. If you don't get out, I'll be around to help. Just don't make any statements to anyone, including your cellmates in the tank there."

"I won't," Bill assured him. Morra pushed his card through a slot in the glass and went back out the door. Bill noticed he walked with a slight limp.

Back in the tank, he got into a desultory game of gin rummy for push-ups in the day room with the older man who slept directly underneath him. The makeup of the jail population was overwhelmingly young black and Latino gangbangers. They paid him no attention, and he kept to himself as much as possible. But the fact that he could no longer relate to people in jail gave him a feeling of loneliness close to desolation.

Tossing and turning that night on the thin mattress and metal bunk, he came to a conclusion. He could no longer just wait like a sitting duck and let things happen to him. If he was lucky enough to be released, he would deal with the Glove by the weekend. If he came back to jail, he didn't want any loose ends out there to worry about.

As he was being processed and released on Wednesday morning, he felt the same exhilaration that he had upon his release after fourteen years. Gail and June were waiting at the jail exit and jumping around like a couple of excited puppies. Both tried to hug and kiss him at the same time. Gail drove them home, and the Bug felt like a limousine.

He called George from the motel and told him he wouldn't be coming back to work. George asked him to reconsider, but Bill detected a note of relief in the man's voice. He didn't want to quit, but after his arrest in the restaurant, along with everything else, he figured his continued employment might do the Ferraros more harm, and he didn't want that. But no sooner had he hung up than Regina called.

"Bill, you've got to stay until I find someone else," she implored.

"Well, I—"

"Bill, Leona's threatening to quit right now if you don't come back. She thinks George fired you. I hope you know that none of us believe you're a murderer," she went on, and her voice was close to tears.

"I'll be there at four," he said. "Tell Leona to have my beer ready."

Going back to work felt good, and it was nice to pretend

that things were as they had been at the start. But no amount of pretending would make the Glove and his family go away. Gail agreed with him that they couldn't go on this way. The strain and stress were getting to them both. She didn't want to hear the details, yet she never tried to dissuade him when he told her he intended to get things over with by the weekend.

25.

Just before noon on Saturday, June sat down beside Bill on the couch and asked him, "If you and my mom get married, will it be okay if my dad comes and stays with us sometimes?"

"He can come anytime he wants. I know he'll be wanting to see you a lot, and he's my friend, too, you know," Bill assured her, and put his arm around her. June sank against him and seemed satisfied with his reply. But the scene brought home to him how much remained unresolved in their lives.

Somehow, thinking about it made him even madder at Fred the Glove. That a man he didn't even know or want to know could keep his life in such turmoil made his blood boil. He got up from the couch, went into the bedroom, and called Richard.

"I'm going to the Glove's bar tonight, and if he's there, one of us is not leaving under his own power," he told Richard.

"Are you taking a gun?" Richard asked.

"I'm not taking anything, and that's why I called. I know he's got friends around with guns. I thought maybe if you and some of your friends are serious about disliking these people, you could get your stuff and be there to pull my slack. Keep his pals from getting involved."

"What time are you going there?" Richard asked.

"Eight o'clock," Bill replied.

"Man, you should have a gun," Richard insisted.

"I can get life under a new federal law for ex-con with a gun. I'd rather have the Glove kill me than do life for carrying a gun that I was thinking about killing him with," Bill said.

"I don't know if anyone else will be there, but Pete, Big Al, and I will be, and we'll be packing nine-millimeters with fourteen-shot clips. Maybe we won't run out of shells."

"I'll see you there, man, and thanks," Bill said, and started to hang up the phone.

"Hold it!" Richard said.

"What is it?" Bill asked.

"Did you hear about that old broad who went into Small Bob's dealership last Sunday and fucked him up with a wine bottle?"

"What?" Bill yelled into the phone.

"Put forty-nine stitches in his head and knocked out two of his teeth. There was a small article in the *Fresno Bee* Monday, but no detail. Bob told the police it was an irate customer and refused to press charges."

"I'll be damned," Bill said.

"Looks like you got some help, man, and if the women are already jumping in, how can we hold back? If they won't let you keep it between you and the Glove, Pete and I will kill every fuckin' wop in the place."

"See you tomorrow," Bill said.

"Man, please don't underestimate that gorilla."

"I won't," Bill assured him and hung up the phone, wondering if he hadn't undersold Fred the Glove already. But there was really only one way to find out.

That fucking Frances, he thought to himself with a smile as he walked back to the living room.

At seven o'clock he went into the bedroom and put on the steel-toed high-top shoes he'd left prison in, along with a pair of Levi's and a long-sleeved cotton pullover. He needed to have clothes on tonight that were comfortable and loose. The shoes were heavy, but he'd worn them for so long in prison that he barely noticed their weight.

Gail walked in and watched him dress. Her eyes were

full of questions and concern, but she held her tongue. He could tell that June was very worried also, even though she watched TV and tried to act indifferent. Gail was shocked out of her silence when he asked to borrow her car.

"Bill, you don't even have a license yet," she said.

"I don't need a license to drive your car," he replied. She left the room to get him the keys.

"I wish you would tell me where you're going and when you'll be back," she said.

"I'm going to Fred the Glove's bar at First and Cedar, and I don't know when I'll be back. If I don't get back, your keys will be under the seat, driver's side," he replied.

"Bill, please," she began.

"I didn't tell you all that so you could argue with me. I love you, woman. Just hang out here till I get back," he said. Before he left he held both her and June in his arms for a long time.

It was a very strange feeling driving the Bug and being alone on the road. Driving a car made him think of the many other things he'd promised himself and hadn't done yet. One of them was a trip to the ocean. As he drove along, he thought of Frances again. There weren't a lot of women like her in the world. His father used to say, "That woman is more of a gangster than I am."

She was such a sweet and loving lady, but some of her inner components were as hard as tempered steel. She had respect for men, but Bill had never seen her intimidated by one. His thoughts turned to the Glove, and the old adrenaline began pumping.

There was no plan to this at all. As far as Bill was concerned, he wanted all the anxiety and pain this affair was causing out of his life for good. The only way he knew was to go directly to the source.

"I'm through, Fred," Small Bob had told his brother Friday evening. "As far as I'm concerned, the family is through, and if you've got any brains at all left in your head you'll realize it's all finished." He was propped up on a chaise longue on his screened porch. A white bandage around his head looked like a turban. He spoke very slowly through the space between his missing front teeth.

"Give it some time, brother," Fred assured him. "You're just down because you got beat up by a woman. There's nothing going on here we can't straighten out. That bitch could have sneaked on anyone with a wine bottle. You'll be back in action in a few days."

But Bob was not to be deterred. "Okay, Fred. I won't argue with you, but I'm out. I'm retiring. The members I made, I'm giving them the option to leave and hook up in L.A. or back East. Or they can stay with you. But with everybody into drugs, the whole show is gonna wind up in a federal prison. It's just a matter of time.

"Look at this deal with this dishwasher," Small Bob continued. "I didn't even know his fuckin' name. He's put your kids in the hospital, burned up your car, had some old broad do a number on me. What we got going with this guy is totally insane, and it's all over a fucked-up drug deal. From what I learned from Freddy, the guy may be in the right. He's fighting us like a fucking madman over a deal he probably wasn't even involved in and you and I damn sure had nothing to do with.

"I mean, there's no win for anyone here. That's what drugs do. You get involved and a lot of ignorant shit begins to happen. I should thank that broad. I needed this ass-whipping to wake me up to what we're doing here. It may take another stretch in prison to wake you up, but I'm done. I'm outta here."

As he spoke, he chopped at the air with his hands. His words did have some impact on the Glove. But he didn't believe things were as drastic as Bob made them out to be.

"Yeah, I know it's not business as usual with this guy Malone. But it's gone too far now. He's made us look real bad. My car looks like a fucking pork skin, and I spent a few hours hiding in bushes and ducking cops that night.

I'm gonna get his ass no matter what else we do about the mess our family is in."

"That's up to you, but I'm moving to Vegas in a couple weeks. I want your word you don't touch him until I'm gone."

"You got it," Fred promised. It wasn't that big a concession, considering he was finally getting control of the family. His mind was already working on ways he could do some weeding out and get things back on track.

"Gimme a few days with Fraschetta to figure out how we divide things up and I'll get back to you," Bob told him. "But take my advice, Fred. If you hurt this guy Malone, watch out for that old broad. That bitch will be on you like a lion, and she's mean as hell."

"Gimme a break," Fred groaned. "I'm supposed to start sweating a fuckin' cunt? Come on, Bob!"

"Okay, okay, brother," Bob calmed him. "Just don't say I never warned you."

When Fred was gone, Bob felt more peaceful than he had in years despite his injuries. Hanging around showgirls in casinos wasn't a bad way to spend one's golden years.

26.

When Malone pulled into a parking space near the bar, another car pulled in behind him, but then kept going toward the department stores at the other end of the shopping center.

Detective Joe Gamboa worked gambling and prostitution on Ray Harrelson's crew. He'd been tailing Malone since last Monday, except for the time Malone was in jail, and he still didn't understand why Harrelson had put him on the guy. Joe didn't press the matter. He was loyal to Harrelson first and the taxpaying public second. The occasional sub rosa assignment he got from Harrelson made him feel honored. It was Harrelson's way of saying that he trusted Gamboa completely.

He watched Malone enter the bar, then got out of his own car, walked to a pay phone, and called Ray at home. This was one of the places that Harrelson had told him to call from immediately if his quarry stopped in.

"Your boy just walked into the Turf Club at First and Cedar."

"Where are you at?" Harrelson asked.

"I'm at those phones in front of Sears," Joe replied.

"Go back to the parking area of the bar and wait in your car. I'm on my way down there," Harrelson told him. Joe could hear that certain edge to his voice that Ray got when he was very excited.

"Hey, Ray! You can tell old Joe. What's up, partner? You've got me tailing this bird for a week now, and it's boring. What the hell are we doing here?"

"Just trust me, Joe. I don't think it will be boring much longer," Harrelson answered.

"All right, I'll see you when you get here. I'm in a gray Plymouth," Gamboa said.

"Joe," Harrelson said before Gamboa could hang up.

"Yeah?" Gamboa responded.

"No matter what happens, don't intervene. Just lay back and wait for me, and don't call anyone unless there's a full-scale war going on."

"Affirmative," Gamboa said. He hung up the phone and walked back to his car.

Harrelson hurriedly finished dressing and almost ran out the door. Of all the rumors and speculation he had heard from stool pigeons the past couple weeks, one bit of information came through consistently. Malone and the Glove had a serious problem with each other. Neither of them was the type to restrain himself for very long. They were like two speeding trains coming together on the same track, and Ray hoped like hell he could be around when they collided.

He knew that what he was doing now wasn't by-the-book police work, but then again it was effective. If one of them killed the other, he would be there to arrest the survivor. It was a no-lose situation for the citizens of Fresno. They were both thugs anyway, even though Malone wasn't near as odious as Fred the Glove. For that reason Harrelson was hoping that if there was a confrontation, Malone would come out on top.

Harrelson had developed a very strong distaste for the Glove over twenty years ago when he began working vice and took on the gamblers with the zeal of a self-righteous rookie. He had learned a lot during the intervening years. The main lesson he had learned is that gambling is here to stay. After all, people had shot dice over the very robe that Jesus wore.

He'd always thought that degenerate gamblers who blew

rent and grocery money were to be pitied. They were like alcoholics: if you could bottle gambling they would buy it by the case. Most gamblers, whether bookies or bettors, were decent enough people who loved walking out on the edge now and then. Gambling did something to the blood pressure that was very similar to cocaine.

Fred the Glove wasn't a gambler, but he controlled and bankrolled many of the bookies in town. Fred would encourage a degenerate gambler to go in way over his head. Then through usurious interest and intimidation, he would milk the guy as long and as thoroughly as possible. He wasn't above pulling the plug and hurting or killing one of his victims.

Over the years, Ray had watched the Glove use every form of extortion and violence he could think of. On four occasions, Harrelson had had him all wrapped up and headed for prison where he belonged, but something always happened, and the Glove would slide away like a hog down a muddy mountain.

From what he had heard about Malone, it was obvious that the Glove had underestimated this one. It was no cinch that anything would happen this night, but he damn sure intended to be there if it did. He drove hard toward the Turf Club.

27.

Bill left Gail's keys under the seat and walked into the Glove's bar. As he entered he thought to himself, I hope I come out as easy as I'm going in.

The Glove was about midway down the bar, leaning over a beer cooler near the back bar, as if he were counting bottles. Bill noted again the size of the man's upper arms, shoulders, and neck. He was built like a bull and still managed to look agile. His daughter, Florence, was at the other end of the bar engrossed in conversation with two women.

The place was packed. There were only three booths along the wall near the back, and they were full. All the bar stools were occupied, and people were standing and drinking in between some of them. Three couples were dancing to a slow Willie Nelson tune on the small dance floor. Pete and Richard were standing at the jukebox, which was situated on the wall near two small quarter-fed pool tables.

Richard looked over at Bill when he entered, nodded slightly, and shifted his eyes back to the selection panel on the jukebox. Bill was relieved to see them both here, but his nerves were wound up to the point where an emotion like relief wouldn't quite register on his senses.

He walked down the bar until he was exactly opposite Fred the Glove. A small woman was sitting on a stool there talking to a man on the right of her. Bill edged up to the bar on her left. He watched Fred intently for a minute or two until he straightened up from the cooler. Bill noticed Fred was wearing a pair of black leather gloves that were shiny and wet from the water in the beer cooler.

"Hey, give me a Budweiser out of there!" he yelled at Fred over the music and babble of the bar patrons.

"Just a minute!" Fred yelled back at him, and started down the bar toward where Florence was standing.

"The fuck are you running here, a bar or a Greyhound bus station?" Bill yelled at Fred's back. Fred spun around, walked back to where Bill stood, leaned his hands on the bar, and said, "Get your loud-mouthed ass out of my bar right now." Fred's jaw was twitching with a barely controlled rage as he spat the words out of tightened lips.

Bill slapped him, but it was no ordinary slap. He came up over the woman's head with a right hand and with all the force he could muster slapped Fred the Glove open-handed across his cheek and ear. The blow sounded like a .22 rifle going off in the bar.

Fred's head snapped around with such force that his feet shuffled when his body followed it. He stumbled toward the back of the bar, and his outflung arm knocked two whiskey bottles to the floor. Somewhere in that instant, either Richard or Pete pulled the plug on the jukebox, and a shocking palpable silence enveloped everyone in the bar.

Bill glanced over toward the jukebox and saw Richard standing by the door looking down the length of the bar with his leather jacket unbuttoned. He assumed that Pete had taken the same position at the other end of the bar. Fred the Glove stood at the back wall as if he were in shock. His features screwed up into a mask of pain and incomprehension.

He had just suffered the worst possible insult that can be imparted to a tough man. He'd been slapped as if he were a woman. Bitch-slapped. The one who does the slapping is saying more forcefully than words can convey, "You're not enough of a man for me to hit, so I'll just slap you like the bitch you are."

Everyone in the bar froze in the deadly silence, some with drinks halfway to their lips, gazing in fascinated horror on the scene unfolding before them. It took a long few seconds for the rage to wipe the Glove's face clear of incomprehension, and he rolled his engorged eyes toward Bill.

"Do you want to come outside, Fred, or do you want me to come over this bar on your big ass?" Bill asked in a normal tone of voice that carried throughout the dive.

"Let's go outside, you cocksucker," Fred spat out. He started walking toward the end of the bar by the door. The livid blotches of Bill's palm and fingers were beginning to show across his cheek.

"The name is Malone, Fred. Bill Malone, and if you call me that again I'm going to stick my dick in your mouth after I beat your ass," Bill told him as he walked on the other side of the bar toward Richard and the door.

Fred the Glove almost stumbled when Bill spoke his name. He watched him closely as more rage poured over his features like hot lava.

Bill wanted the Glove as mad as he could possibly make him. He had decided that his main chance of whipping the man was to outlast him and tire him out. A person in extreme rage is very dangerous because of the added strength he acquires from extra adrenaline pumping through the body. But that adrenaline doesn't pump from a bottomless well. There's only a fixed amount, and when that is used up, fatigue and weakness begin to set in. Bill figured he only had to survive the initial onslaught of the man's fury.

He got out the door quickly as Fred came through the opening at the end of the bar. He was waiting when Fred came out with everyone in the bar following him. Fred looked around and yelled for them to get back inside, and as some men assisted by Pete and Richard began herding the crowd back, the Glove took another look at Bill and rushed him.

Bill threw up his hands as if he were going to meet Fred head on, but at the last moment sidestepped and kicked the Glove as hard as he could in the shin with his steel-toed shoe.

"Goddam!" the Glove yelled in rage and pain as he stumbled past Bill, his punches hitting thin air. He rushed again, and Bill decided to meet him this time and see what he had.

They hit each other at the same time. Fred's fist caught Bill on the forehead and Bill's caught Fred on the bridge of his nose. Bill went down and rolled, thinking that was probably the hardest he'd been hit in his life. He had to get up fast, but as he rolled, he saw that Fred was down also and getting up more slowly than he was.

As Fred got his feet under him, Bill kicked him in the knee, hit him with a vicious uppercut, and stomped the instep of his foot in almost the same motion. Fred hit the ground rolling, and Bill was upon him stomping and kicking. Fred regained his feet, shaking his head while blood ran out his nose. He was unsteady on his feet from the kicks to his shin and knee.

Bill rushed him, leading with a kick that hit Fred's upper thigh. They closed and stood toe to toe, hitting each other with fast, hard punches. Bill had thought he could finish the man, but the Glove was giving back as good as he got. Hard blows were hitting Bill on his eyebrows, jaw, and ears, and he could feel his own punches going home. Blood was dripping to the asphalt from both their heads.

They dropped back and circled each other, looking for an opening. Bill could tell the Glove was winding down now and becoming unsure of himself. Still, he knew he must be careful of becoming overconfident.

There's something about a head-to-head street fight that is like no other situation in the world. Bill felt as if time had stopped momentarily, leaving him and the Glove animated in a freeze-frame photograph. Each was purely focused on the other, each dependent on everything he had learned in a lifetime about survival in the midst of violence. Each understood that his adversary could beat him to death if he lost. That feeling of danger gave the copper taste of blood an added tang on the palate.

Bill felt that this was something he had needed, even though he hadn't wanted it. In the vicious exchange of blows, there was a sense of renewal, a cleansing that can only be found in deadly combat.

The Glove grabbed Bill in a bear hug and took him down, trying to bang his head into the concrete. Bill hooked a leg over the Glove's shoulder, threw him off, and wound up on top. He got to his feet quickly and began stomping and kicking the Glove, who had his arms over his head trying to cover up and get back to his feet at the same time.

Bill caught him in the ribs with a vicious kick and heard bones crack. At the same instant he heard Richard yell, "Put it down, motherfucker!"

Bill glanced around, having to wipe blood from his eyes on the back of his arm to see well. Richard and Pete both had guns out, and Richard was pointing his at a man nearby who had one in his hand. Some of the crowd who had drifted back outside scurried to get back inside when they saw the guns.

Bill looked back at the Glove, who was trying to get up, but his legs weren't working right and he couldn't quite manage to get to his feet. Bill took one step and kicked him in the jaw. The Glove flopped over onto his back, and Bill stomped him twice. Once on the bridge of the nose and another on his neck.

The Glove made a gurgling sound and lay still. His face and head looked like an overripe watermelon that had been stepped on a few times. Blood seeped out onto the parking lot from beneath his head. Bill leaned down, stripped the gloves from Fred's hands, and stuffed them into his mouth.

He pulled his shirt off and began wiping the blood off his own face. As he did so, he looked around and saw that at least eight men had guns in their hands, including Richard and Pete. It was a touchy situation but looked like a standoff, as no one wanted to shoot first.

He looked back at Fred the Glove lying there with blood and glove fingers coming out of his mouth. Out of the corner of his eye, he saw a squad car with lights flashing pulling into the mall from Cedar Street. The armed men saw it also and began walking toward the bar putting away their guns.

"Freeze! Police officers!" he heard a voice yell from beside a gray Plymouth parked nearby. No one froze, though—the men just walked faster into the bar. A squad car was now coming from the other end of the mall, and another was pulling in off Cedar. Bill just stood silently over Fred. He knew he couldn't get lost in a crowd with blood and cuts all over him.

Harrelson took a good look at the Glove and said to an officer emerging from a patrol car, "Get an ambulance out here, and the rest of you arrest every son of a bitch in that bar."

Gamboa was handcuffing Bill's wrists behind his back but was being very gentle about it.

"We've got to take you in, Malone, even if it did look like self-defense," Harrelson told him when the cuffs were in place.

"I understand," Bill replied.

"We've picked up a fucking suitcaseful of guns off the floor in here," one of the patrolmen said as he emerged from the bar.

"Let's see if we can tie them to anyone," Harrelson replied. He and Gamboa walked Bill to a patrol car and deposited him in the backseat.

At the Fresno jail, Bill waited in a bullpen with a crowd of other men who were getting booked. A doctor called him out and told him he needed stitches in his eyebrow. Bill told him to forget it, and the doctor closed the wound with butterfly bandages.

As he was getting booked in, Harrelson walked by and said to the booking officer, "You wouldn't believe it by looking at him, but he won one hell of a fight."

He was booked for assault and battery, and a parole hold was placed on him so he couldn't bail out. He spent the night in an eight-man cell on an upper bunk. When the iron cell door clanked shut behind him, he got an old familiar feeling. But he still felt relieved that his affair with the Glove was over.

On Sunday, Gail and June came to visit but were told at the desk that Bill wouldn't be allowed visits until Monday morning. He talked with them by phone later in the day. They all were relieved that the confrontation with the Glove had finally taken place and Bill was still alive. Yet with the parole hold in place they didn't attempt to make any definite plans for the near future.

A man in his tank had received a copy of the *Sunday Bee*, and the fight at the Glove's bar had made the front page. The article mentioned that more than fifteen pistols had been confiscated and that Fred Sandino was in critical condition. The youngsters in his tank gathered around Bill in the dayroom clamoring to hear all about the fight in detail.

He obliged as well as he could. Most of them had been raised on tales about the Glove and his family. They were thrilled and awed by Bill's account of the fight. One black youngster remarked, "Man, you done spanked that ape like he was a pet monkey."

Another kid said he'd have gladly done an extra ninety days to have been there to watch the fight.

The attention was somewhat embarrassing to Bill, but he enjoyed finding out there was some level on which he could communicate with these young people. They were pretty much the same as the young outlaws of his era except that they leaned more toward impatience, violence, and bad manners than his crowd had.

Campbell called Martin Torres at eight o'clock Monday morning wanting to know who had placed a parole hold on Malone.

"Ray Harrelson had it put on there because he knew he was on parole," Torres told him.

"Well, that's not how it's done. If I want a hold on him, I'll request a warrant from the parole commission. I want that hold taken off immediately," Campbell told him.

"You know, this guy Fred Sandino has about eight broken bones, including two places in his jaw, that Malone inflicted on him," Torres said.

"That's his problem, not mine. I just want that hold dropped," Campbell replied.

"I'll have it off before noon," Torres said and hung up. It was clear there was no use arguing with Campbell any longer.

Bill was called out for a visit a little later on Monday morning. Gail and June were waiting in a partitioned booth on the other side of a sheet of glass. Gail picked up the phone on her side, and Bill picked his up.

"My God, Bill," Gail exclaimed, "you look terrible!"

"You should see the other guy." He smiled through swollen lips, and she smiled back. She put her hand up against the glass, and he put his on the other side as if to touch hers.

"Campbell called me today, and you should have heard what he told me. I couldn't believe it."

"What was that?" he asked.

"He said he was going to put a hold on you. He was going to fax the info to the parole commission and get a warrant. Then he found out Torres or someone had put a hold on you and he went crazy. Said he didn't do their job and didn't want them doing his.

"So now he's going to write up the report and send it by regular mail. That way the commission won't think it's urgent. He wants you to give your word you won't run. He says you may not even get violated, but if you do, you're looking at eight to twelve months."

"I'll give him my word on that," Bill told her.

"I told him you would, and when all the facts are in, I think you'll be okay. I mean, Fred the Glove won't want a trial, and looking at you, it's obvious he was trying to hurt you." She put her hand to the glass as if to touch him, and he wanted to feel her soft fingers on his swollen skin.

"Do you think it's over now?" June asked, and he could tell by her expression she was still very worried.

"I don't know, but I hope so," he told her.

June and Gail left to find Frances, who was arranging bail, and within two hours, he was released. Frances was with Gail and June when he finally walked out into the sunshine. There was a well-dressed man standing just behind them, and Bill watched him warily as he hugged the three women.

"I'm Vic Fraschetta, Fred Sandino's attorney," the man said and stuck out his hand.

Bill hesitated a moment then grasped the hand. "Malone," he mumbled.

"I was going to get an attorney visit with you, but they told me you had bailed, so I waited here. If you could spare five minutes, I'd like to have a word with you in private," the man said.

Bill looked at Gail, she nodded her head, and he made up his own mind.

"I can spare a few minutes," he said.

"Walk with me then," Fraschetta said, and Bill followed him down the sidewalk out of earshot of the women.

"I just talked to the Glove, if you could call it talking. They took out his spleen and wired his jaw shut. I had some more bad news for him. He's about to get indicted on an income tax and racketeering charge, along with Small Bob and a couple of their friends."

"I don't believe that has anything to do with me. He doesn't plan on blaming all that on me also, does he?" Bill asked, and the man smiled before he replied.

"Nope, but he wants me to tell you he's done with you. He's had enough. You can go your way in peace. There won't be any charges filed by him, of course."

"How can I believe what he says?" Bill asked.

"Fred's a funny guy. He's as mean and ornery as they come, but once he gives his word about anything, you can count on what he says. His word is like a fence post."

"I'm happy to be done with the whole mess," Bill told him. "I didn't want it in the first place. But I'm still not sure I know why he's calling it quits."

"Look at it this way, Malone. Fred is no fool. What if he gets ten years on this tax beef and goes to a federal prison? Then what if he runs into you there? Or even if he doesn't run into you, you have plenty of friends in all those joints. What kind of a chance would he have against you and your friends in there?"

"Probably not near as much as I had out here," Bill told him truthfully.

"Well, there it is," Fraschetta said, holding out both hands palms up. "He understands there's no future at all in this deal. And I'm pretty sure he gained a large measure of respect for you last night."

"He's getting too old for fist-fighting," Bill said.

"I believe you made that point quite eloquently last night," the lawyer said with a smile. "Now, if you'll accept my handshake in lieu of his, I will assume we're all in agreement here that this unfortunate affair is settled," Fraschetta said, and stuck out his hand. Bill took it.

"Done," he said, and felt a great sense of relief.

Gail was looking at him anxiously as they walked back to where the women were standing.

"Let's go home," he said, and put his arms around Gail and June.

28.

While a team of doctors were wiring Fred the Glove's jaw shut and debating, among other things, the removal of his spleen, Bullfrog and Cabbage Head debated their own future.

Their conversation took place around the warmth of a good fire. Their camp was at the far end of the vacant lot behind Ferraro's. It was situated near the fence of the junkyard. Bullfrog had cut a hole in the fence with wire cutters so that they could take refuge in a junked-out Dodge van on rainy nights.

A half-gallon coffeepot hung suspended over the fire from a scrap metal-and-wire rigging. Bullfrog sat near the fire, bending toward the light, working on a piece of metal with a small file. Cabbage Head sipped at his coffee and watched him. They were both dead sober.

Their possessions were stacked neatly around them. Bedrolls folded and ready to go. They had decided to leave the coffeepot and some canned goods for whoever came along.

"Hey, Bullfrog, did you ever hear a song by Tom T. Hall called 'Old Dogs and Children and Watermelon Wine'?" Cabbage Head asked.

"Man, you know I don't stay up on that redneck music," Bullfrog replied without looking up from the metal he was filing.

"Well, it's one a' them story songs he sings. It's about a trucker in a Florida bar. There's an old black man cleaning up the bar and he tells the guy that the only thing important in the world is old dogs and children and watermelon wine."

Bullfrog stopped filing and looked up at Cabbage Head. "That ain't hard to figure out, Cabbage. Dogs is loyal, children ain't learned to hate, and even folks like Jesus needs a shot a wine now and again.

"But I know what you be thinkin', and you can forget it. That mangy-ass dog used to live out here won't even bark at us now. June Bug, she ain't no child no more. Something happen to her this last summer. I don't know what, but I know she done lost that magic a child carry around. Now she be feelin' the kinda shit you and me go off in that bottle to forget."

"I just remember how she was four years ago when we met her out here. How she led us around showing us all them bird nests and squirrel holes and stuff," Cabbage Head said.

Bullfrog looked up from his work and could see Cabbage Head's face clearly in the dancing flames playing upon his old beard-stubbled face. There was moisture beneath his eyes.

"Look at this, Cabbage," he said, and held up a lock pick he had just finished making from a piece of a hacksaw blade. It was a sliver of metal with a piece left on the tip that stuck up like a tiny pyramid.

Cabbage nodded, and Bullfrog laid the pick on the ground beside an Allen wrench that he had flattened on the end to use as a tension bar.

"What time it be, Cabbage?" he asked as he rose and brushed grass and dirt from his clean overalls.

"Eleven-fifteen," Cabbage replied, looking intently at a cheap pocket watch.

"Well, get your old ass busy. We been puttin' this score off for three years now because of June Bug. She gone now, man. You may as well face it. So is the dog and most of the wine. It's time to go to work." As he spoke, he leaned down and picked up the lock pick and tension bar. Then he stood there looking expectantly at Cabbage Head.

"Yeah, you're right as usual, Frog," Cabbage Head mumbled as he rose from the ground.

They started across the field toward Ferraro's. At the edge of their campsite, Cabbage Head knelt and picked up a two-foot length of galvanized pipe that was shredded and torn at one end.

The first summer they had come to this field where they had met June Bug, they had noticed an interesting ritual that took place at Ferraro's every Saturday night at eleven-thirty.

A man driving a new Thunderbird pulled up in the rear and walked into the bar. A few minutes later he came out and deposited something in the trunk of the car. Then he went back inside and stayed for an hour or more before leaving.

It didn't take them long to determine what was going on. The man was a runner for a bookmaking operation. He brought the money out to the car then went back inside to help the bartender tally up the betting slips to make sure the amount corresponded with what was in the bag in his trunk.

The reason for the procedure was obvious. In case of a police raid, they didn't want the money and the betting slips in the same place. That's rule number one in a bookie's policy manual. Never keep the money and the betting slips in the same location.

They crouched behind a clump of grass behind Ferraro's, and the T-Bird pulled in at eleven-thirty sharp. The driver entered the bar and came back out five minutes later. They watched as he tossed a cloth sack into the trunk, slammed it down, and walked back inside. They rose and went for the car.

Bullfrog was happy the man was driving a Thunderbird. Ford cars had the easiest trunks to pick. He figured he could do this one in less than five seconds. Cabbage Head took up a position near the door of the bar, fully intending to bust the head of anyone who was unfortunate enough to exit while they were at work.

Bullfrog inserted the pick with the tip up, then inserted the Allen wrench and put tension on the lock as if he were turning a key as he ripped the pick along the upper tumblers. There was a sound like a loud zipper being zipped up. Three zips and the tension bar turned like a key and the trunk popped open. A light came on and Bullfrog saw seven cloth bags lying about the trunk. He scooped them up and slammed the trunk back down. They had hoped the bar was on a route but hadn't dared hope for seven bags. Some of them were pretty full.

"Come on," he said to Cabbage Head, and they walked slowly away so as not to attract attention.

Back at the campsite, Bullfrog dumped all the sacks onto the ground beside the fire. The money made a nice pile of bills in denominations from ones to hundreds. The bulk of the pile was twenties in thousand-dollar stacks with rubber bands around them.

"Jesus, Frog, must be seventy or eighty grand there," Cabbage whispered reverently.

"Take some and leave some," Bullfrog said. He bent down and began scooping the money up and stuffing it into his overall pockets. Cabbage Head followed suit. They never bothered with counting money they made. Whatever they had belonged to them both until it was all gone anyway.

"Leave the bedrolls, canned goods, and everything. We ain't hoppin' no freight tonight. We'll get that Amtrak and a sleeper car," Bullfrog said. He took off toward the Star Motel with Cabbage Head close behind him.

"Hey, Frog, ain't they got a bar car on that Amtrak?" Cabbage Head asked as they walked out onto the motel grounds.

"Yeah, but all they sell is that fancy wine," Bullfrog replied.

"Hell, that will do us till we get to Arkansas," Cabbage Head said.

"Sheeeiiiit, Arkansas your white ass. We getting off in Denver," Bullfrog muttered, and set off down the road toward Roeding Park.